All-Wool Morrison

Holman Day

Contents

To
PERCIVAL P. BAXTER

ALL-WOOL MORRISON

BY

Holman Day

I
HOW "THE MORRISON" BROKE ST. RONAN'S RULE

On this crowded twenty-four-hour cross-section of contemporary American life the curtain goes up at nine-thirty o'clock of a January forenoon. Locality, the city of Marion--the capital of a state.

Time, that politically throbbing, project-crowded, anxious, and expectant season of plot and counterplot--the birth of a legislative session.

Disclosed, the office of St. Ronan's Mill of the city of Marion.

From the days of old Angus, who came over from Scotland and established a woolen mill and handed it down to David, who placed it confidently in the possession of his son Stewart, the unalterable rule was that "The Morrison" entered the factory at seven o'clock in the morning and could not be called from the mill to the office on any pretext whatsoever till he came of his own accord at ten o'clock in the forenoon.

In the reign of David the old John Robinson wagon circus paraded the streets of Marion early on a forenoon and the elephant made a break in a panic and ran into the mill office of the Morrisons through the big door, and Paymaster Andrew Mac Tavish rapped the elephant on the trunk with a penstock and, only partially awakened from abstraction in figures, stated that "Master Morrison willna see callers till he cooms frae the mill at ten."

To go into details about the Morrison manners and methods and doggedness in attending to the matter in hand, whatever it might be, would not limn Stewart Morrison in any clearer light than to state that old Andrew, at seventy-two, was obeying Stewart's orders as to the ten-o'clock rule and was just as consistently a

Cerberus as he had been in the case of Angus and David. He was a bit more set in his impassivity--at least to all appearances--because chronic arthritis had made his neck permanently stiff.

It may be added that Stewart Morrison was thirty-odd, a bachelor, dwelt with his widowed mother in the Morrison mansion, was mayor of the city of Marion, though he did not want to be mayor, and was chairman of the State Water Storage Commission because he particularly wanted to be the chairman; he was, by reason of that office, in a position where he could rap the knuckles of those who should attempt to grab and selfishly exploit "The People's White Coal," as he called water-power. These latter appertaining qualifications were interesting enough, but his undeviating observance of the mill rule of the Morrisons of St. Ronan's served more effectively to point the matter of his character. Stewart Morrison when he was in the mill was in it from top to bottom, from carder to spinner and weaver, from wool-sorter to cloth-hall inspector, to make sure that the manufacturing principles for which All-Wool Morrison stood were carried out to the last detail.

On that January morning, as usual, he was in the mill with his sleeves rolled up.

On his high stool in the office was Andrew Mac Tavish, his head framed in the wicket of his desk, and the style of his beard gave him the look of a Scotch terrier in the door of a kennel.

The office was near the street, a low building of brick, having one big room; a narrow, covered passage connected the room with the mill. A rail divided the office into two small parts.

According to his custom in the past few months, Mac Tavish, when he dipped his pen, stabbed pointed glances beyond the rail and curled his lips and made his whiskers bristle and continually looked as if he were going to bark; he kept his mouth shut, however.

But his silence was more baleful than any sounds he could have uttered; it was a sort of ominous, canine silence, covering a hankering to get in a good bite if the opportunity was ever offered.

It was the rabble o' the morning--the crowd waiting to see His Honor the Mayor--on the other side of the rail. It was the sacrilegious invasion of a business office in the hours sacred to business. It was like that every morning. It was just as well that the taciturn Mac Tavish considered that his general principle of cautious reserve applied to this situation as it did to matters of business in general, other-wise the explosion through that wicket some morning would have blown out the windows. Mac Tavish did not understand politics. He did not approve of politics. Government was all right, of course. But the game of running it, as the politicians played the game! Bah!

He had taken it upon himself to tell the politicians of the city that Stewart Morrison would never accept the office of mayor. Mac Tavish had frothed at the mouth as he rolled his r's and had threshed the air with his fist in frantic protest. Stewart Morrison was away off in the mountains, hunting caribou on the only real vacation he had taken in half a dozen years--and the city of Marion took advantage of a good man, so Mac Tavish asserted, to shove him into the job of mayor; and a brass band was at the station to meet the mayor and the howling mob lugged him into City Hall just as he was, mackinaw jacket, jack-boots, woolen Tam, rifle and all--and Mac Tavish hoped the master would wing a few of 'em just to show his dis-approbation. In fact, it was allowed by the judicious observers that the new mayor did display symptoms of desiring to pump lead into the cheering assemblage instead of being willing to deliver a speech of acceptance.

He did not drop, as his manner indicated, all his resentment for some weeks--and then Mac Tavish picked up the resentment and loyally carried it for the master, in the way of outward malevolence and inner seething. The regular joke in Marion was built around the statement that if anybody wanted to get next to a hot Scotch in these prohibition times, step into the St. Ronan's mill office any morning about nine-thirty.

Up to date Mac Tavish had not thrown any paper-weights through the wicket, though he had been collecting ammunition in that line against the day when noth-ing else could express his emotions. It was in his mind that the occasion would come when Stewart Morrison finally reached the limit of endurance and, with the High-land chieftain's battle-cry of the old clan, started in to clear the office, throwing his resignation after the gang o' them! Mac Tavish would throw the paper-weights. He wondered every day if that would be the day, and the encouraging expectation helped him to endure.

Among those present was a young fellow with his chaps tied up; there was a sniveling old woman who patted the young man's shoulder and evoked protesting growls. There were shifty-eyed men who wanted to make a touch--Mac Tavish knew the breed. There was a fat, wheezy, pig-farm keeper who had a swill contract with the city and came in every other day with a grunt of fresh complaint. There were the usual new faces, but Mac Tavish understood perfectly well that they were there to bother a mayor, not to help the woolen-goods business. There was old Hon. Calvin Dow, a pensioner of David Morrison, now passed on to the considerately befriending Stewart, and Mac Tavish was deeply disgusted with a man who was so impractical in his business affairs that, though he had been financially busted for ten years, he still kept along in the bland belief, based on Stewart's assurances, that money was due him from the Morrisons. Whenever Mac Tavish went to the safe, obeying Stewart's word, he expressed *sotto voce* the wish that he might be able to drop into the Hon. Calvin Dow's palm red-hot coins from the nippers of a pair of tongs. It was not that Mac Tavish lacked the spirit of charity, but that he wanted every man to know to the full the grand and noble goodness of the Morrisons, and be properly grateful, as he himself was. Dow's complacency in his hallucination was exasperating!

But there was no one in sight that morning who promised the diversion or the effrontery that would make this the day of days, and there seemed to be no excuse that would furnish the occasion for the battle-cry which would end all this pestiferous series of levees.

The muffled rackelty-chackle of the distant looms soothed Mac Tavish. The nearer rick-tack of Miss Delora Bunker's typewriter furnished obbligato for the chorus of the looms. It was all good music for a business man. But those muttering, mumbling mayor-chasers--it was a tin-can, cow-bell discord in a symphony concert.

Mac Tavish, honoring the combat code of Caledonia, required presumption to excuse attack, needed an upthrust head to justify a whack.

Patrolman Cornelius Rellihan, six feet two, was lofty enough. He marched to and fro beyond the rail, his heavy shoes flailing down on the hardwood floor. Every morning the bang of those boots started the old pains to thrusting in Mac Tavish's neck. But Officer Rellihan was the mayor's major-domo, officially, and Stewart's pet and protégé and worshiping vassal in ordinary. An intruding elephant might be evicted; Rellihan could not even receive the tap of a single word of remonstrance.

It promised only another day like the others, with nothing that hinted at a climacteric which would make the affairs of the mill office of the Morrisons either better or worse.

Then Col. Crockett Shaw marched in, wearing a plug-hat to mark the occasion as especial and official, but taking no chances on the dangers of that unwonted regalia in frosty January; he had ear-tabs close clamped to the sides of his head.

Mac Tavish took heart. He hated a plug-hat. He disliked Col. Crockett Shaw, for Shaw was a man who employed politics as a business. Colonel Shaw was carrying his shoulders well back and seemed to be taller than usual, his new air of pomposity making him a head thrust above the horde. Colonel Shaw offensively banged the door behind himself. Mac Tavish removed a package of time-sheets that covered a pile of paper-weights. Colonel Shaw came stamping across the room, clapping his gloved hands together, as if he were as cold under the frosty eyes of Mac Tavish as he had been in the nip of the January chill outdoors.

"Mayor Morrison! Call him at once!" he commanded, at the wicket.

Mac Tavish closed his hand over one of the paper-weights. He opened his mouth.

But Colonel Shaw was ahead of him with speech! "This is the time when that fool mill-rule goes bump!" The colonel's triumphant tone hinted that he had been waiting for a time like this. His entrance and his voice of authority took all the attention of the other waiters off their own affairs. "Call out Mayor Morrison."

"Haud yer havers, ye keckling loon! Whaur's yer een for the tickit gillie?" The old paymaster jabbed indignant thumb over his shoulder to indicate the big clock on the wall.

"I can't hear what you say on account of these ear-pads, and it doesn't make any difference what you say, Andy! This is the day when all rules are off." He was fully conscious that he had the ears of all those in the room. He braced back. With an air of a functionary calling on the multitude to make way for royalty he declaimed, "Call His Honor Mayor Morrison at once to this room for a conference with the Honorable Jodrey Wadsworth Corson, United States Senator. I am here to announce that Senator Corson is on the way."

Mac Tavish narrowed his eyes; he whittled his tone to a fine point to correspond, and the general effect was like impaling a puffball on a rat-tail file. "If ye hae coom sunstruck on a January day, ye'd best stick a sopped sponge in the laft o' yer tar-pail bonnet. Sit ye doon and speir the hands o' the clock for to tell when the Morrison cooms frae the mill."

The colonel banged the flat of his hand on the ledge outside the wicket. "It isn't an elephant this time, Mac Tavish. It's a United States Senator. Act on my orders, or into the mill I go, myself!"

The old man slid down from the stool, a paperweight in each hand. "Only o'er my dead body will ye tell him in yer mortal flesh. Make the start to enter the mill, and it's my thocht that ye'll tell him by speeritual knocks or by tipping a table through a meejum!"

"Lay off that jabber, old bucks, the two of ye!" commanded Officer Rellihan, swinging across the room. "I'm here to kape th' place straight and dacint!"

"I hae the say. I'll gie off the orders," remonstrated Mac Tavish; there was grim satisfaction in the twist of his mouth; it seemed as if the day of days had arrived.

"On that side your bar ye may boss the wool business. But this is the mayor's side and the colonel is saying he's here to see His Honor. Colonel, ye'll take your seat and wait your turn!" He cupped his big hand under the emissary's elbow.

Mac Tavish and Rellihan, by virtue of jobs and natures, were foes, but their team-work in behalf of the interests of the Morrison was comprehensively perfect.

"What's the matter with your brains, Rellihan?" demanded the colonel, hotly.

"I don't kape stirring 'em up to ask 'em, seeing that they're resting aisy," returned the policeman, smiling placidly. "And there's nothing the matter with my muscle, is there?" He gently but firmly pushed the colonel down into a chair.

"Don't you realize what it means to have a United States Senator come to a formal conference?"

"No! I never had one call on me."

"Rellihan, Morrison will fire you off the force if it happens that a United States Senator has to wait in this office."

The officer pulled off his helmet and plucked a card from the sweatband. "It says here, 'Kape 'em in order, be firm but pleasant, tell 'em to wait in turn, and'-- for meself--'to do no more talking than necessary.' If there's to be a new rule to fit the case of Senators, the same will prob'bly be handed to me as soon as Senators are common on the calling-list." He put up a hand in front of the colonel's face--a broad and compelling hand. "Now I'm going along on the old orders and the clock tells ye that ye have a scant twenty minutes to wait. And if I do any more talking, of the kind that ain't necessary, I'll break a rule. Be aisy, Colonel Shaw!" He resumed his noisy promenade.

Mac Tavish was back on the stool and he clashed glances with Colonel Shaw with alacrity.

"There'll be an upheaval in this office, Mac Tavish."

"Aye! If ye make one more step toward the mill door ye'll not ken of a certainty whaur ye'll land when ye're upheaved."

After a few minutes of the silence of that armed truce, Miss Bunker tiptoed over to Mac Tavish, making an excuse of a sheet of paper which she laid before him; the paper was blank. "Daddy Mac!" Miss Bunker enjoyed that privilege in nomenclature along with other privileges usually won in offices by young ladies who know how to do their work well and are able to smooth human nature the right way. She went on in a solicitous whisper. "We must be sure that we're not making any office mistake. This being Senator Corson!"

"I still hae me orders, lassie!"

"But listen, Daddy Mac! When I came from the post-office the Senator's car went past me. Miss Lana was with him. Don't you think we ought to get a word to Mr. Morrison?"

"Word o' what?" The old man wrinkled his nose, already sniffing what was on the way.

"Why, that Miss Lana may be calling, along with her father."

"What then?"

"Mr. Morrison is a gentleman, above all things," declared the girl, nettled by this supercilious interrogation. "If Miss Corson calls with her father and is obliged to wait, Mr. Morrison will be mortified. Very likely he will be angry because he wasn't notified. I understand the social end of things better than you, Daddy Mac. I think it's my duty to take in a word to him."

"Aye! Yus! Gude! And tell him the music is ready, the flowers are here, and the tea is served! Use the office for all owt but the wool business. To Auld Hornie wi' the wool business! Politeeks and socieety! Lass, are ye gone daffie wi' the rest?"

"Hush, Daddy Mac! Don't raise your voice in your temper. What if he should still be in love with Miss Lana, spite of her being away among the great folks all this long time?"

Mac Tavish was holding the paper-weights. He banged them down on his desk and shoved his nose close to hers. "Fash me nae mair wi' your silly talk o' love, in business hours! If aye he wanted her when she was here at hame and safe and sensible, the Morrison o' the Morrisons had only to reach his hand to her and say, 'Coom, lass!' But noo that she is back wi' head high and notions alaft, he'd no accept her! She's nowt but a draft signed by Sham o' Shoddy and sent through the Bank o' Brag and Blaw! No! He'd no' accept her! And now back wi' ye to yer tickety-tack! I hae my orders, and the Queen o' Sheba might yammer and be no' the gainer!"

Miss Bunker swept up the sheet of blank paper with a vicious dab and went back to her work, crumpling it. Passing the hat-tree, she was tempted to grab the Morrison's coat and waistcoat and run into the mill with them, dodging Mac Tavish and his paper-weights in spite of what she knew of his threats regarding the use he proposed to make of them in case of need. She believed that Miss Lana Corson would come to the office with the others who were riding in the automobile. She had her own special cares and a truly feminine apprehension in this matter, and she believed that the young man, who was one of the guests at the reopened Corson mansion on Corson Hill, was a suitor, just as Marion gossip asserted he was.

Miss Bunker had two good eyes in her head and womanly intuitiveness in her soul, and she had read three times into empty air a dictated letter while Stewart Morrison looked past her in the direction which the Corson car had taken that first day when Lana Corson had shown herself on the street.

And here was that stiff-necked old watch-dog callously laying his corns so that Stewart Morrison would appear to be boor enough to allow a young lady to wait along with that unspeakable rabble; and when he did come he would arrive in his shirt-sleeves to be matched up against a handsome young man in an Astrakhan top-coat! Under those circumstances, what view would Miss Lana Corson take of the man who had stayed in Marion? Miss Bunker was profoundly certain that Mac Tavish did not know what love was and never did understand and could not be enlightened at that period in his life. But he might at least put the matter on a business basis, she reflected, incensed, and show some degree of local pride in grabbing in with the rest of Mr. Morrison's friends to assist in a critical situation.

And right then the situation became pointedly critical.

The broad door of the office was flung open by a chauffeur.

It was the Corson party.

Colonel Shaw was not in a mood to apologize for anybody except himself. He rose and saluted. "Coming here to herald your call, Senator Corson, I have been insulted by a bumptious understrapper and held in leash by an ignorant policeman. They say it's according to a rule of the Morrison mills. I suppose that when Mayor Morrison comes out of the mill at ten o'clock, following his own rule, he can explain to you why he maintains that insulting custom of his and continues this kind of an office crew to enforce it."

Miss Bunker flung the sheet of paper that she had crumpled into a ball and it struck Mac Tavish on the side of the head that he bent obtrusively over his figures.

The old man snapped stiffly upright and distributed implacable stare among the members of the newly arrived party. He was not softened by Miss Corson's glowing beauty, nor impressed by the United States Senator's dignity, nor won by the charming smile of Miss Corson's well-favored squire, nor daunted by the inquiring scowl of a pompous man whose mutton-chop whiskers mingled with the beaver fur about his neck; a stranger who was patently prosperous and metropolitan.

Furthermore, Mac Tavish, undaunted, promptly dared to exchange growls with "Old Dog Tray," himself. The latter, none else than His Excellency, Lawrence North, Governor of the state, marched toward the wicket, wagging his tail, but the wagging was not a display of amiability. The politicians called North "Old Dog Tray" because his permanent limp caused his coattails to sway when he walked.

"Be jing! I've been on the job here at manny a deal of a morn," confided Officer Rellihan to Calvin Dow, "but here's the first natural straight flush r'yal, dealt without a draw." He tagged the Corson party with estimating squints, beginning with the Governor. "Ace, king, queen, John-jack, and the ten-spot! They've caught the office, this time, with a two-spot high!"

Mac Tavish played it pat! "And 'tis the mill rule; it lacks twal' meenutes o' the hour--and the clock yon on the wall is richt!" Thus referring all responsibility to the clock, the paymaster dipped his pen and went on with his figures.

The Governor cross-creased the natural deep furrows in his face with ridges which registered indignant amazement. "You have lost your wits, but you seem to have your eyes! Use them!"

"It's the mill rule!"

"But we are not here on mill business!"

"Then it canna concern me."

"Officer, do you know what part of the mill Mayor Morrison is in?" The Governor turned from Mac Tavish to Rellihan.

"He is nae sic thing as mayor till ten o' the clock and till he cooms here for the crackin wi' yon corbies!" declared the old paymaster, pointing derogatory penstock through the wicket at "the crows" who were ranged along the settees.

Rellihan shook his head.

"Well, at any rate, go hunt him up," commanded His Excellency.

Rellihan shook his head again; this seemed to be an occasion where unnecessary talking fell under interdiction; for that matter, Rellihan possessed only a vocabulary to use in talking down to the proletariat; he was debarred from telling these dignitaries to "shut up and sit aisy!"

"A blind man, now a dumb man--Colonel Shaw, go and hunt up the man we're here to see!"

The colonel feigned elaborately not to hear.

"And finally a deaf one! Take off those ear-tabs! Go and bring the mayor here!"

Mac Tavish dropped from his stool, armed himself with two paper-weights, and took up a strategic position near the door which led into the passage to the mill.

"Roderick Dhu at bay! Impressive tableau!" whispered the young man of the Corson party in Lana's ear, displaying such significant and wonted familiarity that Miss Bunker, employing her vigilance exclusively in the direction in which her fears and her interest lay, sighed and muttered.

The door of the corridor was flung open suddenly! The staccato of the orchestra of the looms sounded more loudly and provided entrance music. Astonishment rendered Mac Tavish ***hors de combat***. He dropped his weights and his lower jaw sagged.

It was the Morrison--breaking the ancient rule of St. Ronan's--ten minutes ahead of time!

II
THE THREAT OF WHAT THE NIGHT MAY BRING

Allthe Morrisons were upstickit chiels in point of height.

Stewart had appeared so abruptly, he towered so dominantly, that a stranger would have expected a general precipitateness of personality and speech to go with his looks.

But after he had closed the door he stood and stroked his palm slowly over his temple, smoothing down his fair hair--a gesture that was a part of his individuality; and his smile, while it was not at all diffident, was deprecatory. He began to roll down the sleeves of his shirt.

There was the repressed humor of his race in the glint in his eyes; he drawled a bit when he spoke, covering thus the Scotch hitch-and-go-on in the natural accent that had come down to him from his ancestors.

"I saw your car arrive, Senator Corson, and I broke the sprinting record."

"And the mill rule!" muttered Mac Tavish.

"It's only an informal call, Stewart," explained the Senator, amiably, walking toward the rail.

"And you have caught me in informal rig, sir!" He pulled his coat and waistcoat from the hooks and added, while he tugged the garments on, "So I'll say, informally, I'm precious glad to see old neighbors home again and to know the Corson mansion is opened, if only for a little while."

"Lana came down with the servants a few days ago. I couldn't get here till last evening. I have some friends with me, Stewart, who have come along in the car to join me in paying our respects to the mayor of Marion."

Morrison threw up the bar of the rail and stepped through. He clutched the hand of the Senator in his big, cordial grip. "And now, being out in the mayor's office, I'll extend formal welcome in the name of the city, sir."

He looked past the father toward the daughter.

"But I must interrupt formality long enough to present my most respectful compliments to Miss Corson, even walking right past you, Governor North, to do so!" explained Stewart, marching toward Lana, smiling down on her.

Their brief exchange of social commonplaces was perfunctory enough, their manner suggested nothing to a casual observer; but Miss Bunker was not a casual observer. "She's ashamed," was her mental conviction. "Her eyes give her away. She don't look up at him like a girl can look at any man when there's nothing on her conscience. Whatever it was that happened, she's the one who's to blame--but if she can't be sorry it doesn't excuse her because she's ashamed."

Possibly Miss Corson was covering embarrassment with the jaunty grandiloquence that she displayed.

"I have dared to intrude among the mighty of the state and city, Mister Mayor, in order to impress upon you by word of mouth that your invitation to the reception at our home this evening isn't merely an invitation extended to the chief executive of the city. It's for Stewart Morrison himself," ran her little speech.

"I hoped so. This word from you certifies it. And Stewart Morrison will strive to behave just as politely as he used to behave at other parties of Lana Corson's when he steeled his heart against a second helping of cake and cream."

She forestalled her father. "Allow me to make you acquainted with Coventry Daunt, Stewart."

Morrison surveyed the young stranger with frank and appraising interest. Then the big hand went out with no hint of any reservation in cordiality.

"I'm sure you two are going to be excellent friends!" prophesied Lana. "You're so much alike."

The florid giant and the dapper, dark young man swapped apologies in a faint flicker of a mutual grin.

"I mean in your tastes! Mr. Daunt is tremendously interested in water-power," Miss Corson hastened to say. "But father is waiting for you, Stewart."

So, however, was the sniveling old woman waiting!

She had not presumed to break in on a conference with another of her sex--but when the mayor turned from the lady and started to be concerned with mere men, the old woman asserted her prerogative. "Out of me way. Con Rellihan, ye omad-haun, that I have chased manny the time out o' me patch! I'm a lady and I have me rights first!" She struggled and squalled when the officer set his palms against her to push her away.

Morrison dropped the Governor's hand, broke off his "duty speech," and with rueful smile pleaded for tolerance from the Corson party.

"Hush, Mother Slattery!" he remonstrated.

"Ah, that's orders from him as has the grand right to give 'em! Niver a wor-rd from me mouth, Your 'Anner, till I may say me say at your call!"

A prolonged, still more deprecatory smile was bestowed by the mayor on the élite among his guests!

"I was out of town when I was elected mayor, and they hadn't taken the pre-caution to measure me for an office room at the city building. I didn't fit anything down there. Some day they're going to build the place over and have room for the mayor to transact business without holding callers on his knee. In the mean time, what mayoralty business I don't do out of my hat on the street I attend to here where I can give a little attention to my own business as well. Now, just a moment please!" he pleaded, turning from them.

He went to the old woman, checking the outburst with which she flooded him when he approached. "I know! I know, Mother Slattery! No need to tell me about it. As a fellow-martyr, I realize just how Jim has been up against it--again!" He slid something into her hand "Rellihan will speak to the judge!" He passed hastily from person to person, the officer at his heels with ear cocked to receive the orders of his master as to the disposition of cases and affairs. Then Rellihan marshaled the retreat of the supplicants from the presence.

"I do hope you understand why I attended to that business first," apologized the mayor.

"Certainly! It's all in the way of politics," averred the Senator, out of his own experience. "I have been mayor of Marion, myself!"

"With me it's business instead of politics," returned Morrison, gravely. "I don't know anything about politics. Mac Tavish, there, says I don't. And Tavish knows me well. But when I took this job--"

"Ye didna tak' it," protested Mac Tavish, determined then, as always, that the

Morrison should be set in the right light. "They scrabbled ye by yer scruff and whamped ye into a--"

"Yes! Aye! Something of the sort! But I'm in, and I feel under obligations to attend to the business of the city as it comes to hand. And business--I have made business sacred when I have taken on the burden of it."

"I fully understand that, Stewart, and my friend Daunt will be glad to hear you say what I know is true. For he is here in our state on business--business in your line," affirmed the Senator. He put his hand on the arm of the elderly man with the assertive mutton-chop whiskers. "Silas Daunt, Mayor Morrison! Mr. Daunt of the banking firm of Daunt & Cropley."

"Business in my line, you say, sir?" demanded Morrison, pursuing a matter of interest with characteristic directness.

"Development of water-power, Mister Mayor. We are taking the question up in a broad and, I hope, intelligent way."

"Good! You touch me on my tenderest spot, Mr. Daunt."

"Senator Corson has explained your intense interest in the water-power in this state. And this state, in my opinion, has more wonderful possibilities of development than any other in the Union."

Morrison did not drawl when he replied. His demeanor corroborated his statement as to his tenderest spot. "It's a sleeping giant!" he cried.

"It's time to wake it up and put it to work," stated Daunt.

"Exactly!" agreed Senator Corson. "I'm glad I'm paying some of the debt I owe the people of this state by bringing two such men as you together. I have wasted no time, Stewart!"

"Round and round the wheels of great affairs begin to whirl!" declaimed Lana. "The grain of sand must immediately eliminate itself from this atmosphere; otherwise, it may fall into the bearings and cause annoying mischief. I'll send the car back, father. I mustn't bother a business meeting."

A grimace that hinted at hurt wrinkled the candor of the Morrison's countenance. "I hoped it wasn't mere business that brought you--all!" He dwelt on the last word with wistful significance, staring at Lana.

"No, no!" said the Senator, hastily. "Not business--not business, wholly. A neighborly call, Stewart! The Governor, Mr. Daunt, Lana--all of us to pay our respects. But"--he glanced around the big room--"now that we're here, and the time will be so crowded after the legislature assembles, why not let Daunt express some of his views on the power situation? Without you and your support nothing can be done. We must develop our noble old state! Where is your private office?"

"I have never needed one," confessed Stewart; it was a pregnant hint as to the Morrison methods. "I never expected to be honored as I am to-day."

The Hon. Calvin Dow was posted near a window in a big chair, comfortably reading one of Stewart's newspapers. Several other citizens of Marion, sheep of such prominence that they could not be shooed away with the mere goats who had been excluded, were waiting an audience with the mayor.

"You understand, of course, that there is no secrecy--that is to say, no secrecy beyond the usual business precautions involved," protested the Senator. The frank query in Stewart's eyes had been a bit disconcerting. "But to have matters of business bandied ahead of time by the mouth of gossip, on half-information, is as damaging as all this ridiculous talk that's now rioting through the city regarding politics."

"It's all an atrocious libel on my administration," exploded Governor North. "It's damnable nonsense!"

"Old Dog Tray," when he had occasion to bark, was not noted for polite reticence.

Lana took Coventry Daunt's arm and started off with an elaborate display of mock terror. "And now politics goes whirling, too! My, how the ground shakes! Mister Mayor, I'll promise you more serene conditions on Corson Hill this evening."

There was an unmistakable air of proprietorship in her manner with the young man who accompanied her.

The Governor shook his finger before the mayor's face and, in his complete absorption in his own tribulation, failed to remark that he was not receiving undivided attention. "I'm depending on men like you, Morrison. I have dropped in here to-day to tell you that I'm depending on you."

Senator Corson had apparently convinced himself that the mill office of St. Ronan's was too much of an open-faced proposition; it seemed more like an arena than a conference-room. Dow and the waiting gentlemen of Marion showed that they were frankly interested in the Governor's outbreak. Right then there were new arrivals.

The Senator hastily made himself solitaire manager of that particular chess-game and ordered moves: "Lana, wait with Coventry in the car. We'll be only a moment. At my house this evening it will be a fine opportunity for you and Daunt to have your little chat, Stewart, and get together to push the grand project for our good state."

"Yes," agreed Morrison; "I'll be glad to come." He was giving the young woman and her escort his close attention and spoke as if he meant what he said. He blinked when the door closed behind them.

"And what say if you wait till then, Governor, to confer with the mayor--if you really find that there is need of a conference?" suggested the director of moves.

"But I want to tell you right now, Morrison, seeing that you're mayor of the city where our state Capitol is located, that I expect your full co-operation in case of trouble to-night or to-morrow," His Excellency declared, with vigor.

"Oh, there will be no trouble," asserted the Senator, airily. "Coming in fresh from the outside--from a wider horizon--I can estimate the situation with a better sense of proportion than you can, North, if you'll allow me to say so. We can always depend on the sane reliability of our grand old state!"

The Governor was not reassured or placated.

"And you can always depend on a certain number of sore-heads to make fools of themselves here--you could depend on it in the old days; it's worse in these times when everybody is ready to pitch into a row and clapper-claw right and left simply because they're aching for a fight."

The closed door had no more revelations to offer to Morrison; he turned his mystified gaze on the Senator and the Governor as if he desired to solve at least one of the problems that had come to hand all of a sudden.

"I can take care of things up on Capitol Hill, Morrison! I'm the Governor of this state and I have been re-elected to succeed myself, and that ought to be proof that the people are behind me. But I want you to see to it that the damnation mob-hornets are kept at home in the city here, where they belong."

"When father kept bees I used to save many a hiveful for him by banging on mother's dishpan when they started to swarm. As to the hornets--"

"I don't care what you bang on," broke in His Excellency. "On their heads, if they show them! But do I have your co-operation in the name of law and order?"

"You may surely depend on me, even if I'm obliged to mobilize Mac Tavish and his paper-weights," said the mayor, and for the first time in the memory of Miss Bunker, at least, Mac Tavish flushed; the paymaster had been hoping that the laird o' St. Ronan's had not noted the full extent of the belligerency that had been displayed in making mill rules respected.

But the abstraction that had marked Morrison's demeanor when he had looked over the Governor's head at the closed door and the later glint of jest in his eyes departed suddenly. The eyes narrowed.

"You talk of trouble that's impending this night, Governor North!"

"There'll be no trouble," insisted the Senator.

"Fools can always stir a row," declared His Excellency, with just as much emphasis. "Fools who are led by rascals! Rascals who would wreck an express train for the chance to pick pocketbooks off corpses! There's been that element behind every piece of political hellishness and every strike we've had in this country in the last two years since the Russian bear stood up and began to dance to that devil's tune! On the eve of the assembling of this legislature, Morrison, you're probably hearing the blacklegs in the other party howl 'state steal' again!"

"No, I haven't heard any such howl--not lately--not since the November election," said Morrison. "Why are they starting it now?"

"I don't know," retorted the Governor. But the mayor's stare was again wide-open and compelling, and His Excellency's gaze shifted to Mac Tavish and then jumped off that uncomfortable object and found refuge on the ceiling.

"The licked rebels know! They're the only ones who do know," asserted the Senator.

Col. Crockett Shaw, practical politician, felt qualified to testify as an expert. "Those other fellows won't play the game according to the rules, Morrison! They sit in and draw cards and then beef about the deal and rip up the pasteboards and throw 'em on the floor and try to grab the pot. They won't play the game!"

"That's it exactly!" the Governor affirmed.

Senator Corson patted Morrison's arm. "Now that you're in politics for yourself, Stewart, you can see the point, can't you?"

"I don't think I'm in politics, sir," demurred the mayor, smiling ingenuously. "At any rate, there isn't much politics in *me!*"

"But the game must be played by the rules!" Senator Corson spoke with the finality of an oracle.

"If you don't think that way," persisted Governor North, nettled by Morrison's hesitancy in jumping into the ring with his own party, "what *do* you think?"

"I wouldn't presume," drawled Stewart, "to offer political opinions to gentlemen of your experience. However, now that you ask me a blunt question, I'm going to reply just as bluntly--but as a business man! I believe that running the affairs of the people on the square is business--it ought to be made good business. Governor North, you're at the head of the biggest corporation in our state. That corporation is the state itself. And I don't believe the thing ought to be run as a game--naming the game politics."

"That's the only way the thing can be run--and you've got to stand by your own party when it's running the state. You need a little lesson in politics, Morrison, and I'm going to show you--"

The mayor of Marion raised a protesting hand. "I never could get head nor tail out of a political oration, sir. But I do understand facts and figures. Let's get at facts! Is this trouble you speak of as imminent--is it due to the question of letting certain members of the House and Senate take their seats to-morrow?"

"I must go into that matter with you in detail!"

"It has been gone into with detail in the newspapers till I'm sick of it, with all due respect to you, Governor North. It has been played back and forth like a game--and I don't understand games. There has been no more talk of trouble since you and your executive council let it be known that all the members were to walk into the State House and take their seats and settle among themselves their rights."

"We never deliberately and decisively let that be known."

"Then it has been guessed by your general attitude, sir. That's the common talk--and the common talk comes to me like it does to all others. That talk has smoothed things. Why not keep things smooth?"

"Breaking election laws to keep sore-heads smooth? Is that your idea of politics?"

"You cannot get me into any argument over politics, sir! I'm talking about the business of the state. I have found that I could do business openly in this office. It has served me even though it has no private room. I say nothing against you and your council because you have done the state's business behind closed doors at the State House. However--"

"The law obliges us to canvass returns in executive session, Morrison."

"I say nothing against the business you have done there," proceeded Morrison, inexorably. "I can't say anything. I don't know what has been done. I'm in no position, therefore, to criticize. If I did know I'd probably have, good reason to praise you state managers as good and faithful servants of our people. But the people don't know. You have left 'em to guess. It's their business. It's bad policy to keep folks guessing when their own business is concerned. What's the matter with throwing wide the doors to-morrow and saying 'Come along in, people, and we'll talk this over'?"

"That's admitting the mob to riot, to intimidate, to rule!"

"Impractical--wholly impractical, Stewart," the Senator chided.

Calvin Dow came toward the group, stuffing his spectacles back into their case. Given a decoration for his coat lapel, the Hon. Calvin Dow, with his white mustache and his imperial, would have served for an excellent model in a study of a marshal of France. His intrusion, if such it was, was not resented; with his old-school manners and his gentle voice he was the embodiment of apology that demanded acceptance. "Jodrey, you never said a truer word. As old politicians, you and I, we understand just how impractical such an idea is. But I must be allowed to put the emphasis very decidedly on the word 'old.' There seems to be something new in the air all of a sudden."

"Yes, a fresh crop of moonshiners in politics," was the Senator's acrid response. "And the stuff they're putting out is as raw and dangerous as this prohibition-ducking poison."

"The trouble is, Jodrey," pursued the old man, gently, but undeterred, "those honest folks who really do own the country show signs of waking up and wanting to pay off the mortgage the politicians hold on it; and those radicals who think they're going to own the country right soon, now, believe they can turn the trick overnight by killing off the politicians and browbeating the proprietors. It looks to me as if the politicians and the real owners better hitch up together on a clean, business basis."

"Excellent! Excellent!" declared Banker Daunt, who had been shifting uneasily from foot to foot, chafing his heavy neck against the beaver collar, perceiving that his own projects were only marking time. "Hitch up on a better business basis! It should be the slogan of the times. Eh, Mister Mayor?"

"Right you are! crisply agreed Stewart, complimenting Daunt with a cheery smile that promised excellent understanding.

"And harmony among the progressive leaders of city and state! Eh, Mister Mayor? What say, Governor North?" The metropolitan Mr. Daunt was not disposed to allow his commercial proposition to be run away with by a stampeding political team.

"That's what I'm asking for--the co-operation that will fetch harmony," admitted the Governor, grudgingly. "But--"

However, when His Excellency turned to the mayor with the plain intent of getting down to a working understanding, Mr. Daunt broke up what threatened to be an embarrassing clinch. As if carried away by enthusiasm in meeting one of his own kind in business affairs, Daunt grabbed Morrison's hand and pulled the mayor away with him toward the door, assuring him that he was glad to pitch in, heart and soul, with a man who had the best interests of a grand state to conserve and develop in the line of water-power. Then he went on as if quoting from a prospectus.

"When the veins and the arteries of old Mother Earth have been drained of the coal and oil, Mr. Morrison, God's waters will still be flowing along the valleys, roaring down the cliffs, ready to turn the wheels of commerce. On the waters we must put our dependence. They are the Creator's best heritage to His people, in lifting and making light the burden of labor!" was the promoter's pompous declaration.

"You cannot shout that truth too loudly, sir! I have been crying it, myself. But I always add with my cry the warning that if the people don't look sharp, the folks who hogged the other heritages, grabbed the iron, hooked onto the coal, and have posted themselves at the tap o' the nation's oil-can, will have the White Coal, too! God will still make water run downhill, but it will run for the profit of the men who peddle what it performs. I'll be glad to have you help me in that warning!"

"Exactly!" agreed Mr. Daunt. "When you and I are thoroughly *en rapport*, we can accomplish wonders." His rush of the willing Morrison to the door had accomplished one purpose: he had created a diversion that staved off further political disagreement for the moment. "You must pardon my haste in being off, Mister

Mayor. Senator Corson has promised to motor me along the river as far as possible before lunch, so that I may inspect the water-power possibilities. Come, Governor North!" he called.

Daunt again addressed Morrison. "The Senator tells me that your mill privilege is the key power on the river."

"Aye, sir! The Morrison who was named Angus built the first dam," stated Stewart, with pride. "But we have never hoarded the water nor hampered the others who have come after us. We use what we need--only that--and let the water flow free--and we're glad to see it go down to turn other wheels than our own. Without the many wheels a-turning there would not have been the many homes a-building!"

"Exactly! Development--along the broadest lines! Do you promise me your aid and your co-operation?"

"I do," declared Stewart.

"You're the kind of a man who makes a spoken word of that sort more binding than a written pledge with a notarial seal." Again Daunt shook the Morrison hand. "I consider it settled!"

Daunt's wink when he grabbed Morrison had tipped off Senator Corson, and the latter collaborated with alacrity; he hustled the Governor toward the door. "We must show Daunt all we can before lunch, Your Excellency! All the possibilities of the grand old state!"

"I haven't got your promise for myself, Morrison," snapped North over his shoulder. "But I reckon I can depend on you to do as much for your party and for law and order as you'll do for the sake of a confounded mill-dam. And we'll leave it that way!"

"There'll be no trouble, I repeat," promised Senator Corson, making himself file-closer. "North has been sticking too close to politics on Capitol Hill, and he has let it make him nervous. But we'll put festivity ahead of everything else on Corson Hill, to-night, and the girls will be on hand to make the boys all sociable. Come early, Stewart!"

The mayor flung up his hand--a boyish gesture of faith in the best. "Hail to you as a peacemaker! We have been needing you! We're glad you're home again, sir."

For a few moments he turned his back on the business of the city, as it awaited him in the persons of the citizens. He went to the front window and gazed at the Corson limousine until it rolled away; Lana had Coventry Daunt with her in the cozy intimacy afforded by the twin seats forward in the tonneau.

"They make a smart-looking couple, bub," commented Calvin Dow, feeling perfectly free to stand at Stewart's elbow to inspect any object that the younger man found of interest. "Is it to be a hitch, as the gossip runs?"

"There seems to be some gossip that's running ahead of my ken in this city just now, Calvin!" The mayor frowned, his eyes fixed on the departing car. His demeanor hinted that his thoughts were wholly absorbed by the persons in that car. "I hope you're spry enough to catch it. Go find out for me, will you, what the blue mischief they're up to?"

"In politics? Or--"

"In politics! Yes!" returned Morrison, tartly. "What other kind of gossip would I be interested in, this day?"

He snapped himself around on his heels and started toward the men who were waiting. He singled one and clapped brisk hands smartly with the air of a man who wanted to wake himself from the abstraction of bothersome visions. "Well, Mister Public Works, how about the last lap of paving on McNamee Avenue? Can we open up tomorrow? I plan on showing our arriving legislative cousins clean thoroughfares on Capitol Hill, you know!"

"I'm losing fourteen men off the job at noon today, Your Honor! Grabbed off without notice," grumbled the superintendent.

"Grabbed off for what?"

"Well, maybe, to keep our paving-blocks from being thrown through the windows of the State House!"

"Who is taking those men from their work?"

"The adjutant-general. They're Home Guard boys."

"Something busted out in Patagonia needing the attention of a League of Nations army?" inquired the mayor, putting an edge of satire on his astonishment.

The superintendent shot a swift stare past the mayor. "Perhaps Danny Sweetsir, there, can tell you--*Captain* Daniel Sweetsir." The public works man copied the mayor's sarcasm by dwelling on the title he applied to Sweetsir.

The mayor took a look, too.

A young man in overalls and jumper had hurried into the office from the private passage; he was trotting toward a closet in one corner. He had the privileges of the office because he was "a mill student," studying the textile trade, and was a son of the Morrison's family physician.

Sweetsir shucked off his jumper, leaped out of his overalls, threw them in at the closet door, and was revealed in full uniform of O. D. except for cap and sword. He secured those two essentials of equipment from the closet and strode toward the rail, buckling on his sword.

Miss Bunker was surveying him with telltale and proprietary pride that was struggling with an expression of utter amazement.

"The deil-haet ails 'em a' this day!" exploded Mac Tavish. The banked fires of his smoldering grudges blazed forth in a sudden outburst of words that revealed the hopes he had been hiding. His natural cautiousness in his dealings with the master went by the board. "Noo it's yer time, chief! I'll hae at 'em--the whole fause, feth'rin' gang o' the tykes, along wi' ye! Else it's heels o'er gowdie fer the woolen business."

Morrison flicked merely a glance of mystification at Mac Tavish. The master's business was with his mill student. "What's wrong with you, Danny? Hold yourself for a moment on that side of the rail where you're still a man of the mill! I'm afraid of a soldier, like you'll be when you're out here in the mayor's office," he explained, softening the situation with humor. "What does it mean?"

"The whole company of the St. Ronan's Rifles has been ordered to the armory, sir. The adjutant-general just informed me over the mill 'phone."

"What's amiss?"

Captain Sweetsir saluted stiffly. "I am not allowed to ask questions of a superior officer, sir, or to answer questions put by a civilian. I am now a soldier on duty, sir!"

"Come through the rail."

The officer obeyed and stood before Morrison.

"Now, Captain, you're in the office of the mayor of Marion, and the mayor officially asks you why the militia has been ordered out in his city?"

Again Captain Sweetsir saluted. "Mister Mayor, I refer you to my superior officer, the adjutant-general of the state."

Morrison promptly shook the young man cordially by the hand. "That's the talk, Captain Sweetsir! Attend honestly to whatever job you're on! It's my own motto."

"I try to do it, Mr. Morrison. You have always set me the example!"

Mac Tavish groaned. He saw mill discipline going into the garbage along with everything else that had been sane and sensible and regular at St. Ronan's. And the Morrison himself had come from the mill that day ten minutes ahead of the hour!

"So, on with you, lad, and do your duty!" Stewart forwarded Sweetsir with a commendatory clap of the palm on the barred shoulder.

Calvin Dow was lingering. "We mustn't let the youngsters shame us, Calvin," Morrison murmured in the old man's ear. "We all seem to have our jobs cut out for us--and I can't tend to mine in an understanding way till you have attended to yours."

The veteran saluted as smartly as had the soldier and trudged away on the heels of Sweetsir.

"Ain't there any way of your making that infernal old tin soldier up at the State House lay his paws off our paving crew?" asked the superintendent.

"Hush, Baldwin!" chided the mayor, unruffled, speaking indulgently. "We seem to have a new war on the board! Have you forgotten, after all that has been happening in this world, that in time of war we must sacrifice public improvements and private enterprises? Go on and do your best with the paving."

"Hell is paved with good intentions, but I can't put 'em down on McNamee Avenue."

"Of course not, Baldwin! That would be using war material that will be urgently needed, if I'm any judge of these times."

"How's that, Mister Mayor?"

"Why, the hell architects seem to be planning an extension of the premises," drawled Morrison.

III
THE MORRISON ASSUMES SOME CONTRACTS

In the past, each day after lunch, Mac Tavish had been enabled to get back to the sanity of a well-conducted woolen-mill business; in the peace that descended on the office afternoons he put out of his mind the nightmare of the forenoons and tried not to think too much of what the morrows promised.

Stewart Morrison had caused it to be known in Marion that he reserved afternoons for the desk affairs of St. Ronan's mill.

Mac Tavish always brought his lunch; he cooked it himself in his bachelor apartment and warmed it up in the office over a gas-burner at high noon.

While he was brushing the crumbs of an oaten cake off his desk, six men filed in. He knew them well. They were from the Marion Chamber of Commerce; they made up the Industrial Development Committee.

"I'm afraid we're a bit too early to see the mayor," suggested Chairman Despeaux.

"Ye are! Nigh twenty-two hours too early to see the mayor!"

"But we 'phoned the house and were told he had left to come to the office!"

"The mayor--mind ye, the *mayor*--he cooms frae the mill at--"

Mac Tavish remembered the crashing blow to his proud pronunciamiento that forenoon, and his natural caution regarding statements caused him to hesitate. "He is supposed to coom frae the mill at ten o'clock, antemeridian! Postmeridian, Master Morrison, of St. Ronan's--not the mayor--he cooms to his desk yon--well, when he cooms isna the concern o' those who are speirin for a mayor."

The gentlemen of the committee exchanged wise grins, suggestively sardonic grins, and sat down.

Mac Tavish, bristling in silence over his figures, was comforted by the ever-springing hope that this intrusion might serve as the last straw on the overloaded Morrison endurance.

He perked up expectantly when Stewart came striding in. Then he wilted despondently, because Morrison greeted the gentlemen with breezy hospitality, led them beyond the rail, and gave them chairs near his desk.

"Command me! I am at your service!"

"We're on our way to Senator Corson's. We have been invited to meet Mr. Daunt at lunch," said Despeaux; a thin veneer of suavity suited his thin lips.

"Fine!"

"I'm glad to hear you say so. We felt that we'd like your opinion of him and his plans before we commit ourselves,"

"I like his personality," stated Stewart, heartily. "But I have only a general notion of his plans."

"Same here," admitted the chairman, though not in a tone of convincing sincerity. "The Senator brought him into my office for a minute or so before they started up-river. Told me to get the boys together and come for lunch. But if it's to put the water-power of this state on a bigger and broader basis, you and the storage commission are with us, aren't you?" Despeaux demanded rather than queried; his air was a bit offensive.

"I'm a citizen of Marion and a native of this state, body and soul for all the good that can come to us, by our own efforts or through the aid of outsiders," declared Morrison, spacking his palm upon the arm of his chair.

"Well, I guess we don't need any better promise than that, for a starter, at any rate. Of course, we knew it--but there's nothing like having a right-out word of mouth." Despeaux rose and pulled out his watch. "We'd better move on toward the eats, boys!"

"Just a moment, however, Despeaux! My father was a Morrison and my mother a Mac Dougal. I can't help what's in me!"

"What is it that's in you?" inquired Despeaux, pausing in the act of putting back his watch.

"Scotch cautiousness!"

"You don't suspect that a man like the big Silas Daunt, of Daunt and Cropley--"

"I don't suspect. I haven't got as far as that! But I want to know exactly what he means by coming into this state. I have a man out getting me some facts about what kind of a devil's mess is being stirred up all of a sudden to-day in politics. Suppose you get under Daunt's hide and find out whether he wants to *do* us or do *for* us, on the water-power matter."

An observant bystander would have perceived a queer sort of crispness in Morrison's manner from the outset of the interview; the same perspicacity would have detected something hard under the smooth surface of Despeaux's early politeness. Mr. Despeaux was not so elaborately polite when he retorted that he did not propose to play the spy on a guest while eating a host's victuals.

Mr. Morrison promptly put more of a snap into his crispness.

"Having balanced to partners, for politeness's sake, Despeaux, we'll take hold of hands and swing, with both feet on the floor. That was a good job you did in the legislative lobby two years ago for the crowd that called itself 'The Consolidated Development Company.' You're a smart lawyer and we had hard work beating you."

"I'll tell you what you franchise-owners did, Morrison! You beat a grand and comprehensive plan that was going to take in the whole state."

"It did take in a lot of folks for a time, but, thank God, it didn't take in a few of us who were wise to the scheme. I know why you have called on me to-day. But you haven't put me on record. Let no man of you think I have made a pledge or have committed myself till I know what's what!"

"You're Scotch, all right, Morrison. You're canny! You're for yourself and the main chance. Now let me tell you! You caught us foul two years ago because you jumped the newspapers into coming out with broadsides about a thing they didn't understand. Their half-baked scare stuff made the state think somebody was trying to steal the whole water-power."

"According to that general franchise bill, as it was framed, somebody was!"

"Morrison, in the last two years the people have been educated to understand that broad-gaged consolidation of water-power is what we must have."

"You have put out good propaganda. That fellow you have hired is a mighty fine press-agent," admitted Morrison, smiling ingenuously.

"And the men who get in the way and try to trig development this year will be ticketed before an understanding public for what they are," declared Despeaux.

"Try me as a part of the public, and see whether I'll understand! Ticketed as what, Brother Despeaux?"

"As profiting dogs in the manger of manufacturing, sir!"

There were expostulatory murmurs in the group.

"We're rather non-committal as a body on this matter, Despeaux," protested a committeeman. "We're waiting to be shown. In the mean time, we don't like to have a man like Morrison here called any hard names."

"Oh, I don't mind being called a watch-dog, boys! That's what I am. So you think I'm wholly selfish, do you, Despeaux?"

"The water-power franchises of this state were grabbed away from the people years ago, like the timber-lands were, by first-comers, and the state got nothing! The waters belong to the people. The people have a right to realize on their property! Morrison, considering what kind of a free gift you had handed to you, you've got to be careful about the position you take in these enlightened days when the people propose to profit from their own. It's mighty easy to shift public opinion these days!"

"Yes, I have seen tons of sand shifted in no time by a stream from a squirt-gun," confessed Morrison, placidly.

"And that leaves it a fifty-fifty break between us on the name-calling proposition," rejoined Despeaux, "I'll bid you a kind good day!" He strode away and his group trailed him.

A deprecating committeeman turned back, however. "I know you are honest, Morrison. But a lot of us are beginning to think that the general policy in the state regarding outside capital has been a bit too conservative. These are new times."

"Very!" said the mayor, pleasantly. "They're creaking about as loud as Squire Despeaux's new shoes." There was a snarl of ire from the shoes every time the retreating chairman lifted a foot. "I hope they won't pinch us, Doddridge! Good day!" He sat down at his desk.

Mac Tavish held his place on his stool in silence for a long time. The stiffness of his neck seemed to embrace all his members, even his tongue. Miss Bunker came in from her lunch, bringing the afternoon mail. Mac Tavish maintained his silence while Morrison picked out what were patently his personal letters before surrendering the others to the girl to be opened and assorted. Mac Tavish waited till his master had gone through his personal mail. The paymaster maintained a demeanor of what may be termed hopeful apprehension; this baiting, this impugning of honesty must needs turn the trick! No Morrison would stand for it! Mac Tavish found the laird's suppression of all comment promisingly bodeful. The fuse must be sizzling. There would be an explosion!

But Morrison began to play a lively tattoo on his desk with the knob of a paper-slitter and whistled "The Campbells Are Coming, Hurrah, Hurrah!" with the cheery gusto of a man who had not a care to trouble him.

"Snoolin' and snirtlin' o'er it!" spat the old man.

"Eh?" queried Stewart, amiably.

"Do ye let whigmaleeries flimmer in yer noddle at a time like this?"

"Why, Andy, speaking of a day like this, you'd have the crochets whiffed from your head if you'd go out for your lunch in the pep of the air instead of penning yourself in the office."

Mac Tavish leaped from his stool and marched toward this non-combatant. "Whaur's the fire o' yer spunk, Stewart Morrison?"

"Go on, Andy!" permitted the master, leaning back in his chair.

"Do ye allow such feckless loons to coom and beard ye in yer ain castle?"

"Andy, if I were playing their game, as they call it, I'd say that I'm going to give 'em all a chance to lay their cards, face up, on the table. But, putting it in a way you and I understand, I'm touching a match to their goods."

Mac Tavish nodded approvingly. He did understand that metaphor. A burning match will not ignite pure wool; threads of shoddy will catch fire.

"Aye! The fire test o' the fabric! Well and gude! But the toe o' yer boot for 'em. Such was ca'd for when he said ye set yer ainsel' in the way for muckle profeet!"

"Soft! Soft and slow, Andy," reproved the master. "There may be some truth in what he said. I'll have to stop right here and do some thinking about it! A chap gets to slamming ahead in his own line, you know. All of us ought to stop short once in a while and make a cold, calm estimate. Take account of stock! Balance the books! Discover how much of it is for ourselves, personally, and how much for the other fellow! No telling how the figures of debit and credit may surprise us!"

He spun around in his swivel chair.

"Lora, get Mr. Blanchard of the Conawin Mills on the 'phone, that's the girl!"

"Yes, Andy, I'm going to get down to the figures in my case! I hope there's a balance in my favor--but we never can tell!"

He set his elbows on his desk and clutched his hands into the hair above his temples. Mac Tavish tiptoed away. Morrison had apparently prostrated himself in the fane of figures; in the case of Mac Tavish figures were holy.

"Mr. Blanchard on the 'phone, Mr. Morrison," reported Miss Bunker.

Morrison put questions, quickly, emphatically, searchingly. He listened. He hung up. "Memo., Miss Bunker." He was curt. His eyes were hard. One observing his manner and hearing his tone would have realized that quarry had broken cover and that Mr. Blanchard had not been able to confuse the trail by dragging across it an anise-bag; in fact, Morrison had said so over the telephone just before he hung up. "Get me Cooper of the Waverly, Finitter of the Lorton Looms, Labarre of the Bleachery, Sprague of the Bates." He named four of the great textile operators of the river. "One after the other, as I finish with each!"

After he had finished with all, pondering while he waited between calls, he strode to Mac Tavish and brought the old man around on his stool by a clap on the shoulder. "A devil of a mouser, I am! I've been sitting purring on the top and they have hollowed it out underneath me."

"Eh? What?"

"The cheese, Andy, the water-power cheese! They have been playing me for the cat in the case! Left me till the last, left me sitting on an empty shell! The mice have made away with the cheese from under me. They have engineered a combine! There's a syndicate a-forming! It's for me to tumble down among 'em when the shell caves. I was right about Despeaux!"

"He's Auld Bartie, wi'out the horns!"

"Oh no! Not as smart as Satan, Andy! But smart, nevertheless! Very smart. He has shown 'em a good thing. They're ready to run in! And the devil take the hindmost. I'm the hindmost and I'd better get a gait on."

"But the company ye'll be keeping!"

"You don't suppose that I'll run away from the mice instead of after 'em, do you?"

"A thoct has been wi' me, Master Morrison! May I speak it?"

"Out with it!"

"Ye'll ne'er find a better chance to break from the kin o' Auld Cloven Cootie and mind yer ain wi' the claith business! Resign!"

"It's good advice, backed up by a good excuse, Andy!"

"And noo that I may speak freely," rattled on the old man, after a gasp of delight, "I can tell ye how I hae been list'nin' for yer interests till ten o' the clock each forenoon, and the dyvor loons--deil tak' it, and here cooms back one o' the waurst o' the widdifu's."

It was the Hon. Calvin Dow and Morrison hurried to meet him. "Sum it short, Uncle Calvin!"

"They're going to play straight politics, Stewart."

"God save the state--in times like these!"

"They're going to admit to seats only the Senators and Representatives who are clearly and indisputably elected by the face of the returns."

"The picked and the chosen!" scoffed Morrison.

"The matter of the right to take seats is going to be referred to the full bench instead of being left to the legislature--taken out of politics, they say."

"Going to be put into cold storage, with all due respect to our eminent justices!"

"It means the careful weighing of evidence--and the courts are obliged to move with judicial slowness, Stewart!"

"And in the mean time those picked and chosen ones will elect the state officers whom the legislature has the power to name, will have the machinery to distribute all state patronage and to make the legislative committees safe for the big measures. There's no telling when the bench will hand down a decision."

"No telling, Stewart!" admitted the sage.

"After it has been done, it will be hard to undo it, no matter what the judges may decide as to members."

"But we can't throw the law out of the window, my son! On the outside of the thing, the Big Boys on Capitol Hill are playing the game strictly according to the legal rules. The legal rules, understand! On the outside!" Dow's emphasis on certain words was significant. He put up his hand and drew Morrison's head down close to his mouth. He began to whisper.

"Talk out loud, Calvin!" commanded Stewart, jerking away. "Keep in the habit of talking out loud with me! I won't even talk politics in a whisper."

"It really shouldn't be talked out, not at this time," expostulated Dow, wedded to the old ways. "I have had to burrow deep for it. It ought to be saved carefully--to do business with later! To win a stroke in politics it's necessary to jump the people with a sensation!"

"Try it on me! I'm one of the people. See if it will work," insisted Morrison, after the manner of his methods with Despeaux.

"They propose to go according to the strict letter of the law."

"Important but not sensational."

Dow was plainly having hard work to keep his voice above a whisper. "Returns not properly sworn to or not attested in due form by city clerks, returns not signed in open town meeting or otherwise defective on account of strictly technical errors, no matter how plainly the intent of the voters was registered, have been finally and definitely thrown out by North and his executive council, acting as a canvassing board."

"Damn'd picayune hair-splitting! Why can't they use business horse-sense?"

"I'll tell you what they've used! They've used Tim Snell and Waddy Sturges and a few other safe hounds with muffled paws to run around and lug back to cities and towns deficient returns and have 'em quietly and secretly corrected where it was a case of adding a safe man to the legislature. I know that, Stewart. I know how to make some of my close friends brag to me. I know it, but I can't prove it. Clean-scrubbed are the faces of those returns. They'll show up to-morrow like the faces of the good boys on the first day at school."

"That's North's idea of that game he was talking about, is it?" Morrison exploded. "I don't believe that Senator Corson knows about those dirty details, or is a party to 'em."

"Well," asserted the Hon. Calvin Dow, stroking his nose contemplatively, "Jodrey and I used to cut sharp corners on two wheels of the four of the old wagon, in past times when he was a politician. But now that he's a statesman he doesn't like to be bothered by details."

"Do you see any joke to this, Calvin?" demanded Morrison, not relishing the veteran's chuckle.

"I can't help seeing the humor," confessed Dow, blandly. "The other, boys would be grinding the same grist if they had control of the machinery. It's only what I myself used to do." Then his face became grave. "But, confound it! in these days there seems to be an element that can't take a joke in politics. There's trouble in the air!"

"Probably!" agreed Morrison, dryly.

Dow walked to the window and looked out with the air of a man who wanted proof to confirm a statement. "I reckon I'll let you be informed direct from Trouble Headquarters, Stewart. Headquarters was at the Soldiers' Memorial in the park when I came past. I gathered that they were picking out a delegation to call on you. Post-Commander Lanigan of the American Legion was doing the picking. He's heading the bunch that I see coming across the street."

"Resign!" barked Mac Tavish through his wicket. But the mayor of Marion did not appear to hear, nor Calvin Dow to understand.

Morrison faced the door of his office.

Lanigan led in his companions with the marching stride of an overseas veteran and halted them with a top-sergeant's yelp. Click o' heels and snap o' the arm! The salute made Captain Sweetsir's previous effort seem torpid by comparison. That a further comparison with Home Guard methods and morale was in Commander Lanigan's mind became promptly evident.

"Your Honor the Mayor, we represent John P. Dunn Post, American Legion, and the independent young men of this city in general. May we have a word with you?"

"Certainly, Mr. Commander!"

In the stress of his emotions Lanigan immediately sloughed off his official air. "It's a hell of a note when a bunch of sissy slackers can keep real soldiers ten feet from the door of the city armory at the end of a bayonet."

The mayor strolled over and placed a placatory palm on the shoulder of the spokesman. "What's, all the row, Joe? Let's not get excited!"

"I have been away fighting for liberty and justice and I don't know what's been going on in politics at home. I don't know anything about politics."

"Nor I, Joe, so let's not try to discuss 'em. What else?"

"They've got three machine-guns up in our State House. What for? They are going to put in them sissy slackers--"

"Let's not call names, Joe. Those boys would have followed you across if you boys hadn't been so all-fired smart that you cleaned it all up in a hurry! What else?"

"Why have a gang of politicians got to barricade our State House against the people?"

"Let's keep cool, Joe, my boy, and find out."

"They won't let us in to find out. How are we going to find out?"

"Why, I was thinking of doing something in that line--thinking about it just before you came in."

Lanigan looked relieved, also a bit ashamed. "Excuse me for being pretty hot, Mr. Morrison. But the boys have been saying we couldn't depend on anybody to stand up for the people. By gad! I told 'em we'd come to you. Says I, 'All-Wool Morrison is our kind!'"

"I hope the name fits the goods, Joe! Suppose you boys keep all quiet and calm for the good name of the city and let me find out how the thing stands?"

He was assured of support and compliance by a chorus of voices.

Lanigan trailed the chorus in solo. "Does that settle it? I'll say it does. It's up to you--the whole thing. You've given us the word of a square man! We can depend on you. And we thank you for taking the full responsibility for seeing to it that the people get theirs--and not in the neck, either!"

But the mayor looked like a man who had stretched forth his hand to take a kitten and had had an elephant tossed at him. "It's a pretty big contract, that! See here, Joe--"

"You're good for any contract you take on, sir! We should worry after what you promise!" He whirled on his heels. "'Bout face! Forward, march!" He followed them and turned at the door. "All the rest of the Big Ones seem to be too almighty busy to bother with the common folks to-day, sir! The Governor with his politics, the adjutant-general with his tin soldiers, and the high and mighty Senator Corson with that party he's giving to-night so as to spout socially the news that his daughter is engaged to marry a millionaire dude. Thank God, we've got a man who 'ain't taken up with anything of that sort and can put all his mind on to a square deal!"

Morrison did not turn immediately to face the three persons, his familiars in the office of St. Ronan's. He clasped his hands behind him and went to the window, as if to survey the departure of the delegation.

"What with one thing and another, they're loading the boy up--they're piling it on," observed Dow to Mac Tavish in sympathetic undertone.

"He'll resign out o' the meeser-r-rable pother," growled Mac Tavish. "The word he just gied the gillies! It was as much as to say, 'I'll be coomin' along wi' ye from noo on.'" The old man's hankerings were helping his persistent hope, in spite of his respect for the Morrison trait of devotion to duty.

"Resign, Andy! Confound it, he's only nailing his grit to the mast and planning on what end of the row to tackle first. You'll see!"

Stewart walked slowly, meditating deeply, went through the opening in the rail, sat down at his desk and fumbled in a drawer and sought deeply under many papers. He brought out a book, a worn volume.

Calvin Dow, daring to peer more closely than Miss Bunker or Mac Tavish had the courage to venture, noted that the place to which Morrison opened was marked by a slip of paper, a snapshot photograph.

"Miss Bunker!" called the master. "A memo.!"

She came with her note-book and sat at the lid of the desk, facing him.

"His resignation, I tell ye," whispered Mac Tavish. "I ken the look o' detar-rmination!"

"I want it typed on a narrow strip that I can slip into my pocketbook," stated Stewart. Then, to all appearances entirely unconcerned with the listening veterans, he dictated:

"Meanwhile I was thinking of my first love, As I had not been thinking of aught for years. Till over my eyes there began to move Something that felt like tears."

Mac Tavish bent on Dow a wild look and swapped with the old pensioner of the Morrisons a stare of amazement for one of bewildered concern.

"I thought of the dress that she wore last time
When we stood 'neath the cypress-tree together
In that lost land, in that soft clime,
In the crimson evening weather.

"Of that muslin dress (for the eve was hot)
And her warm white neck in its golden chain,
And her full, soft hair, just tied in a knot,

And falling loose again.

"I thought of our little quarrels and strife,

And the letter that brought me back my ring. And it all seemed then, in the waste of life,

Such a very little thing."

The girl dabbed up her hand under pretense of fixing a lock of hair; she scrubbed away tears that were trickling. So this was it! The powwow over business and politics had not been stirring even languid interest in her. Now her emotions were rioting. Here seemed to be something worth while in the life of the master!

"But I will marry my own first love   With her primrose face; for old things are best. And the flower in her bosom I prize it above--

"My God!" Mac Tavish gasped. "Next he'll be playing jiggle-ma-ree wi' dollies on his desk! His wits hae gane agley!"

In the horror of his discovery he flung his arms and knocked off the desk his full stock of paperweight ammunition. Then he was convinced beyond doubt that the Morrison was daft. Stewart did not even raise his eyes from the book; he kept on dictating above the clatter of the rolling weights; his intentness on the matter in hand was that of a business man putting a proposition on paper for the purpose of making it definite and cogent and clear.

But Stewart's thoughts were not at all clear, he was confessing to himself; in spite of his assumed indifference, he was embarrassed by the focused stares of Dow and Mac Tavish. He wondered what sudden, devil-may-care whimsy was this that was galloping him away from business and politics and every other sane subject! He was conscious that there was in him a freakish and juvenile hankering to astonish his friends.

He heard Dow say: "Oh, don't worry about the boy, Andy! We do strange things in big times! Even Nero fiddled when Rome was burning!"

Stewart finished the dictation and closed the book.

"Losh! I canna understand!" mourned Mac Tavish, not troubling to hush his tones.

The girl hesitated, her gaze on her notes. Then she looked full into Morrison's face, all her woman's intuitive and long-repressed sympathy in her brimming eyes. "But I understand, sir!" She arose. She extended her hand and when he took it she put into her clasp of his fingers what she did not presume to say in words.

"Thank you!" said Morrison.

Then he left his chair and strolled across to the old men, while Miss Bunker rattled her typewriter. "It begins to look, boys, like we're going to have quite a large evening!" he remarked, sociably.

IV
ANSWERING THE FIRST ALARM

After his dinner with his mother, Stewart went to the library-den, his own room, the habitat consecrated to the males of the Morrison menage. He was in formal garb for the reception at Senator Corson's. He removed and hung up his dress-coat and pulled on his house-jacket; he was prompted to make this precautionary change by a woolen man's innate respect for honest goods as much as he was by his desire for homely comfort when he smoked. He lighted a jimmy-pipe and marched up and down the room. He was determined to give the situation a good going-over in his mind.

He had settled many a problem in that old room!

He was always helped by Grandfather Angus and Father David.

When he walked in one direction he was looking at the portrait of Angus on the end wall of the long narrow room; Angus bored him with eyes as hard as steel buttons and out from the close-set lips seemed to issue many an aphorism to put the grit into a man.

From the opposite wall, when Morrison whirled on his heels, David looked down. David's eyes had little, softening scrolls at the corners of them; the artist had painted from life, in the case of David, and had caught the glint of humor in the eyes. The picture of Angus had been enlarged from a daguerreotype and seemed to lack some of the truly human qualities of expression. But it was a strong face, the face of a pioneer who had come into a strange land to make his way and to smooth that way for the children who were to have life made easier for them. "Tak' it! Wi' all the strength o' ye, reach oot and tak' it for yer ainsel' else ithers will gr-rasp ahead and snigger at ye!" So said Angus from the wall, whenever Stewart pondered on problems.

But David, though the pictured countenance was resolute enough, always put in a shrewd and cautionary amendment, whenever Stewart came down the room, stiffened by the counsel of Angus, "Mind ye, laddie, when ye tak', that the mon wha tak's slidd'ry serpents to tussle wi' 'em, he haes nae hand to use for his ainsel' whilst the slickit beasties are alive; and a deid snake serves nae guid."

That evening Stewart was distinctly getting no help from either Angus or David. They did not appear to understand his new and peculiar mood. He had been in the habit of fusing their clashing arbitraments by a humor of his own which he knew was fantastic, yet helpful according to his whimsical custom, welding their judgments twain into one dominant counsel of determination, softened by the spirit of fairness.

But after he had plucked a certain slip of paper from his waistcoat pocket, squinting at it through the pipe smoke, as he walked to and fro, mumbling as if he were engaged in the task of memorizing, he ceased to look up to Angus and David for assistance. He was sure they would not know! Here were warp and woof of a fabric beyond their ken. He would not admit to himself that he understood in full measure this emotion that had come surging up in him, overwhelming and burying all the ordinarily steadfast landmarks by which he regulated his daily thoughts and actions. "I had built a dam," he muttered, using the metaphor that was natural, "and I've been thinking it was safe and sure. Whether it wasn't strong enough--whether it was undermined, I don't know. It has given way."

There was a tap on the door and he hastily tucked the paper back into his pocket. He knew it was his mother, trained in the way of the Morrisons to respect the sanctuary of the family lairds when they were paying their devotions at the shrine of business.

"I'm saying my gude nicht to ye, bairnie, for ye're telling me ye'll no' be hame till late," she said when he flung open the door.

He copied affectionately her Scotch "braidness" of dialect when they were alone together. "No, wee mither, not till late."

He stepped out into the corridor and kissed her. She patted his cheek and walked on.

More of that whimsy into which he had been allowing his troubled emotions to lead him! He realized it fully! His brow wrinkled, he shook his head, but he called to her. He went to meet her when she returned.

"It's like it is at the office, these days! I'm Morrison of St. Ronan's on one side o' the rail; I'm the mayor of Marion on t'other! Here in the corridor, ye're wee mither!" He put his arm about her and lifted her into the library. "Coom awa' wi' ye, noo!" he cried. He threw himself into a big chair and pulled her upon his knee. "Ye're Jeanie Mac Dougal--only a woman. I need to talk wi' a woman. I canna talk wi' Mac Tavish or sic as he. He thinks I'm daft. He said so. I canna get counsel frae grands'r or sire yon on the walls. They don't understand, Jeanie Mac Dougal. I'm in love!"

"Aye! Wi' the lass o' the Corsons!"

"But ye shouldna sigh when ye say it, Jeanie Mac Dougal."

"A gashing guidwife sat wi' me to-day in the ben, bairnie, and said the lass brings her ain laddie wi' her frae the great town."

"I tak' no gossip for my guide!" he protested. "In business I tak' my facts only frae the lips o' the one I ask. I'll do the same in love."

She did not speak.

"I know, Jeanie Mac Dougal! Ye canna forget ye are wee mither and it's hard for ye to be only woman richt noo. I know the kind of wife ye hae in mind for me. The patient wife, the housewife, the meek wife wi' only her een for back-and-ben, for kitchen and parlor. But I love Lana."

"She promised and she took her promise back! Again she promised, and again she took it back!" The proud resentment of a mother flamed. "And I'm no' content wi' the lass who once may win my laddie's word and doesna treasure it and be thankfu' and proud for all the years to come."

"Oh, I know, mither! But she was young. She must needs wonder what there was in the world outside Marion. I loved her just the same."

"But noo that she is hame they tell me that her heid 'tis held perkit and her speech is high and the polished shell is o'er all."

Stewart looked away from his mother's frank eyes. He was too honest to argue or dispute. "I love her just the same!"

"She ca'd wi' her father at the mill this day, eh? The guidwife said as much."

"Aye, in the way o' politeness!" He remembered that the politeness seemed too elaborate, too florid, altiloquent to the extent of insincerity. "To see her again is to love her the more," he insisted. "I have never been to Washington. Probably I'd be able to understand better the manners one is obliged to put on there, if I had been to Washington. I ought to have gone there on my vacation, instead of into the woods. I'm afraid I have been keeping in the woods too much!"

"But did she talk high and flighty to you, bairnie?"

"It meant nowt except it's the way one must talk when great folks stand near to hear. The Governor was there!" he said, lamely.

"That was unco trouble to mak' for hersel' in the hearing o' that auld tyke whose tongue is as rough as his gruntle!"

"Still, he's the Governor in spite of his phiz, and that shows her tact in getting on well with the dignitaries, Jeanie Mac Dougal, and you're a woman and must praise the wit of the sex. She has seen much. She has been obliged to do as the others do. But good wool is ne'er the waur for the finish of it! My faith is in her from what I know of the worth o' her in the old days. And now that she has seen, she can understand better. Yes, back here at home she'll be able to understand better. Listen, Jeanie Mac Dougal!" He fumbled in his pocket. "Here's a bit of a poem. I have loved it ever since she recited it at the festival when she was a little girl. You have forgotten--I remember! And here's one verse:

"And I think, in the lives of most women and men, There's a moment when all would go smooth and even,   If only the dead could find out when   To come back and be forgiven."

"But I would change it to read, 'If only we all could find out when,'" he proceeded. "It wasn't all her fault, mother. I was younger, then. I'm old enough now to be humble. She is home again, and I'm going to ask to be forgiven!"

Then the telephone-bell called.

He lifted her gently off his knee and stood up. "As to the lad who is here with his father! Gossip is playing all sorts of capers this day, wee mither! And do not be worried if gossip of another sort comes to you after I'm gone this evening. There may be matters in the city for me to attend to as mayor. If I'm not home you'll know that I'm attending to them."

He went to the telephone, replied to an inquiring voice and listened intently, and then he assented with heartiness.

"It's Blanchard of the Conawin Mills! He has a bit of business with me and offers to take me along with him to the reception. Tell Jock he'll not have to bother with my car!" he said, coming to her where she waited at the door. She had picked up the slip of paper which he had dropped in his haste to attend to the telephone.

"I daured to peep at yer bit poem, Stewart, so that my ear might not seem to be put to o'erhearing your business discourse," she apologized, stanch in her adherence to the rules of the Morrisons. "And I'll tell ye that Jeanie Mac Dougal says aye to one sentiment I hae found in it."

"Good! Read it aloud to me, that's my own girlie!" He folded his arms and shut his eyes. She read in tones that thrilled with conviction:

"The world is filled with folly and sin   And love must cling where it can, I say;   For Beauty is easy enough to win,   But one isn't loved every day."

She tucked the paper into the fingers of his hand that lay lightly along his arm. He opened his eyes and gazed down into her straightforward ones.

"Whoever may be the lass my bairnie loves will be honored by that love; aye, and sanctified by that love! And sic a lass will deserve from Jeanie Mac Dougal a smile at our threshold and respect in our hame." She went away. Her eyes were dim with unshed tears; but she held her chin high and trailed her bit of a train with dignity.

Morrison folded the paper and put it away. He took a turn up and down the long room, confronting the portrait faces in turn. He eyed them as if he were approaching them on a matter where there now could be a better understanding than on the subject suggested by the slip of paper. "I don't know whether Blanchard ought to be kicked or coddled," he confessed. "He's a fair sample of the rest. They don't kick so often in these days, Grands'r Angus, as you did in yours. On the other hand, Daddy David, there has been too much coddling in this country, lately, by the cowardice of men who ought to know better and the coddling has continued to the hurt of all of us!"

He sat down and looked at the clock; the face of that would, at least, tell him something definite: Blanchard said that he was talking from the club, around the corner, and would be along in five minutes.

And Blanchard arrived on time!

"I suppose I ought to be offended by what you said to me over the 'phone today, Morrison. I was hurt, at any rate!"

"So was I!" retorted Stewart, promptly. "Hurt and offended, both! So we start from the scratch, neck and neck!"

"But why do you assume that attitude on account of what I told you?"

"I was obliged to put questions to you in order to get the news that you propose to hitch up with a dominating water-power syndicate!"

"Only following out your proposition that we must get down to development in this state."

"The development is taking care of itself, Brother Blanchard. As chairman of the water-power commission, I shall submit my report to the incoming legislature. And in that report I propose to make conservation the corollary of development."

Blanchard blinked inquiringly. "What do you mean?"

"Why, I mean just this! Putting it in business terms, I propose to ask for legislation that will make the public the partners of the men who handle and control the water-power."

"I don't know how you're going about to do that in any sensible way," grumbled the other. "There have been a good many rumors about that forthcoming report of yours, Morrison. What's the big notion in keeping it so secret?"

"I have been ordered to report to the legislature, Blanchard! I have prepared my case for that general court, and customary deference and common politeness in such matters oblige me to hold my mouth till I do report officially."

"Nothing to be hidden, then?" probed the magnate.

"Not a thing--not when the proper time comes!"

"But we have been left guessing--and I don't like the sound of the rumors. You must expect big interests to get an anchor out to windward. There's no telling what a damphool legislature will do in case a theory is put up and there are no sensible business arguments to contradict it."

"As owners of water-power, Blanchard--you and I--let's bring our business arguments into the open this year, in the committee-rooms and on the floor of the House and Senate, instead of in the buzzing-corners of the lobby or down in the hotel button-holing boudoirs! Now we'll get right down to cases! You have been leaving me out of your conferences ever since I refused to drop my coin into the usual pool to hire lobbyists. I take the stand that these times are more enlightened and that we can begin to trust the people's business to the people's general court in open sessions."

Blanchard showed the heat of a man whose conscience was not entirely comfortable. "Just what is this **people** idea that you're making so much of all of a sudden, Morrison? People as partners, people as judges--people--people--" Blanchard hitched over the word wrathfully.

"People be damned?" inquired Stewart, with a provocative grin.

"There's too much of this soviet gabble loose these days. It all leads to the same thing, and you've got to choke it for the good of this government!"

"Right you are to a big extent, Blanchard! But just now we are talking of a vital problem in our own state and it has nothing to do with sovietism."

"But you spoke of making the people our partners!"

"I merely put the matter to you in a nutshell, for we'll need to be moving on pretty quick!" He glanced at the clock. He threw off his jacket and pulled on his coat.

"Partners how?"

"It will be explained in my official report, as chairman of the power and storage commission."

"I don't relish the rumors about what that report is likely to recommend."

"Rumors are prevalent, are they?"

"Prevalent, Morrison, and devilish pointed, too!"

"I suppose that's why the old horned stags of the lobby are whetting their antlers," surmised Morrison, giving piquant emphasis to his remark by a gesture toward a caribou head, a trophy of his vacation chase. "I have heard a rumor, too, Blanchard. Are they going to introduce legislation to abolish my commission and turn the whole water-power matter over to the public utilities commission?"

Blanchard flushed and said he knew nothing about any such move.

"I'm sorry that syndicate isn't taking you into their confidence," sympathized Morrison. "I know just how you feel. The boys who ought to train with me are not taking me into their conferences, either!"

"You spoke of coming down to cases!" snapped Blanchard, his uneasy conscience getting behind the mask of temper. "I don't ask you to reveal any official report. But can you tell me what this 'people-partners' thing is?"

"I can, Blanchard, because it isn't anything that is specifically a part of the report. It's principle, and principle belongs in everything. I merely apply it to the case of water-power in this state."

He went close to his caller and beamed down on him in a sociable manner. "I rather questioned my own good taste and the propriety of my effort to get on to the commission and be made its chairman. As an owner of power and of an important franchise I might be considered a prejudiced party. But I hoped I had established a bit of a reputation for square-dealing in business and I wanted to feel that my own kind were in touch with me and would have faith that I was working hard for all interests. You and I can both join in damning these demagogues and radicals and visionaries and Bolshevists. We must be practical even when we're progressive, Blanchard."

"Now you're talking sense!"

"I hope so!" But his next statement, made while the millman glared and muttered oaths, fell far short of sanity in Blanchard's estimation. "I'm fully convinced that one of the inalienable rights of the people is ownership of water-power. We franchise-proprietors ought to content ourselves with being custodians, managers, lessees of that power that comes from the lakes that God alone owns."

"Are you putting that notion in your confounded report?"

"I am."

"Are you sticking in something about confiscating the coal and the oil and the iron and--"

"Oh no!" broke in Morrison, calm in the face of fury. "Those particular packages all seem to be nicely tied up and laid on the shelf out of the people's reach. And whether they are or not is not my concern now. I'm only a little fellow up here in a small puddle, Brother Blanchard. I'm not undertaking the reorganization of the world. I'll say frankly that I don't know just what kind of legislation in regard to the already developed water-power in this state can be passed and be made constitutional. But now when coal is scarcer and high, or monopolized, at any rate, to make it high and scarce in the market, the exploiters are turning to water-power possibilities with hearty hankering, and the people are turning with hope."

"I'm afraid I'm getting hunks out of that report of yours, ahead of official time."

"You're getting the principle underlying it--and you're welcome."

"Morrison, the idea that the people have any overhead right and ownership in franchise-granted and privately developed water-power is ridiculous and danger-ous nonsense."

"It does sound a bit that way, considering the fact that the people of this state have never even taxed water-power, as such. The ideas of the fathers, who gave away the power for nothing, seem to have come down to the sons, who haven't even woke up to the fact that it's worth taxing--yes, Blanchard, taxing even to the extent that the people will get enough profits from the taxation to make 'em virtual partners! And as to the millions of horse-power yet to be developed, let the profits be called lease-money instead of taxation. Then we'll be going on a business basis without having the matter everlastingly muddled and mixed and lobbied in poli-tics!"

Blanchard knew inflexibility when he saw it; and he knew Stewart Morrison when it came to matters of business. He did not attempt argument. "Well, I'll be good and cahootedly condemned!" he exploded.

"No, you'll be helped and I'll be helped by putting this on a business basis where the radicals, if they grab off more political power, won't be able to rip it up by crazy methods; the radicals don't know when to stop when they get to reforming."

"Radicals! Confound it, it looks to me as if we had one of 'em at the head of that power commission! Morrison, have you turned Bolshevik?"

"My friend," expostulated Stewart, gently, "when you opposed the principle of prohibition the fanatics called you 'Rummy.' The name hurt your feelings."

"They had no right to impugn my motives!"

"Certainly not! It's all wrong to try to turn a trick by sticking a slurring name on to conscientiousness."

"You're turning around and hammering your friends and associates, no matter what name you put on it."

"It has always been considered perfectly proper to lobby for the big interests in this state for pay! Why shouldn't I lobby for the people for nothing?"

"You and I are the people! The business men are the people. The enterprising capitalists who pay wages are the people. The people are--"

He halted; the telephone-bell had broken in on him.

Morrison apologized with a smile and answered the call. He sprawled in his chair, his elbow on the table, and listened for a few moments. "But don't stutter so,

Joe!" he adjured. "Take your time, now, boy! Say it again!"

He attended patiently on the speaker.

"They won't take your word on the matter, you say? Why, Joe, that's not courteous in the case of an American Legion commander! Hold on! I can't come down there! I have to attend the reception at Senator Corson's."

He listened again to what was evidently expostulation and entreaty, and, while he listened, he gazed at the sullen Blanchard with an expression of mock despair.

"Joe, just a word for myself," he broke in. "I'm afraid you have pledged me a little too strongly. You went off half cocked this afternoon! Oh no! I don't take it back. I'm not a quitter to that extent. But I really didn't undertake to run the whole state government, you know! Those folks up on Capitol Hill don't need my advice, they think!"

With patience unabated he listened again. "If it's that way, Joe, I'll have to come down. I'll certainly never put an honest chap in bad or leave him in wrong, when a word can straighten the thing. Hold 'em there! I'll be right along!" He hung up.

"As I was saying," persisted Blanchard, "the people--"

Morrison put up his hand and shook his head.

"I guess we'd better hang up the joint debate on the people right here, Blanchard! What say if you come along with me and pick up a few facts? The facts may give you a new light on your theories." He hastened to a closet and secured his top-coat and his silk hat.

"Come where?"

"Down to the Central Labor Union hall. There's a big crowd waiting there."

Blanchard surveyed his own evening apparel in a mirror. "I'm headed for a reception--not the kind I'd get as the head of the Conawin corporation from a labor crowd."

"Nevertheless, I urge you to come with me. I believe that a little contact with the people in this instance will clear your thoughts."

"Another one of your riddles!" snorted the manufacturer. "What's it all about?"

"Blanchard," declared Morrison, setting his jaws grimly while he pondered for a moment and then coming out explosively, "it's about what we may expect from the people when damned fools try to play politics according to the old rules in these new times. It's about what we may expect of the people when they're denied a showdown by men at the head of public affairs. There's trouble brewing in the city of Marion to-night. What would you do if you happened to glance out of your office window and saw a leak spurting big as a lead-pencil from the base of the Conawin dam? You'd know the leak would be as big as a hogshead in a few minutes, wouldn't you?"

"Yes!" admitted the other.

"You'd get to that leak and plug it mighty quick, wouldn't you?"

"No need to ask!"

"Well, this is a hurry call and I need your help."

"I don't stand in well with the labor crowd--" demurred Blanchard.

"I know all that! You're hiring too many aliens and Red radicals in your mill! But you ought to have some influence with your own gang, such as they are! I suspect that they're the leading troublemakers down in that hall. Blanchard, if you're not afraid of your own men, come along!" He clapped the millman on the shoulder and led the way toward the door.

"If there are scalawags starting that 'state steal' howl again somebody ought to tell 'em that there are three machine-guns and plenty of loaded rifles on Capitol Hill to-night, and the men behind 'em propose to shoot to kill," stated Blanchard, vengefully, shaking his silk hat.

Morrison whirled on him. "You're just the man to go down there and tell 'em so! You probably have inside information. All I know is hearsay! I'll advise 'em and you threaten 'em. Come along, Blanchard! We'll make a good team!"

V
THE MEN WHO WERE WAITING TO BE SHOWN

While Commander Lanigan talked with the mayor from a telephone-booth in a drugstore under Central Labor Union hall, Post-Adjutant Demeter stood with his nose pressed against the glass door, waiting anxiously.

Lanigan pushed open the door with one hand while he hung up the receiver with the other, and by his precipitate exit nigh bowled his adjutant over; Mr. Lanigan, it was plain to be seen, was wound up tightly that evening and his mainspring was operating him by jumps.

"He's the boy! He's coming! Tell the world so! And I'll go back up-stairs and tell them blistered sons o' seefo that there are such things as truth and a bar o' soap in this country, spite o' the fact they have never used either one!"

Demeter followed his commander into the street.

In spite of his haste, Lanigan was halted; he gazed up into the heavens, his breath streaming on the crackly-cold air.

The skies were blazing with shuttlings of lambent flame. From nadir to zenith the mystic light shivered and sheeted. Never had Lanigan beheld a more vivid display of the phenomenon of the aurora borealis. He seemed to be waiting for something. He sighed and shook his head.

"Peter, my heart jumped at first glimpse! 'Tis like the flash of the Argonne big guns! Thank God, the thunder of 'em isn't following!"

"Yes, thank God!" murmured Demeter, his soul in his tones!

They stood there for a few minutes, shoulder to shoulder, the contact of arm with arm serving for an exchange of thoughts between those veterans in a silence that would have been profaned by words.

The phantasmagoria overhead was shifting infinitely and rapidly; there were flashes that seemed to presage a thunderous roar of an explosion and were more bodeful because the hush aloft in the heavenly spaces remained unbroken; then the filaments and streamers of light made one mighty oriflamme across the skies, an expanse of woven hues, wavering and lashing as if a great wind were threshing across the main fabric and flinging its attendant bannerets.

"It's in the air; it's in the nerves! It puts hell into a man, doesn't it, Peter?"

"Yes!"

"It was in that telephone back there! It crackled and snapped! A lot of it may be in those poor fools up in that hall--and they ain't knowing what the matter is with 'em! You and I have been over in the Big Bow-wow, boy, and we have had some good lessons in how to handle rattled nerves. I guess it's up to us to hold things steady, as experts. Soothe 'em and smooth 'em! It was All-Wool Morrison's lesson to me to-day! Soft and careful with 'em, seeing that they're full of what's in the air this night, and don't know just what ails 'em!"

He lowered his gaze from the skies. A man was passing on his way toward the door of the hall.

Lanigan had just laid down a general rule of diplomatic conduct for the evening, but he made a prompt exception. He leaped on the man, struggled with him for a moment, and yanked off a red necktie, taking with it the man's collar and a part of his shirt, "But some stuff that they're full of can't be smoothed out--it's got to be whaled out!" panted Lanigan. He did not release his captive. "The nerve o' ye, parading your red wattles on a night like this, ye Tom Gobbler of a Bullshevist!"

"I have the right to pick the color of my own necktie!" snarled the man.

"Not for the reason why you picked it! Not to wear it up into that hall, my bucko boy!"

When the man expostulated with oaths, Lanigan tripped him and held him on the sidewalk. "Hush your yawp! You can't fool me about your taste in ties! I know what's behind that color like I'd know what's behind an Orangeman's yellow! I don't need to wait for him to hooray for the battle o' the Boyne ere I get my brick ready! Peter, frisk his pockets!"

Demeter obeyed.

A crowd was collecting. Through the press rushed a young man. "Need help,

Commander?"

"Only keep your eye peeled to see that another Bullshevist don't sneak up and kick me from behind, after the like o' the breed!"

Demeter's exploration produced a bulldog revolver, a slungshot, a packet of pamphlets, and several small red flags.

"What's your name?" demanded the commander.

"No business of yours!"

Lanigan kneeled on the captive and roweled cruel thumbs into the man's neck. "Out with it before I dig deeper for it."

"Nicolai Krylovensky!"

"I knew it must be bad, but I didn't think it was as bad as that! I don't blame ye for trying to keep it mum! And ye look as though it tasted bitter coming up. I'll not poison me own mouth." He stood up and yanked the man to his feet. "So I'll call ye Bill the Bomber! Where do ye work, or don't ye work?"

"Conawin!"

"I thought so! One of that bunch down there that's trying to undermine the best government on the face of the earth. Come along! I've got a bit o' business on hand right now and I need you in it."

Then he turned, pushing the man ahead of him.

Lanigan became aware that the young fellow who had proffered aid was muttering in a derogatory fashion.

"What's on your mind, Jeff?" demanded the commander, recognizing a member of the post.

"Nothing!"

"I'm in an inquiring turn o' mind right now," rasped Lanigan. "And ye have just seen me go after information. I heard ye damning something. Ye'd best make me understand that you wasn't damning *me*!"

"I sure wasn't, sir! But as for this government being the best, I want to say--"

Lanigan's yelp broke in like an explosion. "Hold this Bullshevist, Peter! I want both hands free!"

"I wasn't saying anything against our government, Commander Lanigan! Not a word!" wailed the overseas man. "So help me!"

"I'm in a soothing frame of mind this night," returned the ex-sergeant. "I have been having some good lessons in soothing from the mayor of Marion, God bless him! I was nigh making a fool of myself till he showed me that the soothing way is the best way. And I shall keep right on soothing. But this is a night when the plain truth and the word of man-to-man have got to operate to prevent trouble! And I want the truth out o' ye, Jeff Tolson, or else ye'll be calling for toast, well soaked, in the hospital in the morning!"

"I went up to one of them sissy slackers--"

"Mind the kind of a name ye stick on to a soldier of the government! Do ye see who's listening?" He grabbed his prisoner again and shook him. "Be careful of what you say as an American citizen in the hearing of rats like this, Tolson! It encourages 'em. They think we mean it. Get the bile out of your system in a strictly family fuss! Spit out a lot you don't mean, if it's going to make you feel better! But first slam down the windows so that the outsiders can't overhear. I'll see you later!"

"But I want you to get me right, Commander," Tolson pleaded. "I went up to one of the boys to show him how to hold his gun and he banged me with the butt of it!"

"He did!" Lanigan clicked his teeth and showed that he was having hard work to control his own resentment.

"I was only trying to be helpful. I tried to take his gun and show him. And he insulted an overseas veteran!"

Lanigan had himself in hand again. "Tried to take away his gun, you say! You in civics and he in uniform and on duty! Jeff, if it's that hard to wake up and know that you're no longer a soldier, I reckon your wrist-watch is acting too much like a reminder-string around a Jane's finger! Better hang it from the end of your nose. It's a wonder he didn't give you the bayonet!"

"The butt was aplenty, sir!"

"I can stand it better to be banged on the knob by a gun-butt by a good American than batted in the eye by this color on a Bullshevist!" asserted Lanigan, waving the red necktie that he still retained in his clutch. He gave the owner of it another push. "Along with you, Bill the Bomber."

Tolson trailed. "But what are they trying to do up on Capitol Hill, sir? What does it all mean?"

"I don't know," confessed the commander. He drove his way through the bystanders. "You see, boys, I have started in along the way of telling the truth to-night. So I own up that I don't know! We're going to find out what it means!" He kept on toward the door of the hall with his prisoner. "I've arranged to have a man come down here and tell us what it means and tell us how to act."

"Well, he'll know more than anybody else I have tackled on the subject to-night," said Tolson, sourly. "He's a wonder, if he does know!"

"He's All-Wool Morrison--and that's your answer, buddie," retorted Lanigan. And that answer did seem to suffice for Tolson.

There were many men on the stairs leading up to the hall, and the elbowing throng at the door of the auditorium furnished further evidence of the overflowing nature of the gathering.

"Gangway!" commanded Lanigan at the top of his voice. "Make way, there! I'm bringing something straight in my mouth and something crooked in my mit, and neither one of 'em will ye have till free passage is made to the platform."

The crowd's curiosity served effectively to clear that passage.

Lanigan's captive went along, sullenly unresisting. There was no opportunity for rebellion in that mob that opened a narrow passage grudgingly, only to pack together again in a solid mass. But certain men whom Krylovensky passed or men who caught his eye by swift motions spat whispers at him in a language that Lanigan did not understand.

"Is it three cheers that your brother rattlesnakes are giving ye in the natural hissing way of 'em?" inquired the captor. "They're a fine bunch!"

With his hand twisted tightly into the slack of the man's coat and the torn shirt, the ex-sergeant forced the prisoner up the short stairs that conducted to the platform; Demeter followed.

Tobacco smoke streamed up in whirls from the banked faces that filled the hall from side to side, and the eddying clouds floated in strata above the rows of heads. Lanigan peered sternly at the crowd through the haze. "Here I am back! And I'm thanking the good saints for the few mouthfuls of fresh air I got outside and the news I got, and for this here I found and fetched along. I need him. I was on a jury once, in a murder case, and they had the tool that done the job and the lawyers tagged it Exhibit A. This is it! He's got a name, but if I tried to say it, it would cramp my jaws and hold my mouth open so long that I'd get assifixiated with this smoke.

This is Bill the Bomber! Demeter, hold up the goods we found on him!"

The post-adjutant obeyed the order.

"Now, Bill the Bomber," demanded Lanigan, "tell me and the bunch what's the big idea of the arsenal, in a peaceful American city?"

"Is it peaceful?" screamed the captive, at bay. "There are soldiers marching with guns. There are men threatening and cursing! There are--"

"Hold right on--right where you are! Are you naturalized?"

"No!"

"Well, let me tell you, you red-gilled Bullshevist, that till you're a voting American citizen, our private and personal and strictly family rows are none of your damn' business! All American citizens kindly applaud!"

He was answered by cheers, stamping feet, and clapping hands.

"Contrary-minded?" he invited in the silence that followed.

"Hiss a few hisses, you snakes!" he urged. "Or show those red flags you're carrying in your pockets!"

There was no demonstration, either by act or by word.

Lanigan pushed his captive to the rear of the platform and jolted him down into a chair behind which, on the wall, was draped a large United States flag. "Set there and see if you can't absorb a little of the white and blue into your system, along with the red that's already there," counseled the patriot. "You're going to hear some man-talk in a little while, and I hope 'twill do you good!"

A man in the audience rose to his feet when Lanigan marched back to the front of the rostrum.

"I am a voter here, yet I was born in another country. Will you allow me to ask a question, Commander Lanigan?"

"Sure! But let's start even on names. What's yours?"

"Otto Weisner!"

Lanigan made a grimace. "But even at that I'm going to keep my word and I call on all present to back me up."

"See here!" bawled a voice from a far corner. "Let that Hun wait! How about your word to us in another matter? Where's the mayor of Marion?"

"The mayor of Marion is on his way to this hall!" The soldier's face was set into a grim expression and deep ridges lined his jaws. "I gave you all once tonight his word to me that he'd stand up for us on Capitol Hill, whatever it is they're trying to put over. I got the hoot from you when I said it. You wouldn't take my word and I just told him so. Now he's coming down here for himself! I say it. If some gent would like to hoot another hoot on that subject will he kindly step up here and hoot?" He doubled his fists.

There was no indication that anybody wanted to accept the invitation.

"Very well, then!" proceeded Lanigan. "I'm in a soothing frame of mind, myself, and I hope you're all soothed, too. And so that we won't be wasting any time on a busy evening I'll state that the meeting is now open for that question, Mister Weisner. Shoot!"

VI
THE MAN'S WORD OF THE MAYOR OF MARION

Commander Lanigan had constituted himself the presiding officer of the assemblage that had been gathered under no special auspices and by no formal call. It was a flocking together of those uneasy persons who had been informing one another that they wanted to be shown! Mr. Lanigan's unconventional methods in the chair were tolerated because he had displayed much alacrity in putting the mob in the way of securing information from such high authority as the mayor of Marion. Chairman Lanigan's compelling methods in pumping this time-filler kept up the interest of the auditors.

"I belong to der Socialist party," stated Weisner.

"We don't want no Boche speeches!" warned a voice.

In his absorption in affairs, Lanigan was still hanging on to the captured red necktie. He noted that fact and held the danger signal aloft. "I don't approve of this color at this time," he remarked. "But when I have seen it waved in times past I have known that it meant a blast going off or a train coming on, and I have never taken foolish chances. Does the objecting gent down there in the corner need any further instruction from here, or shall I come down and whisper in his ear?"

Silence assured him and again he ordered Mr. Weisner to ask his question.

The querist ceased from showing deference to the volunteer in the chair; Weisner turned his back on Lanigan and addressed all in hearing, shaking his fist over his head: "Who tells me dis vhat I don'd know? Does Karl Trimbach his seat haf in der State House vhere der Socialists haf elected him?"

"If he has been elected, sure he'll have his seat," declared Lanigan, loyally. "That's the way we do things in this country! Why shouldn't he have his seat?"

"Den vhere--vhere is dot zertificate dot should show to Karl Trimbach dot he shall valk into der State House und sit on his seat? He don't get it. Why don'd dey send it?" Weisner bellowed his questions. He threshed his arms wildly about him.

"This is no time to be starting anything, Weisner! Don't stand there and be a Dutch windmill--be an American citizen! Soothe yourself!"

Another gentleman arose. He was distinctly Hibernian. He wore an obtrusive ribbon-knot of green, white, and yellow, the colors of the flag of the Irish Republic. "Lanigan, ye may not be able to reply satisfact'rily to th' questions o' the sour-krauters, but when I ask ye whether or not the Hon'rable Danyel O'Donnell, riprisent'thive-ilict, put in that high office be th' votes o' th' Marion pathrits of a free Ireland, takes his sate, what does th' blood o' yer race say to me?"

Lanigan blinked and hesitated. He felt the sudden Celtic surging of a natural impulse to run with his kind, to swing the cudgel valiantly for the cause, and to ask questions after the shindy was over.

"You know th' principles o' th' Hon'rable O'Donnell," insisted the speaker in loud tones. "Tis his intint to raise his voice in th' halls o' state and shout ear-rly and late, 'Whativer it is ye're about, gents, it all may be very well, but what will ye be doing for the cause o' free Ireland?' That's th' kind of a hero we're putting in th' State House en the hill."

"Putting a pest there, ye mean!" returned Lanigan.

"Is that the blood o' yer race speaking?"

"No, it's the common sense up here," declared the commander, tapping his knuckles against the side of his head. "Look, here, Mulcahy, my man! You're spouting about a subject that's too big for me to understand or you to explain. And that's why you're muddling yourself and mixing up the minds of others with your questions. I ask you no questions. I'm going to tell you something--and it's so! If the kids in your family was down with the measles, and the missus was all snarled up with the tickdoolooroo and you wasn't feeling none too well yourself, what with a hold-over, a black eye, and a lot o' bumps, what would you--Hold on! I say, I ask no questions! I know the answer. If Tommy O'Rourke came howling and whooping into your back door and asked you to go out and shin up a tree and fetch down his tomcat, ye'd tell Tommy to bounce along and mind his own matters till ye'd settled your own--and if he didn't go you'd kick him out."

"I'm discussing th' rights and wrongs of a suffering people."

"And playing safe for yourself because the subject is so big--and putting others in wrong because they can't settle all the troubles of the universe offhand to suit ye! My family is America, Mulcahy! It ought to be yours, first, last, and all the time. But we've got our own aches to mind, right now! And the way I'm putting it, a plain man can understand. If the tomcat don't know enough to come down all by himself, leave him be up there till the doctor tells us we can be out and about."

Weisner put his demand again and Mulcahy made the affair a vociferous duet; other men were on their feet, shouting. But a top sergeant has a voice of his own and a manner to go with the voice: Lanigan yelled the chorus into silence.

While he was engaged in this undertaking a diversion at the door assisted him. The crowd parted. Men shouted, pleading, "Make way for the mayor!"

Morrison came up the aisle toward the platform, Blanchard at his heels.

There were cheers--plenty of them!

But sibilantly, steadily, ominously the derogatory hisses were threaded with the frank clamor of welcome; hisses whose sources were concealed.

The mayor ran up the steps of the platform and marched to Lanigan, doffing the silk hat and extending his hand cordially.

With his forearm the commander scrubbed off the sweat that was streaming down into his eyes. "It's been like hauling a seventy-five into action with mules, Your Honor! For the love o' Mike, shoot!"

The hisses continued along with the applause when Stewart faced the throng.

Lanigan leaped off the platform, not bothering with the stairs. "I'm going to wade through this grass," he yelped. "God pity the rattlesnake I locate!"

A shrill voice from somewhere dared to taunt, "Pipe the dude!"

Morrison smiled. He had unbuttoned his topcoat, and his evening garb, in that congress of the rough and ready, made him as conspicuous as a bird of paradise in a rookery. "I seem to be double-crossed by my scenic effects, Blanchard," he stated in an aside to the magnate, who had stepped upon the platform because that elevation seemed safer than a position on the floor. "We must fix that! Furthermore, it's hot up here!" He pulled off his top-coat. He realized that the full display of his formal dress only aggravated the situation. In St. Ronan's mill he mingled with men in his shirtsleeves. He turned and saw Nicolai Krylovensky in the chair where Lanigan had thrust him. There was no other chair on the platform. Stewart hastily laid the coat across the alien's knees. "Keep 'em out of the dirt for me, will you, brother? I'm notional about good cloth!" He pushed his silk hat into the man's hand and then he stripped off the claw-hammer and white waistcoat, piled them upon the overcoat; and whirled to face his audience.

All eyes were engaged with the mayor.

Krylovensky, unobserved, let the garments slip to the floor and dropped the hat.

"Now, boys, we'll get down to business together in an understanding way! What's it all about?" Stewart invited, cheerily.

"Just a minute!" cried Lanigan, heading off all the possibilities that were threatening by a general powwow. "I've just been up against the bunch here, Mister Mayor, and they're trying to turn it into a congress-of-nations debate, and it ain't nothing of the kind. And I know you're in a hurry, and we don't expect a speech!"

"You won't get one!" retorted the mayor, tartly. "I have dropped down here merely in a business way to find out what's wanted of me as the executive head of this city."

"Your Honor, I have been preaching the notion of telling the truth to-night, and I'm going to come across with something about myself," confessed Lanigan, manfully. "I've gone off half cocked twice to-day. I've been thinking it over and I realize it. In your office I grabbed in on a word or two you said and took it for granted that you were going to lift the whole load of the people's case up at the State House and stop anything being put over on the people, whatever it is the Big Boys are planning. But you didn't promise me to do it."

"I did not, Joe!"

"And I've been telling this gang that you did promise me and that I'd get you down here to back up my word. I don't ask you to back up my lie. You're too square a proposition, Mayor Morrison!"

"After that man-talk, Joe, I've just naturally got to make a little of my own. And the boys can't help seeing that both you and I mean all right. I did give you good reasons for jumping at conclusions as you say you did, Joe! Understand that, boys! But my head isn't swelled to the extent that I believe I can settle everything.

"Now that I'm down here I'll say this. I'll do everything I can, as mayor of Marion, to straighten things out to-night so that the people won't be left guessing.

Guessing starts gabble and gabble starts trouble! Don't do any more shouting about 'state steal,' and don't allow others to shout. Most of us don't know what it means, anyway, and others don't care, so long as it gives 'em a chance to stir up riots and grab off something for themselves under cover of the trouble. There are a lot of outsiders in this country, standing ready to make just such plays! Don't let your ears be scruffed by mischief-makers, boys. Let's have our city come through with a clean name! I'm going to do my part as best I can. But you've all got to do yours-- understand that!" He smacked his fist down into his palm.

"Do you bromise me dot Karl Trimbach gets dot seat?" boomed Mr. Weisner.

"The same question goes as to th' Hon'rable Danyel O'Donnell," said Adherent Mulcahy.

"I cannot promise."

Then sounded that voice of the unknown troublemaker, sneeringly shrill, the senseless, passion-provoking common, human fife of the mob spirit, persistently present and consistently cowardly in concealment. "Of course you don't promise anything to the people! Dudes stand together! Go back and dance!"

Lanigan began to claw a passage for himself.

"Stand where you are, Joe!" commanded Stewart. "Don't flatter a fool by making any account of him!"

"Those kinds of fools are going to make trouble in this city before the night is over, Your Honor!"

"That's the trouble with politics," declared Mulcahy. "Ye can't get a square promise in politics fr'm th' Big Boys!"

Morrison put up a monitory forefinger.

"But you can get a square promise from me in business--and I can see that it's time to give that promise and make it specific. That's the way a business contract must be drawn. Hear me, then! It's the business of this city to see that no man abuses its good name or its hospitality, no matter whether he's a resident or comes here because it's the capital of the state. And I'll see to it that the men up at the State House end understand that they must play fair for the good of all of us. You must understand the same at this end. I'll take no sides in politics. The men who are entitled to their seats in this legislature will have those seats. I'm only one man, boys! But one man who is perfectly honest and is depending on the right will find the whole law of the land behind him--and wise men and good men have attended to the law. Will you take my word and let it stand that way between us?"

A chorused yell of assent greeted him.

"All right! It's a contract! Mind your end of it!"

He turned sharply from them and faced Krylovensky. The alien leaped up and kicked the mayor's garments to one side.

"Say! See here, my friend!" expostulated Stewart.

"Down with rulers!" screamed the man. "I'll be a martyr, but not a hat-rack!"

The mayor walked toward the frantic person. "I'm sorry! I was thoughtless!"

"You and your kind think of nothing but yourselves. You try to make slaves of free citizens of the world!" Krylovensky had been buffeted and had controlled himself. But the fires of his narrow fanaticism were now whirling in his brain; sitting there on high before the eyes of his fellows, the men to whom he had been preaching the doctrines of soviet sovereignty--the supremacy of the people--he had just suffered what his distorted views held as the enormity of ignominy; he had been used as a clothes-tree for discarded garments. Used by a ruler!

When Morrison, not realizing that the man had become little short of a maniac, stooped to pick up the garments Krylovensky dove forward and struck the mayor's face with open hand. "Now throw me to your dogs! I'll die a martyr to my cause!" he squalled.

The mayor snapped upright and laid restraining hands on the man who was threatening him with doubled fists.

A roaring mob came milling toward the platform.

"I'll be a martyr!" insisted the alien.

"I can't humor you to that extent," replied Morrison, in the tone of a father denying indulgence in the case of a wilful child.

He got between the man and the mob. He held Krylovensky from him with one hand and put up the other protestingly, authoritatively.

"No man that's a real man lets another man bang him in the face," declared Lanigan with fury.

"That's a nice point, to be argued later by us when things are quieter, Joe. Stand back!"

"I'm going to kill him even if you haven't got the grit to do it." Lanigan was showing the bitter disappointment of a worshiper kicking among the fragments of a shattered idol.

"I won't allow you to do that, Joe! A dead man can't answer questions. Stand back, all of you, I say!" He twisted the grip of his hand in the man's collar until Krylovensky ceased his struggles.

"Do you work in this city?" asked the mayor.

"He works in the Conawin," shouted Lanigan. "And I shook him down this evening for a gun, a knob-knocker, and a lot of red flags."

Blanchard was backed against the big Stars and Stripes, apprehensively seeking refuge from the crowd massing on the platform. Morrison caught his eye. "Seems to be one of your patriots, Blanchard! Shall I hand him over to you?"

"I never saw the renegade before."

"I'm sorry you don't get into your mill the way I do into mine. I'd like to know something about this gentleman who doesn't show any inclination to speak for himself."

"I'm not afraid to speak," declared the captive, all cautiousness burned out of him by the fires of his martyr zeal. "I'm an ambassador of the grand and good Soviet Government of Russia."

The mayor preserved his serenity.

"Ah, I think I understand! One of the estimable gentlemen who have been coming to us by the way of the Mexican border of late! When you picked up such a good command of our language, my friend, it's too bad you didn't pick up a better understanding of our country. I haven't any time just now to give you an idea of it, sir. I'll have a talk with you to-morrow."

The mayor had seen Officer Rellihan at the door of the hall. As a satellite, Rellihan was constant in his attendance on his controlling luminary in public places, even though the luminary issued no special orders to that effect; Morrison's intended visit to the hall had been quickly advertised down-town.

Stewart glanced about him and found Rellihan at his elbow.

"Here's the honorable ambassador of Soviet Russia, Rellihan," said his chief. "Take him along with you, keep harm from him on the way, and see that he is well lodged for the night in a place where enemies can't get at him."

"I know just the right place, Your Honor," stated the policeman, pulling his club from his belt and waving it to part the throng.

Morrison broke in upon Lanigan's mumbled threats. "Mind your manners, Joe!"

"But he hit you!"

The mayor picked up his garments, one by one, inspected them, and dusted them with his palm; then he pulled them on. The crowd gazed at him.

"He hit you!" Lanigan insisted, bellicosely. "When a man hits me, I lick him!"

"You're a good fighter, Joe," agreed His Honor, running his forearm about his silk hat to smooth the nap. "But let me tell you something! Unless you put yourself in better shape there'll be a fellow some day that you'll want to lick, and you won't be able to lick him, and you'll be almighty sorry because you can't turn the trick."

"Show me the feller, Mister Mayor!"

"Go look in the glass, Joe."

"Lick myself--is that what you mean, sir?"

"Sure! If you can do it when it ought to be done, you'll have the right to feel rather proud of yourself."

He invited Blanchard with a side wag of his head and led the way from the hall.

"Morrison, let me say this," blurted the mill magnate, when they were on their way in the limousine. "By reason of this people-side-partner notion of yours, you have gone to work and got yourself into an infernal fix. How do you expect to make good that promise?"

"I suppose I did sound rather boastful, but I had to put it strong. A mealy-mouthed promise wouldn't hold them in line!"

"But that promise only encourages such muckers in the belief that they have a right to demand, to boss their betters, to call for accountings and concessions. You have put the devil into 'em!"

"I hope not! Faith in a contract--that's what I tried to put into 'em. They'll wait and let me operate!"

"Operate! You're one man against the whole state government and you're defying single-handed the political powers! You can't deliver the goods! That gang down-town will wait about so long and then 'twill be hell to pay to-night!"

Morrison had found his pipe in his overcoat pocket. He was soothing himself with a smoke on the way toward the Corson mansion.

"But why worry so much when the night is still young?" he queried, placidly.

VII
THE THIN CRUST OVER BOILING LAVA

Senator Corson, at the head of the receiving-line, attended strictly to the task in hand as an urbane and assiduous host.

Wonted by long political usage to estimate everything on the basis of votes for and against, he was entirely convinced, by the face of the returns that evening, that the reception he was tendering was a grand success, unanimously indorsed; he would have been immensely surprised to learn that under his roof there was a bitterly incensed, furiously resentful minority that was voting "No!"

The "Yes!" was by the applausive, open, *viva voce* vote of all those who filed past him and shook his hand and thronged along toward the buffet that was operated in *de luxe* style by a metropolitan caterer's corps of servants.

The Senator's mansion was spacious and luxuriously appointed, and the millions from the products of his timber-land barony were lavishly behind his hospitality. Consoled by the knowledge that Corson could well afford the treat, his guests, after that well-understood quality in human nature, relished the hospitality more keenly. At the buffet all the plates were piled high. In the smoking-room men took handfuls of the Senator's cigars from the boxes. And the pleasantry connected with Governor Lawrence North's custom in campaigning was frequently heard. It was related of North that he always thriftily passed his cigars by his own hand and counseled the recipient: "Help yourself! Take all you want! Take two!"

The guests adopted the comfortable attitude that Corson had dropped down home to Marion to pay a debt which he owed to his constituents, and they all jumped in with alacrity to help him pay it.

While the orchestra played and the ware of the buffet clattered, the joyous voices of the overwhelming majority gave Senator Corson to understand that he was the idol of his people and the prop of the state.

The minority kept her mouth closed and her teeth were set hard.

The minority was racked by agony that extended from finger-tips to shoulder.

The minority was distinctly groggy.

This minority was compassed in the person of a single young and handsome matron who was Mrs. J. Warren Stanton in her home city Blue Book, and Doris in the family register of Father Silas Daunt, and "Dorrie" in the good graces of Brother Coventry Daunt.

In addition she was the close friend, the social mentor, the volunteer chaperon for Lana Corson, whose mother had become voicelessly and meekly the mistress of the Corson mausoleum, as she had been meekly and unobtrusively the mistress of the Corson mansion.

Miss Lana had suddenly observed warning symptoms in the case of Mrs. Stanton.

Mrs. Stanton, according to a solicitous friend's best judgment, was no longer assisting in the receiving-line; Mrs. Stanton needed assistance!

Therefore, sooner than the social code might have permitted in an affair of more rigorously formal character, Lana left the receiving job to her father and the Governor and the aides, and rescued Mrs. Stanton and accompanied the young matron to the sanctuary of a boudoir above-stairs.

Mrs. Stanton extended to the tender touch of her maid a wilted hand, lifted by a stiffened arm, the raising of which pumped a groan from the lady. The white glove which incased the hand and arm was smutched liberally in telltale fashion.

"Pull it off, Hibbert! But careful! Don't pull off my fingers unless they are very loose and beyond hope. But hurry! Let me know the worst as soon as possible."

"I realize that the reception--" began Lana.

"Reception!" Mrs. Stanton snapped her head around to survey her youthful hostess. The flame on the matron's cheeks matched the fire in her tones.

"Reception, say you? Lana Corson, don't you know the difference between a reception and a political rally?"

"I'm sorry, Doris! But father simply must do this duty thing when the legislature meets. The members expect it. It keeps up his fences, he says. It's politics!"

"I'm glad my father is a banker instead of a United States Senator. If this is what a Senator has to do when he comes back to his home, I think he'd better stay in Washington and send down a carload of food and stick a glove on the handle of the town pump and let his constituents operate that! At any rate, the power wouldn't be wasted in a dry time!"

Lana surveyed her own hand. The glove was not immaculate any more, but it covered a firm hand that was unweary. "Father has given me good advice. It's to shake the hand of the other chap, not let yours be shaken."

"Those brutes gave me no chance!"

"I noticed that they were very enthusiastic, Doris. I'm afraid you're too handsome!"

But that flattery did not placate Mrs. Stanton. "It's only a rout and a rabble, Lana! The feminine element does not belong in it. My father dines his gentlemen and accomplishes his objects. And I think you have become one of these political hypocrites! You actually looked as if you were enjoying that performance downstairs."

"I was enjoying it, Doris! I was helping my father as best I could, and at the same time I was meeting many of my old, true friends. I'm glad to be home again." The girl was unaffectedly sincere in her statement.

The glove was off and Mrs. Stanton was surveying her hand, wriggling the fingers tentatively.

"And they all seemed so glad to see me that I'm a bit penitent," Lana went on. "I'm ashamed to own up to myself that I have allowed California and Palm Beach to coax me away from Marion these last two winters. I ought to have come down here with father. I'm not talking like a politician now, Doris. Honestly, I'm stanch for old friends!"

"I trust you don't think I'm an ingrate in the case of my own old friends, Lana!" Mrs. Stanton, unappeased, was willing to take issue right then with anybody, on that topic. "But the main trouble with old friends is, they take too many liberties. Your old friends certainly did take liberties with my poor hand, and they took liberties with your own private business in my hearing."

"How--in what way?"

"I overheard persons say distinctly, over and over again, that one feature of this--no, I'll not muddle my own ideas of society functions by calling it a reception-

-they declared that your father proposes to announce to-night in his home town your engagement to Coventry."

The question that she did not put into words she put into the searching, quizzical stare she gave Lana.

"Ah!" remarked Miss Corson, revealing nothing either by tone or countenance.

"It looks to me as if you've been receiving other lessons from your father, outside of the hand-shaking art. You are about as non-committal as the best of our politicians, Lana dear!"

For reply the Senator's daughter smiled. The smile was so ingenuous that it ought to have disarmed the young matron of her petulance.

But Mrs. Stanton went on with the sharp insistence of one who had discovered an opportunity and proposed to make the most of it. "Seeing that the matter has come up in this way--quite by chance--" Mrs. Stanton did not even blink when she said it--"though I never would have presumed to speak of it to you, Lana, without good and sufficient provocation--I think that you and Coventry should have confided in me, first of all. Of course, I know well enough how matters stand! I really believe I do! But I think I'm entitled to know, officially, to put it that way, as much as your highly esteemed old friends here in Marion know."

"Yes," agreed Miss Corson.

"But *first*, Lana dear! To know it first--as a sister should! I'm not blaming you! I realize that you met some of those aforesaid old, true friends while you were out around the city to-day. One does drop confidences almost without realizing how far one goes, when old friends are met. I'm sure such reports as I overheard couldn't be made up out of whole cloth."

Mrs. Stanton's air and tone were certainly provoking, but Miss Corson's composure was not ruffled. "Out of the knowledge that you profess in regard to old friends, Doris, you must realize that they are energetic and liberal guessers." She turned toward the door.

"Where are you going?"

"To my room for a fresh pair of gloves, dear."

"Do you mean to tell me that you're going back for another turn among those jiu-jitsu experts?"

"We're to have dancing later."

"For myself, I'd as soon dance with performing bears. I must be excused. I'll do anything in reason, but I have reached my limit!"

Lana walked back to her, both hands extended. "You have been a dear martyr to the cause of politics. But now you are going to be the queen of our little festival. Listen, Doris! All the political buzzing bees will be thinning out, right soon. Those elderly gentlemen from the country who shook hands with a good Grange grip-- they'll be wanting to get plenty of sleep so as to be wide awake to-morrow to hear the Governor's inaugural address. The other vigorous gentlemen who are so deeply in politics will be hurrying back to their hotels for their caucuses, or whatever it is they have to attend to in times like these. And the younger folks, who have no politics on their minds, will stay and enjoy themselves. There are some really dear folks in Marion!"

"I thank you for the information," returned Mrs. Stanton, dryly. "It's important if true. But there's other information that's more important in my estimation just now and you don't allow me the opportunity to thank you for it."

"I have been thinking, Doris! I really don't feel in the mood, when all those friends are under my roof, to stand here and brand them as prevaricators. Mayn't we let the matter stand till later?"

"Until after it has been officially announced?" queried Mrs. Stanton, sarcastically.

"I'm afraid that father's lessons have trained me better in political methods than I have realized," said Lana, meekly apologetic. "Because, right now, I'm obliged to run the risk of offending you, Doris, by quoting him and making his usual statement my rule of conduct."

"Well?"

"'Nothing can be officially declared until all the returns are in.'"

"What am I to understand from that?"

"It isn't so awfully clear, I know! But let's not talk any more about it."

Lana had dropped her friend's hands. She took them again in her grasp and swung Mrs. Stanton's arms to and fro in girlish and frolicsome fashion. "Now go ahead and be your own jolly Doris Stanton! You're going to meet folks who'll understand you and appreciate all your wit. One especially I'll name. I don't know why he's so late in coming, for he had a special invitation from my own mouth. He's the mayor of Marion!"

"What?" demanded Mrs. Stanton, irefully, pulling away from the girl who was trying to coax back good nature. "Picking out another politician for my special consideration, after what I have been through?"

"Oh, he's not a politician, Doris dear! Father says he isn't one; he says so himself and his party newspaper here in the city says regularly that he isn't, in a complimentary way, and the opposition paper says so in a sneering way--and I suppose that makes the thing unanimous. He is one of my oldest friends; he was my hero when I was a little girl in school; he is tall and big and handsome and--"

Mrs. Stanton narrowed her eyes.

She broke in impatiently on the panegyric. "I'm so thoroughly disgusted with the ways of politics, Lana, that I draw the line at a speech of nomination. You said you'd name him! Who is he?"

"Stewart Morrison."

"I thought so!" Mrs. Stanton's tone was vastly significant.

Lana flushed. The composure that she had been maintaining was losing its serenity and her friend noted that fact and became more irritable.

"My dear Lana, I gathered so much enlightenment from the twittering of those old friends of yours down-stairs that you'll not be obliged, I think, to break your most excellent rule of reticence in order to humor my impertinent curiosity in this instance!"

"Don't be sarcastic with me, Doris! I don't find it as funny as when you're caustic with other folks."

"There does seem to be a prevailing lack of humor in the affairs of this evening," acknowledged Mrs. Stanton. "We'll drop the subject, dear!"

"I don't like you to feel that I'm putting you to one side as my dearest friend--not in anything."

"If you haven't felt like being candid with me in a matter where I'd naturally be vitally interested, I can hardly expect you to pour out your heart about a dead-and-gone love-affair with a rustic up in these parts. I understood from the chatter of your old friends that it *is* dead and gone. I can congratulate you on that proof of your newer wisdom, Lana. It shows that my counsels haven't been entirely wasted on you."

"It was dead and gone before you began to counsel me, Doris. It's not a matter of withholding confidence from you. Why should I talk about such things to anybody?"

"Oh, a discreet display of scalp-locks decorates a boudoir and interests one's friends," vouchsafed the worldly matron.

"Such confidences are atrocious!" Miss Corson displayed spirit.

"Now both of us are getting peppery, dear Lana, and I always reserve that privilege exclusively for myself in all my friendly relations. I have to keep a sharp edge on my tongue because folks expect me to perform the social taxidermy in my set, and it's only brutal and messy if done with a dull tool. Run and get your gloves! But take your own time in returning to me. There are still two of my fingers that need a further period of convalescence."

Mrs. Stanton promptly neglected her duties as a finger nurse the moment Miss Corson was out of the room. "Hibbert, ask one of the servants to find my brother and tell him I want to see him here. He will undoubtedly be located in some group where there is a rural gentleman displaying the largest banner of beard. My brother has an insatiable mania for laying bets with sporting young men that he can fondle any set of luxuriant whiskers without giving the wearer cause for offense."

Coventry answered his sister's call with promptitude.

"I'll keep you only a moment from your whisker-parterres, Cov! When you go back into that downstairs garden please give some of those beards a good hard yank for my sake."

But young Mr. Daunt was serious and rebuked her. "This isn't any lark we're on up here, Dorrie! Dad needs to have everybody's good will and I'm doing my little best on the side-lines for him. And he isn't tickled to pieces by your quitting. It's a big project we're gunning through this legislature!"

"It may be so! It probably is! But I'm not sacrificing four fingers, a thumb, and a perfectly good arm for the cause and I'm not allowing public affairs to take my mind wholly off private matters. So here's at it! Are you and Lana formally engaged?"

"Well, I must say you're not abrupt or anything of the sort!"

"Certain semi-coaxing methods haven't seemed to succeed, and therefore I'm shooting the well, as our oil friend Whitaker puts it!"

"Simply for the sake of keeping our affectionate brother-and-sister relations on the safe and approved plane, I'll say it's none of your blamed business," declared Coventry. "On the other hand, in a purely tolerant and friendly way, I'll say that Lana and I are proceeding agreeably, I think, and dad told me the other day that the Senator talked as if the matrimonial bill might receive favorable consideration when duly reported from committee--meaning Lana and myself and--"

"Gas!" broke in Mrs. Stanton. "I shot and I get only gas! I'm looking for oil! Is there an actual and formal engagement, I ask?"

"Oh, say!" expostulated her brother, registering disgust. "The motion pictures have spoiled that sort of thing. They have to propose bang outright in the films because the fans can't be bothered by the nuances of courtship. But for a chap to get down on his knees these days in real life would make the girl laugh as loud as the fans would whoop if the hero in reel life stood on his head and popped the question. Nothing of that kind of formal stuff in my case, sis! Of course not!"

"There better be! You go ahead this very night and attend to it!"

"Where do you get your appointment as general manager of the matter, Dorrie? You certainly don't get it from me!"

"Leaving it to be inferred--"

"I leave nothing to be inferred," declared her brother, righteously indignant. "Dorrie, you absolutely must get off that habit of carving your own kin in order to keep up the edge of your tongue. I wouldn't as much as intimate it, by denying it, that you get your meddling commission from Lana. If this is all you wanted to talk about, I'll have to be going. This is my busy evening!"

"Just one moment! It's always the busiest man who has time to attend to one thing more! I'm assuming that you love Lana."

"Conceded! You always did have a good eye in that line, Dorrie!"

"Then my advice, as an expert, ought to be respected. You go ahead and get a promise from Lana Corson. Then you'll have somebody working for your interests day and night."

"Who?"

"Her New England conscience!"

Young Mr. Daunt gave his sister a long, searching, and sophisticated stare. "I think I have a little the advantage of you, Dorrie. I met to-day this Mr. Stewart Morrison you're speaking of!"

"I haven't spoken of him! I haven't mentioned his name!"

"Oh, didn't you?" purred the brother. "Then I must have anticipated what you were going to say, or else I read your mind for the name--and that only shows that the Daunt family's members are thoroughly *en rapport*, to use dad's favorite phrase when he's showing the strawberry mark on ideas and making the other fellow adopt 'em as his own children. And I have heard how Lana and Morrison have been twice engaged and twice estranged. So, how about her New England conscience in the matter of a promise in love?"

"As I understand it, the New England conscience grows up with the possessor and comes of age and asserts itself. You can't expect an infant or juvenile conscience to boss and control like a grown-up conscience. Coventry, what kind of a man is Morrison?"

"A big, opinionated ramrod of a Scotchman who'd drive any girl to break her engagement a dozen times if she had promised as often as that."

Mrs. Stanton relaxed in her chair and sighed with relief. "Oh, from what she said about him--But no matter! I think you do know men very well, Cov! I'll do no more worrying where he's concerned. Forgive me for advising you so emphatically."

"He'd boss any girl into breaking her engagement," continued Coventry, with conviction. "Any dreaming, wondering, restless girl, curious to find out for herself and afraid of restraint."

"I know the type. Impossible as husbands," averred Mrs. Stanton, a caustic and unwearying counselor of sex independence.

"But there are some girls who grow up into real women, though you probably have hard work to believe that," said her brother, equally caustic in stating his opinions, "and they are waiting for the right man to come along and take sole possession of them, body and soul and affairs--when they are women! Then it isn't bossing any more! It's love, glorified! Letting 'em have their own way would seem like neglect and indifference, and their hearts would be broken. They eat it up, sis, eat it up, that kind of love!"

His sister leaped from her chair. "How anybody with an ounce of brains can take stock in this caveman nonsense is more than I can understand!"

"It has nothing to do with brains, sis! It's in here!" He tapped his finger on his breast. "It was put in when the first heart started beating."

"But you listen to reason! No woman wants a--"

He put his hand up and broke in on her furious remonstrance. "If I listen to reason, sis, you'll have me against the ropes in thirty seconds. I admit that there's no reason why a woman should want it that way! Brains can argue us right out of the notion. I won't argue. But I don't want you to think I'm keeping anything away from you that a sister ought to know. As my sister and as Lana's good friend, I'm sure you'll be glad to know that I love her with all my heart and I hope I haven't misunderstood her feelings in regard to me. I don't want to be too complacent, but I think she's still girl enough to welcome my kind of love and to take me for what I am."

He and his sister were thoroughly absorbed in their dialogue. Having summed up the situation in his final declaration, he turned hastily to leave the room and was assured, to his dismay, that Miss Corson had heard the declaration; she was at the threshold, her lips apart; she was plainly balancing a desire to flee against a more heroic determination to step in and ignore the situation and the words which had accompanied it.

Young Mr. Daunt manfully did his best to get that situation out of the chancery of embarrassing silence.

"Lana, the three of us are too good friends to allow this foozle to make us feel altogether silly. Despite present appearances I don't go around making speeches on a certain subject. Nor will I lay it all on Dorrie by saying, 'The woman tempted me and I fell.'"

"Yes, we may as well be sensible," affirmed Mrs. Stanton. In spite of her momentary embarrassment her countenance was displaying bland satisfaction. This was an occasion to be grasped. "I'll say right out frankly that I consider I'm one too many in this room just now!"

Lana retreated across the threshold. She was distinctly frightened.

Young Mr. Daunt laughed and his merriment helped to relieve the situation still more. "Oh, I say, Lana! This isn't a trap set by the Daunts. You come right in! I'm leaving!"

"I didn't mean to overhear," the girl faltered.

"You and I have nothing to apologize for--either of us! I take nothing back, but this is no kind of a time to go forward. I'd be taking advantage of your confusion."

"Well, of all the mincing minuets!" blurted the young matron. "One word will settle it all. I tell you, I'm going!"

But Daunt rushed to the door, seized Lana's hands, and swung her into the room. "This is a political night, and we'll go by the rules. The gentleman has introduced the bill and on motion of the lady it has been tabled. But it will be taken from the table on a due and proper date and assigned at the head of the calendar. I think that's the way the Senator would state it. It ought to be good procedure." He released her hands.

"And speaking of the calendar, Lana, may I have a peep at your dance-list?"

She gave him the engraved card.

"All the waltzes for me, eh?" he queried, wistfully. "I note that you're free."

"One, please, Coventry--for now! No, please select some of the new dances. You know them all! Some of my Marion friends are old-fashioned and I must humor them with the waltzes." Her hands were trembling. She laughed nervously. "I feel free to task your good nature."

"Thank you," he returned, gratefully, accepting the implied compliment she paid him. He dabbed on his initials here and there and hurried away.

Mrs. Stanton had plenty of impetuous zeal for all her quests, but she had also abundance of worldly tact. "One does get so tremendously interested in friends and family, Lana! Affection makes nuisances of us so often! But no more about it! I feel quite happy now. I'm even so kindly disposed toward politics that I'm ready to go down and dance for the cause, whatever it is your father and mine are going after. These men in politics--they always seem to me to be like small boys building card houses. Piling up and puffing down! Putting in little tin men and pulling out little tin men. And to judge by the everlasting faultfinding, nobody is ever satisfied by what is accomplished."

Miss Corson plainly welcomed this consoling shift from an embarrassing topic. And, in order to get as far from love as possible, she turned to business. When she and her friend descended the broad stairway of the mansion Lana was discoursing on the need of coaxing men of big commercial affairs into politics. Her views were rather immature and her fervor was a bit hysterical, but the subject was plainly more to her taste than that on which Mrs. Stanton had been dwelling.

The crowd below them, as they stood for a moment on the landing, half-way down the stairs, gave comforting evidence that it had thinned, according to Lana's prophecy. The receiving-line was broken. Senator Corson was sauntering here and there, saying a word to this one or that in more intimate manner than his formal post in the line permitted. Governor North, also released from conventional restrictions as a hand-shaker, was on his rounds and wagged his coattails and barked and growled emphatically.

The word "Law," oft repeated, fitted itself to his growls; when he barked he ejaculated, "Election statutes!"

"It's a pity your state is wasting such excellent material on the mere job of Governor, Lana. What a perfectly wonderful warden he would make for your state prison," suggested Mrs. Stanton, sweetly. But she did not provoke a reply from the girl and noted that Lana was frankly interested in somebody else than the Governor. It was a new arrival; his busy exchange of greetings revealed that fact.

"Ah! Your dilatory mayor of Marion!" said the matron, needing no identification.

Nor did Stewart require any word to indicate the whereabouts of the hostess of the Corson mansion. His eyes had been searching eagerly. As soon as he saw Lana he broke away from the group of men who were engaging him. The Governor accosted Morrison sharply, when the mayor hurried past on the way to the stairway. But again, within a few hours, Stewart slighted the chief executive of the state.

"I am late, I fear," he called to Lana, leaping up the stairs. "And after my solemn promise to come early! But you excused me this morning when I was obliged to attend to petty affairs. Same excuse this time! Do I receive the same pardon?"

The girl displayed greater ease in his presence at this second meeting. She received him placidly. There were no more of those disconcerting and high-flown forensics in her greeting. There was the winning candor of old friendship in her smile and he flushed boyishly in his frank delight. She presented him to Mrs. Stanton and that lady's modish coolness did not dampen his spirits, which had become plainly exuberant. In fact, he paid very little attention to Mrs. Stanton.

"It has got to you, Lana--this coming home again, hasn't it?" he demanded, with an unconventionality of tone and phraseology that caused the metropolitan matron to express her startled emotions by a blink. "I knew it would!"

"I am glad to be home, Stewart. But I have been tiring Mrs. Stanton by my enthusiasm on that subject," was her suggestive move toward another topic. "You're in time for the dancing. That's the important feature of the evening."

"Certainly!" he agreed. "May I be pardoned, Mrs. Stanton, for consulting my hostess's card first?"

He secured Lana's program without waiting for the matron's indifferent permission.

"A waltz--two waltzes, anyway!" he declared. "They settle arrearages in your accounts, Lana, for the two winters you have been away. And why not another?" He was scribbling with the pencil. "It will settle the current bill."

"It is a business age," murmured Mrs. Stanton, "and collections cannot be looked after too sharply."

"Will you not permit me to go in debt to you, madam?" he asked. "I'll be truly obligated if you'll allow me to put my name on your card."

"As a banker's daughter, I'll say that the references that have been submitted by Miss Corson in regard to your standing are excellent," said Mrs. Stanton, with a significance meant for Lana's confusion. But while she was detaching the tassel from her girdle Governor North interrupted. He was standing on the stairs, just below the little group.

"Excuse me for breaking in on the party, but I'm due at the State House. I'll bother you only a second, Morrison. Then you won't have a thing to do except be nice to the ladies."

"I know I'll be excused by them for a few moments, Governor." He started to descend. His Excellency put up his hand.

"We can attend to it right here, Mister Mayor!"

"But I have a word or two--"

"That's all I have!" was the blunt retort. "And I'm in a hurry. Have you got 'em smoothed down, according to our understanding?"

"I have, I think! But whether they'll stay smooth depends on you, Governor North!"

"And I can be depended on! I told you so at the office." He turned away.

"I think I ought to have a few words with you in private, however," Morrison insisted. "That general understanding is all right. But I need to know something specific."

The Governor was well down the stairs; he trudged energetically, his coattails wagging in wide arcs. It was not premeditated insolence; it was the usual manner of Lawrence North when he did not desire an interview prolonged to an extent that might commit him. "I'll be at the State House in case there's any need of my attention to something specific. I'll attend to it over the telephone--over the telephone, understand!"

The diversion on the stairs had attracted a considerable audience and produced a result that interfered further with Stewart's immediate social plans.

Senator Gorson came across the reception-hall, beckoning amiably, and the three descended obediently.

"Stewart, before you get too deep into the festivities with the girls, I want you to have a bit of a chat with Mr. Daunt. We arranged it, you know."

"But Stewart isn't up here to attend to business, father," protested the daughter, with a warmth that the subject of the controversy welcomed with a smile of gratitude.

"There is an urgent reason why Mr. Daunt should have a few words with Stewart to-night--before the legislature assembles." The Senator assumed an air of mock autocratic dignity. "I command the obedience of my daughter!" He saw the banker approaching. "I call on you, sir, to put down rebellion in your own family! These daughters of ours propose to spirit away this young gentleman."

"I'll keep you from the merrymaking only a few moments, Mayor Morrison," apologized Daunt. "But I feel that it is quite essential for us to get together on that matter we mentioned in the forenoon. I'm sure that only a few words will put us thoroughly *en rapport*."

Mrs. Stanton lifted her eyebrows. "That phrase means that father will do the talking, Mister Mayor. I recommend that you go along with him. You won't have to do a thing except listen. You can come later and dance with us with all your energy unimpaired."

"Yes!" urged Lana. "The waltzes will be waiting!"

"Use my den, Daunt! If I can get away from my gang, here, I'll run in on you," stated the Senator. He smacked his palm on Stewart's shoulder. "I know you always put business ahead of pleasure, though it may be hard to do it in this case, my boy!

But after you and my friend Daunt get matters all tied up snug you won't have a thing to do for the rest of the night but enjoy yourself and be nice to the girls--not another thing, Stewart."

VIII
A ROD IN PICKLE

With great promptitude Attorney Despeaux fastened upon Blanchard, of the Conawin, the moment the latter left the company of Mayor Morrison on the arrival of the twain at the Corson mansion; and Mr. Blanchard seemed alertly willing to break off his companionship with the passenger he had brought in his limousine.

"What's that bull-headed fool been stirring up down-town?" demanded Despeaux when he had Blanchard safely to himself in a corner.

"Have you heard something about it?"

"I was called on the 'phone a few minutes ago."

"Who called you?"

"No matter! But hold on, Blanchard! I may as well tell you that I'm using a part of our fund to have Morrison shadowed. I suppose the reason you went along was to get a line on him. But it was imprudent. It looked like lending your countenance."

Blanchard explained sullenly why he did accompany Morrison to the meeting.

"Well, I'm glad you were there and heard him inflaming the mob," admitted the syndicate's lobbyist and lawyer. "I want to have Senator Corson fully informed on the point and it will come better from you than from a paid detective. Give it to Corson, and give it to him strong!"

"I don't know that I can justly say that he was inflaming the mob," demurred Blanchard.

"But you've got to say it! You must make it appear that way! Blanchard, it has come to a clinch and we must smash Morrison's credit in every direction. I didn't realize till to-day that he is out to blow up the whole works. Didn't he preach to you on the text of that infernal people-partner notion of his?"

"Yes! He's crazy!"

"The people own the moon, if you want to put it that way! But they can't do anything sensible with it, any more than they can with ownership of the state's water-power."

The Conawin magnate exhibited bewilderment. "Despeaux, I'm a business man. I suppose you lawyers go to work in a different way than we do in business. But as I have read the propaganda you're putting out--as I understand it--*you* are shouting for the people's rights, too!"

"I am! Strongly! Right out open! I even preached on people's rights to Morrison this very day--and looked him right in that canny Scotch eye of his while I preached. I like to keep in good practice!"

"Then why is Morrison so dangerous, if he's only doing what you do?" inquired the business man, with an artlessness that the attorney greeted with an oath.

"Because the infernal ramrod means what he says, Blanchard!"

"But if you don't mean it--if you have put yourself on record--and if you're obliged to step up and honor the draft you've sanctioned--what's going to happen in the showdown?"

Attorney Despeaux moderated his mordancy and became tolerantly patient in enlightening the ignorance of one of his employers. "The people are hungry for some kind of fodder in this water-power proposition. I've been telling all you power-owners so! We'll have to admit it, Blanchard! The time is played out when you can drive the people in this country. You've got to be a nice, kind shepherd and get their confidence and lead 'em. I'm a shepherd! See?" He patted himself on the breast. "There are two cribs!"

"You'll have to name 'em to me, Despeaux. I'm apt to be pretty dull outside of matters in my own line."

"I guess I'd do better to designate the chaps who are managing the cribs." The two men were in a window embrasure. Despeaux pointed to one side of the niche. "Over there, behold Morrison and his 'storage and power' crowd, made up of pig-headed engineers and scientific experts who are thinking only of how much power can be developed for the people as proprietors; over here, the public utilities commission made up of safe men, judiciously appointed, tractable in politics, consistently on the side of vested interests and right on the job to see to it that the state keeps its contracts with capital. I propose to be something of a shepherd and lead the people to the public utilities crib! And I'm going to show folks that they'll be eating poison-ivy out of the Morrison crib--even if I have to put the poison-ivy in there myself. This is no time to be squeamish, Blanchard! You've got to do your part in nailing a disturber like Morrison to the cross. Speak like a business man and say that he is dangerous in good business. We've got a Governor who is safe; we've got to have a legislature that will see to it that the committees are all right. And that's why we're standing no monkey business from any mob up on Capitol Hill to-night! Down at that hall, so my man told me, Morrison talked as if he's going to take hold and run the state! Didn't he?"

"Well, one might draw some such conclusions, I suppose, by stretching his words!"

"Blanchard, you must stretch words when you talk to Senator Corson and to all others who need to be stirred up and can help us. If that wild Scotchman butts into this plan he's inviting trouble, and we've got to see that he gets it. He's got to be choked now or never! Don't have any mercy! Just look at it this way! Talk it this way! He's turning on his own, if he does what he threatens! He played the sneak, he, a mill-owner, getting on to that commission! And he proposes to shove in a report that will smother development by outside capital. Play up the reason for his interest in the thing along that line! A hog for himself! It's easy to turn public sentiment by the right kind of talk! If I really start out to go the limit I can have him tarred and feathered as a chief conspirator, rigging a scheme to have our big industries knocked in the head."

Despeaux spoke low, but his tone conveyed the malice and the menace of a man who had been nursing a grudge for a long time. "Two years ago his newspaper letters and his rant killed that Consolidated project, and I had a contingent fee of fifty thousand dollars at stake; as it was, I got only a little old regular lobby fee and my expense money. And the power hasn't been developed by the infernal, dear, protected people, has it?" he sneered. "If the Consolidated folks had been let alone and given their franchise, we'd now be marketing over our high-tension wires two millions of horse-power in big centers two or three hundred miles from this state."

"Well, I'm not so awfully strong, myself, for making a mere power station of our own state, and letting outsiders ship our juice over the border."

"But you ought to be devilish strong against a man who is proposing to have the state break existing contracts, take back power rights and franchises and make you simply a lessee of what you already own! You've got yours! Give the outsiders a show! It's all snarled up together, Blanchard, and you've got to kill him and his crowd and their whole mushy, socialistic scheme and eliminate him from the proposition. Then we can go ahead and do something sensible in this state!" affirmed Mr. Despeaux, with the lustful ardor of one who foresaw the possibility of eliminating, also, the hateful word "contingent" in the case of fees.

But Business-man Blanchard was displaying symptoms of worriment.

The lawyer viewed with concern this evidence of backsliding, but his attention was suddenly diverted from his companion; then Despeaux nudged Blanchard and directed the latter's gaze by a thumb jerk.

They saw Morrison hurry up the stairs to greet Lana Corson when she appeared with her house guest. The attorney seemed to be vastly interested in the scene.

"I don't mean to scare you," went on Despeaux, his manner milder. "I'm not planning to commit murder or steal a state! It's Morrison right now! He's the one we're after! This whole thing may be taken care of in another way--so easily that it may make us smile. I've been keeping my eyes open, Blanchard--ears, too! Did you see Morrison rush to the Senator's daughter? A fellow can work himself into a terrible state of worry over the dear, unprotected people, when he has nothing else better to take up his mind. But after a Scotchman goes crazy over a girl--well, when the whole of 'em hold Poet Bobby Burns up as the type of their race, they know what they're talking about!"

"I can hardly conceive of Morrison being a poet or relishing poetry or the ways of a poet," returned Blanchard, dryly.

"And he probably has never read a line of it in his whole life," agreed Despeaux. "But that isn't the point! You may think I've gone off on a queer tack, all of a sudden, but I know human nature! That girl is back here with a slick young fellow, and he's the pepper in a certain mess of Scotch broth that has been heated up all over again, if I'm any guesser. That girl has been living in Washington, Blanchard. It's a great school! I've been watching her shake hands. You saw her just now when she shook with our friend, the mayor. That girl isn't down here on this trip simply to see whether the care-takers have been looking after the Corson mansion in good shape," opined the cynical Mr. Despeaux, having excellent personal reasons to distrust everybody else in the matter of motives.

"That sort of a trick is beneath Senator Corson and his daughter."

"Well," drawled the lawyer, "that all depends how closely he and Silas Daunt are tied up in a common interest in this water-power question and other matters. I suspect everybody in this world. I go on that principle. It eases my mind about slipping something over on the other fellow when I get the chance. I'm talking out pretty frankly, Blanchard, to a man who has his money in the syndicate pool, as you have! But I play square with the crowd I take money from, so long's I'm with 'em. The fee makes me yours to command, heart and soul! There's something--some one thing--that can control every man, according to his tastes. Stewart Morrison can be controlled right now by that black-eyed Corson girl more effectually than he can by any other person or consideration on God's earth. I've known him ever since he was a boy--I have watched the thing between 'em--and now that she's back here where he can see her, be near her, and be worried by the sight of another fellow trailing her, he'll be doing more thinking about her than he will about the partner-people, as he calls that dream of his about something that isn't so! I wish I could know just how sly the Senator is! I wish I could get a line on what's underneath that girl's curly topknot," he said, fervently.

Apparently absorbed by that speculation, Lawyer Despeaux again gave close attention to the tableau on the landing presented by Lana, Mrs. Stanton, and Morrison.

When Governor North marched up the stairs, said his vociferous say, and marched down again Despeaux grunted his satisfaction. "That's the talk, old boy! Show him where he gets off!"

The manner in which Senator Corson handed Morrison over to Silas Daunt elicited further commendation from the lawyer. "He's being pulled into camp smoothly and scientifically, Blanchard! The Senator is on to his job, but did you see Morrison's mug when he had to leave the girl?"

"I'll admit that it's the first time I ever saw him make up a face when he was called on to tend to business!"

"The Senator is a wise old bird! He knows human nature down to the ground. He's got the right kind of a daughter to help him, and he's making her useful. It's a case of shutting Morrison's mouth, and Corson is hep to the right play. I don't think the Senator needs any advice from us, but a little of the proper kind of information about Morrison's latest demfoolishness will make Corson understand that he needs to put some hot pep as well as sugar into his politeness. We'll get to him as soon as we can. Make it strong, Blanchard, make it strong!"

As soon as opportunity offered, Blanchard did make it strong. He was harboring a pretty large-sized grudge of his own in the case of Morrison, and it was easy to put malice into the report he gave the Senator.

"But hold on!" protested Corson. "You're making Stewart out to be a radical as red as any of them!"

"I can't help that, Senator," retorted the millman. "He dragged me down to his cursed meeting over my protest and he made a speech that put himself in hand in glove with 'em."

Corson pursed his lips and displayed the concern of a friend who had heard bad news regarding a favorite. "I always found the boy a bit inclined to mix high-flown notions in with the business practicality of his family. But I didn't realize that he was going so far wrong in his theories. That's the danger in permitting even one unsound doctrine to get into a level-headed chap's apple-basket, gentlemen! First thing you know, it has affected all the fruit. I'm glad you told me. I'm not surprised that your arguments have had no effect, Despeaux. He's naturally headstrong. Do you know, these fellows with poetic, chivalrous natures are hard boys to bring to reason in certain practical matters?"

"I was just telling Despeaux that I never saw much poetry sentiment in Stewart Morrison," affirmed the millman.

Senator Corson's condescending smile assured Mr. Blanchard that he was all wrong. "He was much in our family as a boy. Very sentimental if approached from the right angle! Very! And I think this is a matter to be handled wholly by Stewart's closest friends. Sentiment has led him off on a wrong slant. He'll only fight harder if he's tackled by a man like you, Despeaux. That's the style of him. But in his case sentiment can be guided by sentiment. And all for his best good! He mustn't run wild in this folly! I believe there's no one who can approach him with more tact than my daughter Lana." Despeaux found an opportunity to dig his thumb suggestively into Blanchard's side. "They have been extremely good friends, I believe, in boy-and-girl fashion; between us three old townsmen, I'll go as far as to say they were very much interested in each other. But in the case of both of 'em their horizons are naturally wider these days; however, first-love affairs, even if rather silly, are often the basis for really sensible and enduring friendships. And friendship must handle this thing. We'll leave it to Lana. I'll speak to her."

He went on his way toward the ballroom, pausing to chat with this or that group of constituents.

"There!" exclaimed the lawyer, relieving his high pressure by a vigorous exhalation of breath. "What did I tell you?"

"It's mighty kind and sensible of the Senator! Morrison is making a big mistake and the way to handle him is by friendship."

"Friendship hell!"

"Say, look here, Despeaux, I don't believe in spoiling my teeth by biting every coin that's handed to me in this world."

"Are you as devilish green as you pretend to be, Blanchard? If you had ever hung around in Washington as I have, you'd have wisdom teeth growing so fast that they'd keep your jaws propped open like a country yap's unless you kept 'em filed by biting all the coin of con! Now I know what's in the Senator's dome and what's under his girl's topknot! But let's not argue about that. Let's take a look at the probabilities in regard to the water-power matter--that's of more importance just now. I doubt that even friendship"--he dwelt satirically on the word--"can shut Morrison up on the storage report that he will shove into the legislature. But we're going to have safe committees this year, thanks to the election laws and guns, and that report will be pocketed. Then if Morrison keeps still about making the dear people millionaires by having 'em peddle their puddles to the highest bidders, capital can go ahead and do business in this state. I think his mouth is going to be effectively shut! The right operators are on the job!"

Despeaux took a peep at his watch.

"Time slipped by while we were waiting to get at Corson. Daunt has had half an hour for laying down the law to Morrison. And Daunt can do a whole lot of business in half an hour."

"He'll only stir up Morrison's infernal scrapping spirit by laying down the law," objected Blanchard, sourly.

Despeaux took both of the millman's coat lapels in his clutch. "He'll lay down in front of Morrison the prospect of the profits to be made by the deal that is proposed. And if you had ever heard Silas Daunt talk profits as a promoter you would reckon just as I'm reckoning, Blanchard--to see our Scotch friend come out of that conference walking like the man who broke the bank at Monte Carlo, instead of bobbing around astraddle of that damnation hobby-goat of his! Daunt can talk money in the same tone that a Holy Roller revivalist talks religion, Blanchard! And he makes converts, he sure does!"

A moment later the mayor of Marion strode across the reception-hall.

Lawyer Despeaux, giving critical attention, was not ready to affirm that Morrison's gait was that of a man who had broken a bank. But the manner in which he marched, shoulders back and chin up, and the dabs of color on his cheeks, would have suggested to a particularly observant person that the mayor had broken something. He pushed past those who addressed him and went on toward the ballroom, staring straight ahead; the music was pulsing in the ballroom; he seemed to be thoroughly entranced by the strains; at any rate, he was attending strictly to the business of going somewhere! He passed Senator Corson, who was returning to the reception-hall; the mayor gave his host only a nod.

While the Senator stood and gazed at the precipitate young man, Banker Daunt, following on Morrison's trail, arrived in front of Corson.

Lawyer Despeaux stepped from the window embrasure to get a good view and was not at all reassured by Daunt's looks. The banker displayed none of the symptoms of a victor. There was more of choler than complacency in his air. He hooked his arm inside the Senator's elbow and they went away together.

"Blanchard," said the lawyer, after a period of pondering, "that infernal Scotch idiot says that he isn't interested in politics and now he seems to have put promoting in the same class. Our hope is that he's interested in something else. Suppose we stroll along and see just how much interested he is."

By the time they reached the ballroom Morrison was waltzing with Lana.

He was distinctly another person from that tense, saturnine, defiant, brusk person who strode through the reception-hall. He was radiantly and boyishly happy. He was clasping the girl tenderly. He directed her steps in a small circle outside the throng of dancers, and waltzed as slowly as the tempo would allow. He was talking earnestly.

"Look at him! There you have it!" whispered Despeaux, recovering his confidence. "Every man has his price--but it's a mistake to think that the price must always be counted down in cash. Daunt didn't act as if he had captured our friend. He's dancing to a girl's tune now. Corson will whistle a jig when he gets ready and Morrison will dance to that tune, too!"

IX
MAKING IT A SQUARE BREAK

In the privacy of Senator Corson's study Mr. Daunt had allowed himself to raise his voice and express some decided opinions by the way of venting his emotions.

In his heat he disregarded the amenities that should govern a guest in the presence of his host. In fact, Mr. Daunt asserted that the host was partly responsible for the awkward position in which Mr. Daunt found himself.

The Senator, whenever he was able to make himself heard, put in protesting "buts." Mr. Daunt, riding his grievance wildly, hurdled every "but" and kept right on. "Confound it, Corson, I accepted him as your friend, as your guest, as a gentleman under the roof of a mutual friend. Most of all, I accepted him as a safe and sane business man. I talked to him as I would to the gentlemen who put their feet under my table. I know how to be cautious in the case of men I meet in places of business. But you bring this man to your house and you put me next to him with the assurance that he is all right--and I go ahead with him on that basis. I was perfectly and entirely honest with him. I disregarded all the rules that govern me in ordinary business offices," the banker added, too excited to appreciate the grim humor flashed by the flint and the steel of his last, juxtaposed sentences.

"You say you told him all your plans in full?" suggested Corson, referring to the outburst with which Daunt began his arraignment of the situation.

"Of course I told him! You gave me no warning. I dealt with him, gentleman with gentleman, under your roof!"

"I didn't think it was necessary to counsel a man like you about the ordinary prudence required in all business matters."

"I had his word in his own office that he was heartily with me. You told me he was as square as a brick when it came to his word. I went on that basis, Corson!"

"I'm sorry," admitted the Senator. "I thought I knew Stewart through and through. But I haven't been keeping in touch as closely as I ought. I have heard things this evening--" He hesitated.

"You have heard things--and still you allowed me to go on and empty my basket in front of him?"

"I heard 'em only after you were closeted here with him, Daunt. And I can't believe it's as bad as it has been represented to me. And even as it stands, I think I know how to handle him. I have already taken steps to that end."

"How?"

"Please accept my say-so for the time being, Daunt! It isn't a matter to be canvassed between us."

"I suppose you learn that sort of reticence in politics, even in the case of a friend, Corson," growled the banker. "I wish I had taken a few lessons from you before talking with one of your friends this evening."

"Was it necessary for you to do so much talking before you got a line on his opinions?"

"Confound it, Corson, with that face of his--with that candor in his countenance--he looks as good and reliable as a certified check--and in addition I had your indorsement of him."

"I felt that I had a right to indorse him." The Senator showed spirit. "Daunt, I don't like to hear you condemn Stewart Morrison so utterly."

"Not utterly! He has qualities of excellence! For instance, he's a damnation fine listener," stated the disgusted banker.

"But he couldn't have thrown down your whole proposition--he couldn't have done that, after the prospects you held out to him, as you outlined them to me when we first discussed the matter," Corson insisted. "Morrison has a good business head on him. He comes of business stock. He has made a big success of his mill. He must be on the watch for more opportunities. All of us are."

"Well, here was the offer I made to him, seeing that he is a *friend* of yours," said Banker Daunt, dilating his nostrils when he dwelt on the word "friend." "I offered to double his own appraisal of his properties when we pay him in the preferred stock of the consolidation. I told him that he would receive, like the others, an equal amount of common stock for a bonus. I assured him that we would be able to pay dividends on the common. And he asked me particularly if I was certain that dividends would be paid on the common. I gave him that assurance as a financier who knows his card." Daunt had been attempting to curb his passion and talk in a business man's tone while on the matter of figures. But he abandoned the struggle to keep calm. He cracked his knuckles on the table and shouted: "But do you know--can you imagine what he said after I had twice assured him as to those dividends on common, replying to his repeated questions? Can you?"

"No," admitted Corson, having reason to be considerably uncertain in regard to Stewart Morrison's newly developed notions about affairs in general.

"He told me I ought to be ashamed of myself--then he pulled out his watch and apologized for monopolizing me so long on a gay evening, hoped I was enjoying it, and said he must hurry away and dance with Miss Corson. What did he mean by saying that I ought to be ashamed of myself? What did he mean by that gratuitous insult to a man who had made him a generous proposition in straight business--to a guest under your roof, Senator Corson?"

"By gad! I'll find out what it means!" snapped the Senator, pricked in his pride and in his sense of responsibility as a go-between. He pushed a button in the row on his study table. "This new job as mayor seems to be playing some sort of a dev-il's trick with Stewart. I'll admit, Daunt, that I didn't relish some of the priggish preachment on politics mouthed by him in his office when we were there. But I didn't pay much attention--any more than I did to his exaggerated flourish in the way he attended to city business. The new brooms! You know!"

"Yes, I know!" The banker was sardonic. "I could overlook his display of impor-tance when he neglected gentlemen in order to parade his tuppenny mayor's busi-ness. I paid no attention to his vaporings on the water question. I've heard plenty of franchise-owners talk that way for effect! He's an especially avaricious Scot, isn't he? Confound him! How much more shall I offer him?"

"I'll admit that Stewart seems to be different these days in some respects, but unless he has made a clean change of all his nature in this shift of some of his ideas, you'd better not offer him any more!" warned the Senator. "I never detected any 'For Sale' sign on him!"

The Senator's secretary stepped into the study.

"Find Mayor Morrison in the ballroom and tell him I want to see him here."

"Corson, you're a United States Senator," proceeded the banker when the man had departed, "and your position enables you to take a broad view of business in general. But naturally you're for your own state first of all."

"Certainly! Loyally so!"

"I think you thoroughly understand my play for consolidated development of the water-power here. Every single unit should be put at work for the good of the country. Isn't that so?"

"Yes, decidedly."

"To set up such arbitrary boundaries as state lines in these matters of development is a narrow and selfish policy," insisted Daunt. "It would be like the coal states refusing to sell their surplus to the country at large. If this Morrison proposes to play the bigoted demagogue in the matter, exciting the people to attempt impractical control that will paralyze the whole proposition, he must be stepped on. You can show due regard for the honor and the prosperity of your own state, but as a statesman, working for the general welfare of the country at large, you've got to take a broader view than his."

"I do. I can make Stewart understand."

Daunt paced up and down the room, easing his turgid neck against a damp collar. The Senator pondered.

The secretary, after a time, tapped and entered.

"Mayor Morrison is not in the ballroom, sir. And I could not find him."

"You should have inquired of Miss Corson."

"I could not find Miss Corson."

The Senator started for the door. He turned and went back to Daunt. "It's all right! I gave her a bit of a commission. It's in regard to Morrison. She seems to be attending to it faithfully. Be easy! I'll bring him."

The father went straight to the library. He knew the resources of his own mansion in the matter of nooks for a tete-a-tete interview; now he was particularly assisted by remembrance of Stewart's habits in the old days. He found his daughter and the mayor of Marion cozily ensconced among the cushions of a deep window-seat.

Stewart was listening intently to the girl, his chin on his knuckles, his elbow propped on his knee. His forehead was puckered; he was gazing at her with intent seriousness.

"Senator Corson," warned the girl, "we are in executive session."

"I see! I understand! But I need Stewart urgently for a few moments."

"I surrendered him willingly a little while ago. But this conference must not be interrupted, sir!"

"Certainly not, Senator Corson!" asserted Stewart, with a decisive snap in his tone. "We have a great deal of ground to go over."

"I'll allow you plenty of time--but a little later. There is a small matter to be set straight. 'Twill take but a few moments."

"It's undoubtedly either business or politics, sir," declared Lana, with a fine assumption of parliamentary dignity. "But I have the floor for concerns of my own, and I'll not cede any of my time."

"It is hardly business or politics," returned the Senator, gravely. "It concerns a matter of courtesy between guests in my home, and I'm anxious to have the thing straightened out at once. I beg of you, Stewart!"

The mayor rose promptly.

"I suppose I must consider it a question of privilege and yield," consented Lana, still carrying on her little play of procedure. "But do I have your solemn promise, Senator Corson, that this gentleman will be returned to me by you at the earliest possible moment?"

"I promise."

"And I want your promise that you will hurry back," said the girl, addressing Stewart. "I'll wait right here!"

"But, Lana, remember your duties to our guests," protested her father.

"I have been fulfilling them ever since the reception-line was formed." She waved her hand to draw their attention to the distant music. "The guests are having a gorgeous time all by themselves. I'll be waiting here," she warned. "Remember, please, both of you that I am waiting. That ought to hurry your settlement of that other matter you speak of."

"I'll waste no time!" Morrison assured her. He marched away with the Senator.

In the study Corson took his stand between his two guests. Daunt was bristling; Morrison displayed no emotion of any sort.

"Mr. Daunt, I think you'd better state your grievance, as you feel it, so that Mr. Morrison can assure both of us that it arises from a misunderstanding."

The banker took advantage of that opportunity with great alacrity. "Now that Senator Corson is present--now that we have a broad-minded referee, Mr. Morrison, I propose to go over that matter of business."

"Exactly on the same lines?" inquired Stewart, mildly.

"Exactly! And for obvious reasons--so that Corson may understand just how much your attitude hurt my feelings."

"Pardon me, Mr. Daunt. I have no time to listen to the repetition. It will gain you nothing from me. My mind remains the same. And Miss Corson is waiting for me. I have promised to return to her as soon as possible."

"But it will take only a little while to go over the matter," pleaded Corson.

"It will be time wasted on a repetition, sir. I have no right to keep Miss Corson waiting, on such an excuse."

"You give me an almighty poor excuse for unmannerly treatment of my business, Morrison," Daunt stated, with increasing ire.

"I really must agree in that," chided the Senator.

"Sir, you gave your daughter the same promise for yourself," declared Stewart.

"Now let's not be silly, Stewart. Lana was playing! You can go right on with her from where you left off."

"Perhaps!" admitted the mayor. "I hope so, at any rate. But I don't propose to break my promise." He added in his own mind that he did not intend to allow a certain topic between him and Lana Corson to get cold while he was being bullyragged by two elderly gentlemen in that study.

"By the gods! you'll have to talk turkey to me on one point!" asserted Daunt, his veneer of dignity cracking wide and showing the coarser grain of his nature. "I made you a square business proposition and you insulted me--under the roof of a gentleman who had vouched for both of us."

"Thank you! Now we are not retracing our steps, as you threatened to do. We go on from where we left off. Therefore, I can give you a few moments, sir. What insult did I offer you?"

"You told me that I ought to be ashamed of myself."

"That was not an insult, Mr. Daunt. I intended it to be merely a frank expression of opinion. Just a moment, please!" he urged, breaking in on violent language. He brought his thumb and forefinger together to make a circle and poised his hand over his head. "I don't wear one of these. I have no right to wear one. Halo, I mean! I'm no prig or preacher--at least, I don't mean to be. But when I talk business I intend to talk it straight and use few words--and those words may sound rather blunt, sometimes. Just a moment, I say!"

He leaned over the table and struck a resounding blow on it with his knuckles. "This is a nutshell proposition and we'll keep it in small compass. You gave me a layout of your proposed stock issue. No matter what has been done by the best of big financiers, no matter what is being done or what is proposed to be done, in this particular case your consolidation means that you've got to mulct the people to pay unreasonably high charges on stock. It isn't a square deal. My property was developed on real money. I know what it pays and ought to pay. I won't put it into a scheme that will oblige every consumer of electricity to help pay dividends on imaginary money. And if you're seriously attempting to put over any consolidation of that sort on our people, Mr. Daunt, I repeat that you ought to be ashamed of yourself."

"And now you have heard him with your own ears," clamored the banker. "What do you say to that, Mr. Corson?"

"All capitalization entails a fair compromise--values to be considered in the light of new development," said the Senator. "Let's discuss the proposition, Stewart."

"Discussion will only snarl us up. I'm stating the principle. You can't compromise principle! I refuse to discuss."

"Have you gone crazy over this protection-of-the-people idea?" demanded Corson, with heat.

"Maybe so! I'm not sure. I may be a little muddled. But I see a principle ahead and I'm going straight at it, even though I may tread on some toes. I believe that the opinion doesn't hold good, any longer, as a matter of right, that because a man has secured a franchise, and his charter permits him to build a dam across a river or the mouth of a lake, he is thereby entitled to all the power and control and profit he can get from that river or lake without return in direct payment on that power to the people of the state. We know it's by constitutional law that the people own the river and the lake. I'm putting in a report on this whole matter to the incoming legislature, Senator Corson."

"Good Heavens! Morrison, you're not advocating the soviet doctrine that the state can break existing contracts, are you?" shouted the Senator.

"I take the stand that charters do not grant the right for operators of water-power to charge anything their greed prompts 'em to charge on ballooned stock. I assert that charters are fractured when operators flagrantly abuse the public that way! I'm going to propose a legislative bill that will oblige water-power corporations to submit in public reports our state engineers' figures on actual honest profit-earning valuation; to publish complete lists of all the men who own stock so that we may know the interests and the persons who are secretly behind the corporations."

Corson displayed instant perturbation.

"Such publication can be twisted to injure honest investors. It can be used politically by a man's enemies. Stewart, I am heavily interested financially in Daunt's syndicate, because I believe in developing our grand old state. I bring this personal matter to your attention so that you may see how this general windmill-tilting is going to affect your friends."

"I'm for our state, too, sir! And I'll mention a personal matter that's close to me, seeing that you have broached the subject. St. Ronan's mill is responsible for more than two hundred good homes in the city of Marion, built, owned, and occupied by our workers. And in order to clean up a million profit for myself, I don't propose to go into a syndicate that may decide to ship power out of this state and empty those homes."

"You are leaping at insane conclusions," roared Daunt. He shook his finger under Morrison's nose.

"I'll admit that I have arrived at some rather extreme conclusions, sir," admitted Stewart, putting his threatened nose a little nearer Daunt's finger. "I based the conclusions on your own statement to me that you proposed to make my syndicate holdings more valuable by a legislative measure that would permit the consolidation to take over poles and wires of existing companies or else run wires into communities in case the existing companies would not sell."

"That's only the basic principle of business competition for the good of the consuming public. Competition is the demand, the right of the people," declared

Daunt.

"I'm a bit skeptical--still basing my opinion on your own statements as to common-stock dividends--as to the price per kilowatt after competitors shall have been sandbagged according to that legislative measure," drawled the mayor. He turned to the Senator. "You see, sir, your guest and myself are still a good ways apart in our business ideas!"

"We'll drop business--drop it right where it is," said the Senator, curtly. "Mr. Daunt has tried to meet you more than half-way in business, in my house, taking my indorsement of you. When I recommended you I was not aware that you had been making radical speeches to a down-town mob. I am shocked by the change in you, Stewart. Have you any explanation to give me?"

"I'm afraid it would take too long to go over it now in a way to make you understand, sir. I don't want to spoil my case by leaving you half informed. Mr. Daunt and I have reached an understanding. Pardon me, but I insist that I must keep my promise to Miss Corson."

The father did not welcome that announcement. "I trust that the understanding you mention includes the obligation to forget all that Mr. Daunt has said under my roof this evening."

"I have never betrayed confidences in my personal relations with any man, Senator Corson," returned Morrison.

"Then your honor naturally suggests your course in this peculiar situation."

"Let's not stop to split hairs of honor! What do you expect me to do?" demanded Morrison, bruskly business-like.

"I'll tell you what I expect," volunteered Daunt. "You have possession of facts----"

"I did not solicit them, sir. I was practically forced into an interview with you when I much rather would have been enjoying myself in the ballroom."

"Nevertheless, you have the facts. Under the circumstances you have no right to them. I expect you to show a gentleman's consideration and keep carefully away from my affairs."

"I, also, must ask that much, as your mutual host," put in Corson.

"Gentlemen," declared Stewart, setting back his shoulders, "by allowing myself to stretch what you term 'honor' to that fine point I would be held up in a campaign

I have started--prevented from going on with my work, simply because Mr. Silas Daunt is among the men I'm fighting. I'm exactly where I was before Mr. Daunt talked to me. I propose to lick a water-power monopoly in this state if it's in my humble power to do it. If you stay in that crowd, Mr. Daunt, you've got to take your chances along with the rest of 'em."

"Stewart, your position is outrageous," blazed Corson. "You're not only throwing away a wonderful business opportunity on lines wholly approved by general usage--simply to indulge an impractical whim for which you'll get no thanks--taking a nonsensical stand for a mere dream in the way of public ownership--but you're insulting me, myself, by the inference that may be drawn."

"I don't understand, sir."

"Well, then, understand!" said the Senator, carried far by his indignation. "You know how I made my fortune!"

"I do!"

"Was I not justified in buying in all the public timber-lands at the going price?"

"Yes, seeing that the people of the state were fools enough to stay asleep and let lands go for a dollar or so an acre--lands to-day worth thousands of dollars an acre for the timber on 'em!"

"I paid the price that was asked. That's as far as a business man is expected to go."

"Certainly, Senator. I'm glad for you. But, I repeat, the people were asleep! Now I'm going to wake 'em up to guard their last great heritage--the water-power that they still own! I'll keep 'em awake, if I've got strength enough in this arm to keep on drumming and breath enough to keep the old trumpet sounding!"

"The corporations in this state are organized, they will protect their charters, they will make you let go of your wild scheme," bellowed the banker. "By the jumped-up Jehoshaphat, they will make you let go, Morrison! By the great--"

"Hush!" pleaded their host. "They can hear outside. No profanity!"

Stewart had started toward the door; he paused for a moment when he had his hand on the knob. "We will not let go!" he said, calmly. "We won't let go--and this is not profanity, Senator Corson--we won't let go of as much as one dam-site!"

X
A SENATOR SIZES UP A FOE

After Stewart had closed the door behind himself Senator Corson rose hastily. For a few moments he surveyed the panels of the oaken portal with the intentness of one who was studying a problem on a printed page. Then, plainly, his thoughts went traveling beyond the closed door. But he appeared to be receiving no satisfaction from his scrutiny or from his thoughts. He scowled and muttered.

He stared into the palms of his soiled gloves; the suggestion they offered did not improve his temper. He ripped them from his hands. "What the mischief ails 'em, down here? They're all more or less slippery, Daunt! I've been sensing it all the evening! I feel as if I'd been handling eels."

Banker Daunt was calming himself by a patrol of the room.

"I can view matters like a statesman when I'm in the Senate Chamber," Corson asserted, "but down here at home these days I can't see the forest on account of the trees! I don't know what tree to climb first, Daunt, I swear I don't! What with North getting the party into this scrape it's in, and playing his sharp politics, and this power question fight and--and--"

He gazed at the door again. It now suggested a definite course of procedure, apparently. He crumpled his gloves into a ball and threw them on the table. There was a hint in that action; the Senator was showing his determination to handle matters without gloves for the rest of the evening. "There's one thing about it, Daunt, a man can't do his best in public concerns till he has freed his mind of his private troubles. You wait here. I'll be right back."

"Where are you going, Senator?"

"I'm going to regain my self-respect! I'm going to assert myself as master of my own home. I'm going to tell Stewart Morrison that I have business with him, and that I'll attend to it in a strictly business office, later, where he can't insult my friends and abuse my hospitality!"

"Wait a minute! I've had an acute attack of it, too, this evening--the same ailment, but I'm getting over it. Don't lose your head and your temper, both at the same time. You're not in the right trim just now to go against that bullhead. Let's estimate him squarely. That's always my plan in business." Mr. Daunt plucked a cigar from a box on the table and lighted up leisurely, soothing himself into a matter-of-fact mood. Corson waited with impatience, but his politician's caution began to tug on the bits, moderating the rush of his passion, and he took a cigar for himself.

"Outside of this petty mayor business, does Morrison cut any figure--have any special power in state politics?" the banker asked.

"Not a particle--not as a politician. He doesn't know the A B C's of the game."

"How much influence can he wield as an agitator, as he threatens to become?"

Corson's declaration was less emphatic. "We're conservative, the mass of us, in these parts. Starting trouble isn't wielding influence, Daunt. He'll be going up against the political machine that has always handled this state safely and sanely-- and we know what to do with trouble-makers."

"This communistic stand of his certainly discredits him with the corporations, also. Despeaux has been doing good work, and practically all of 'em have come over to the Consolidated camp. Of course, Morrison is antagonizing the banking interests, too. Is he a heavy borrower?"

"He doesn't borrow. He works on his own capital. St. Ronan's is free and clear," admitted the Senator, crossly.

"That's too bad! Calling loans is always effective in improving a radical's opinions. Then this friend, whom you have held up to me as so important in our plans----"

"I did consider him important, Daunt! I do now. I know him. I have seen him go after things, ever since he was a boy. That storage-commission scheme is his own device and, as the head of it, he occupies a strategic position."

"But it's only a scheme; he has no actual organization of the people behind it."

"Confound it! I'm afraid he will have!"

"It's an impractical dream--trying to establish such shadowy ownership of what vested capital under private control must naturally possess and develop. We have sound business on our side."

"It may not seem so much like a dream after he puts that report into the legislature," complained the Senator. "I tell you, I know Stewart Morrison. He indulges in visions, but he'll back this particular one up with so many facts and figures that it will make a treasury report look like a ghost-story by comparison. Talk about sound business! That's Morrison's other name!"

"What's going to be done with that report, Corson?"

The Senator hesitated a few moments.

"Understand that I'm no kin of old Captain Teach, the buccaneer, either in politics or business, Daunt. But I'm not fool enough to believe that the millennium has arrived in this world, even if the battle of Armageddon has been fought, as the parsons are preaching. We still must deal with human conditions. The tree is full of good ideas, I'll admit. But we've got to let 'em ripen. Eat 'em now--and it's a case of the gripes for business and politics, both. Therefore"--the Senator paused and squinted at the end of his cigar. "Well, Daunt, we'll have to apply a little common sense to conditions, even though the opposition may squeal. That ownership of the water-power by the people isn't ripe. The legislative committee will pocket Morrison's report, or will refer the thing to the public utilities commission."

"Both plans meaning the same thing?"

"I won't put it as coarsely as that. It only means handling the situation with discretion. Discretion by those in power is going to save us a lot of trouble in times like these."

"You are sure of the right legislative committee, are you?"

"Certainly! North is on the job up at the State House. I'll admit that he isn't tactful. He's very old-fashioned in his political ideas. But he doesn't mind clamor and criticism, and he isn't afraid of the devil himself. Between you and me, I think," continued the Senator, judicially, "that North is skating pretty near the edge this time. I would not have allowed him to go so far if I had been in better touch with conditions down here. But it's too late to modify his plans much at this hour. He must bull the thing through as he's going. I can undo the mischief to the party by the selection of a smooth diplomat for the gubernatorial nomination next year. But jumping back to the main subject--Stewart Morrison! Seeing what he is, in the water-power matter, I hoped I could smooth things by your getting next to him. I'm sorry you have been so much annoyed, Daunt! He may make it uncomfortable by his mouth, but he cannot control anything by direct political influence. Absolutely not!" The Senator was recovering his confidence in himself as a leader; he started up from his chair and stamped down an emphatic foot. "He is a nonentity in that direction. Politics will handle the thing! The legislature will be all right! The situation on Capitol Hill is safe. However, I think I'll pass a word or two with North!"

He went to the wall of the study, slipped aside a small panel, and lifted out a telephone instrument. "A little precaution I've held over from the old days," Corson informed his guest, with a smile. "A private line to the Executive Chamber."

From where he sat Daunt could hear the Governor's voice. The tones rasped and rattled and jangled in the receiver, which, for the sake of his eardrum, Senator Corson held away from his head. The puckers on his countenance indicated that he was annoyed, both by the news and by the discordant violence of its delivery.

"But it's not as threatening as all that! It can't be!" the listener kept insisting.

"Well, I'll come up," he promised, at last. "I'll come, but I think you're overanxious, North!"

There was a sound as if somebody were banging on a tin pan at the other end of the line; His Excellency had merely put more vigor into his voice.

"I think--I'm quite sure that he's still here--in my house," Corson replied. "Yes--yes--I certainly will!" He hung up.

"You seemed to think, Daunt, that I didn't have a good and a sufficient reason for saying a few words to Morrison when I started to hunt him up a few minutes ago. However, this time you'll have to excuse me. I'm going to him."

"But you're not intending to make him of any especial importance in affairs, are you? You said he could be ignored."

"Yes! But I don't propose to ignore his efforts to stir up the mob spirit in a city of which he happens to be mayor. He has been up to that mischief! I have heard straight reports from various sources this evening. The Governor has been posted and he is very emphatic on the point." Corson rubbed the ear that was still reminding him of that emphasis.

"That's the trouble with men like Morrison, when they begin to talk people's rights these days, Senator! They go up in the air and jump all the way over into Bolshevism. I'm sorry now because I counseled you to smooth your temper. Go at him. I'll sit here and finish my smoke."

At the head of the broad staircase Senator Corson came upon Mrs. Stanton and Coventry Daunt.

They wore expressions of bewilderment that would have fitted the countenances of explorers who had missed their quest and had lost their reckoning.

Mrs. Stanton put out her fan, and the striding father halted at the polite barrier with a greeting, but evinced anxiety to be on the way.

"I'm so glad to see you, Senator Corson!" This with delight. "But isn't Lana with you?" this with anxiety. "I mean, hasn't she been with you?"

"My dance contracts with Miss Corson have been shot quite all to pieces," said Coventry.

"I have searched everywhere for her--I think I have," supplemented the sister. "But we guessed she must be with you, and we didn't venture to intrude."

"And you are sure she is not in the ballroom?"

"Absolutely!" Young Mr. Daunt plainly knew what he was talking about.

"Coventry, if you and Mrs. Stanton will go there and wait a few moments, I am positive that Lana will come to you very promptly!"

Senator Corson also seemed to know what he was talking about!

XI
FLAREBACKS IN THE CASE OF LOVE AND A MOB

Again was Stewart a close listener, his chin resting on his knuckles, his serious eyes searching Lana's face while she talked.

A cozy harbor was afforded by the bay of the great window in the library. When Stewart had returned to the girl he noticed that she had provided the harbor with a breakwater--a tall Japanese screen; waiting there she had found the room draughty, she informed him.

He was placid when he returned. His demeanor was so untroubled and his air so eagerly invited her to go on from where she had left off that she did not bother her mind about the errand which had called him away.

"I'm really glad because we adjourned the executive session for a recess," she confided. "I've had a chance to think over what I was saying to you, Stewart. While I talked I found myself getting a bit hysterical. I realized that I was presumptuous, but I couldn't seem to stop. But I have been going over it in my mind and I'm glad now that my feelings did carry me away. Friendship has a right to be impetuous on some occasions. I never tried to advise you in the old days. You wouldn't have listened, anyway."

"I've always been glad to listen to you," he corrected.

"But it makes a friend so provoked to have one listen and then go ahead and do just as one likes. I want to ask you--while you have been away from me have you been reflecting on what I said?"

He stammered a bit, and there was not absolute candor in his eyes. "To tell the truth, Lana, I allowed myself to be taken up considerably with other matters. But I did remember my promise to hurry back to you, just the minute I could break away," he added, apologetically.

"I'm a little disappointed in you, just the same, Stewart! I've been hoping that you were putting your mind on what I said to you. I was hoping that when you came back----"

"Well, go on, Lana!" he prompted, gently, when she paused.

"It's so hard for me to say it so it will sound as I mean it," she lamented. "To make my interest appear exactly what it is. To find the words to fit my thoughts just now! I know what they're saying about me these days in Marion. I know our folks so well! I don't need to hear the words; I have been studying their faces this evening. You, also, know what they're saying, Stewart!"

He confined his assent to a significant nod; Jeanie MacDougal's few words on the subject had been, for him, a comprehensive summary of the general gossip.

"When I was speechifying to you in St. Ronan's office you thought I had come back here filled with airs and lofty notions. I knew how you felt!"

He shook his head and allowed the extent of his negation to be limited to that! "I'll tell you how I felt--some time--but now I'll listen to you."

"I was putting all that on for show, Stewart! I felt so--so--I don't know! Embarrassed, perhaps! And I felt that you--" her color deepened then in true embarrassment. "And--and--they were all there!" It was naïve confession, and he smiled.

"So I said to my wee mither, Lana, by way of setting her right as to meddlesome tongues."

"I am sincere and honest still, Stewart, where my real friends are concerned. I've just complained because I can't find words to express my thoughts to you. Well, I never was at a loss when we were boy and girl together." She paused and they heard the sound of music.

"There's a frilly style of talk that belongs with that--down there," she went on. There was a hint of contempt in her gesture. "But you and I used to get along better--or worse--with plain speech." The flash of a smile of her own softened her *moue*.

"I make it serve me well in my affairs," agreed Morrison.

"Do you think I'm airy and notional and stuck up?"

"No!"

"Do you think I'm posing as a know-it-all because I have been about in the world and have seen and heard?"

"No!"

"But you do think I'm broader and wiser and more open-minded and have better judgment on matters in general than I had when I was penned up here in Marion, don't you?"

"Yes!"

"Stewart, you're not helping me much, staring at me and popping those noes and yesses at me! You make me feel like--but, honestly, I'm not! I don't intend to seem like that!"

"Eh?"

"Why, like an opinionated lecturer, laying down the law of conduct to you! I don't mean to do all the talking."

"You'd better, Lana--for the present," he advised, seriously; "If you have something to say to me, take care and not let me get started on what I want to say to you."

She flushed. She drew away from him slightly. In her apprehensiveness she hurried on for her own protection. "I hoped you were coming back just now, Stewart, and put out your hand to me as your friend, a good pal who had given sensible advice, and say to me, 'Lana, you have used your wits to good advantage while you have been out and about in the world, and your suggestions to me are all right.' Aren't you going to say so, Stewart?"

"As I understand it, putting all you said to me awhile back in that plain language we have agreed on, you tell me that I'm missing my opportunities, have gone to sleep down here in Marion, am allowing myself to be everlastingly tied up by petty business details that keep me away from real enjoyment of a bigger and better life, and that there's not the least need of my spending my best years in that fashion."

"You state it bluntly, but that is the gist of it!"

"Yes, I was blunt. I'm going to be even more blunt! What do I get out of this prospective, bigger life, Lana?" He drew a deep breath. "Do I get--you?"

"Stewart, hush! Wait!" He had spread his hands to her appealingly. "I am talking to you as your friend--I'm talking of your business, your outlook. I must say something further to you!"

He set as firm a grip on his emotions as he had on his anger earlier in the evening when Krylovensky's hand had dealt him a blow. Her demeanor had thrust him away effectually. The fire died in his eyes. "Go on, Lana! I have promised to allow you to have your say. And, once I start, only a 'Yes!' can stop me."

She displayed additional apprehension and plunged into a strictly commercial topic with desperate directness. "I'm positive that you have no further need of making yourself a slave to details of business. I know that you can be free to devote yourself to the higher things that are worthy of your real self and your talents, Stewart. Father says that through Mr. Daunt there will come to you the grandest opportunity of your life. I suppose that's what Mr. Daunt explained to you when you were with him this evening. Even though you may not consider me wise in men's business affairs, Stewart, you must admit that my father and Mr. Daunt know. You haven't any silly notions, have you? You're ready to seize every opportunity to make a grand success in business, the way the great men do, aren't you?"

There was a very different light in Morrison's eyes than had flamed in them a few moments before. He stared at her appraisingly, wonderingly. His demanding survey of her was disconcerting, but his somberness was that of disappointment rather than of any distrust.

"Has your father asked you to talk to me on the subject of that business?"

She did not reply promptly. But his challenge was too direct.

"I confess that father did intimate that there'd be no need of mentioning him in the matter."

"He asked you to talk to me, then?"

"Yes, Stewart!"

"And I thought you were talking only for yourself when you begged me to step up into that broader life!" His voice trembled. She did not appear to understand his emotion.

"But I *am* talking for myself," protested the girl.

"You're talking only your father's views, his plans, his ambition, his scheme of life--talking Daunt's project for his own selfish ends!"

"I don't understand!"

"I hope you don't! For the sake of my love for you, I hope so!" He was striving to control himself. "In the name of what we have been to each other in days past, I hope you are not their--that you don't realize they are making you a----But I can't say it! I want proof from you now by word o' mouth! I don't want any more prattle of business! I want you to show me that you are talking for yourself. Lana Corson, say to me some word from your own heart--something for me alone--something from old times--to prove that you are what I want you to be! I love you. You are mine! I don't believe their gossip. I have never given you up. I've been waiting patiently for you to come back to me. Can't you go back to the old times--and speak from your own soul?"

The intensity of his appeal carried her along in the rush of his emotion. "Stewart, I have been speaking for myself, as best I knew how! I'm back to the old times! If you need further words from me, you shall have them."

Senator Corson stepped around the end of the screen. "You will postpone any further words to Mr. Morrison! I have some words of my own for him! Lana, Coventry Daunt is waiting for you in the ballroom and I have told him that you will be there at once."

"Mr. Daunt must continue to wait, father. I have something to tell Stewart, and you must allow me to say it--say it to him, alone."

"You shall never speak another word to him on any subject with my permission. I have been listening and--"

"Father, do you confess that you have been eavesdropping?"

"My present code of manners is perfectly suited to the tactics of this fellow who has flouted me and insulted an honored guest under my roof this evening. Morrison, leave the house!"

"He shall stay at the request of his hostess," declared the girl, defiantly.

"On with you to your guests--that's where your hostess duties are!" Corson reached to take her arm.

Stewart hastily raised Lana's hand and bent over it. "I am indebted to you for a charming evening." He stood erect and his demeanor of manly sincerity removed every suggestion of sarcasm from the conventional phrase he had spoken quietly. "The charm, Senator Corson, has outweighed all the unpleasantness."

When he turned to retire Corson halted him with a curt word.

"Lana, I command you to go and join your partner."

But Miss Corson persisted in her rebelliousness. She did not relish the ominous threat that she perceived in the situation. "I shall stay with you till you're in a better state of temper, father."

"You'll hear nothing to this man's credit if you do stay," said the Senator, acridly. "I have just talked on the 'phone with the Governor, Mayor Morrison. He asked me to notify you that your mob which you have stirred up in your own city, by your devilish speeches this evening, is evidently on the war-path. He, expects you to undo the mischief, seeing that your tongue is the guilty party!"

Lana turned startled gaze from her father to Morrison; amazement struggled with her indignation. Her amazement was deepened by the mayor's mild rejoinder.

"Very well, Senator. I have an excellent understanding with that mob."

"Making speeches to a mob!" Lana gasped. "I'll not allow even my father to say that about you, Stewart, and leave it undisputed."

"Your father is angry just now, Lana! Any discussion will provoke further unpleasantness!"

"Confound you! Don't you dare to insult me by your condescending airs," thundered Corson. "You have your orders. Go and mix with your rabble and continue that understanding with 'em, if you can make 'em understand that law and order must prevail in this city to-night."

The library was in a wing of the mansion, far from the street, and the three persons behind the screen had been entirely absorbed in their troubled affairs. They had heard none of the sounds from the street.

Somebody began to call in the corridor outside the library. The voice sounded above the music from the ballroom, and quavered with anxious entreaty as it demanded, over and over: "Senator Corson! Where are you, Senator Corson?"

"Here!" replied the Senator.

The secretary rushed in. "There's a mob outside, sir! A threatening mob!"

"Ah! Morrison, your friends are looking you up!"

"They are radicals--anarchists. They must be!" panted the messenger. "They are yelling: 'Down with the capitalists! Down with the aristocrats!' I ordered the shades pulled. The men seemed to be excited by looking in through the windows at the dancers in the ballroom!"

"There'll be no trouble. I'll answer for that," promised the Mayor, marching away.

Before he reached the door the crash of splintered glass, the screams of women and shouts of men; drowned the music.

Stewart went leaping down the stairs. When he reached the ballroom he found the frightened guests massed against the wall, as far from the windows as they could crowd. A wild battle of some sort was going on outside in the night, so oaths and cries and the grim thudding of battering fists revealed.

Before Stewart could reach a window--one of those from which the glass had been broken--Commander Lanigan came through the aperture with a rush, skating to a standstill along the polished floor. Blood was on his hands. His sleeves hung in ribbons. In that scene of suspended gaiety he was a particularly grisly interloper.

"They sneaked it over on us, Mister Mayor!" he yelled. "I got a tip and routed out the Legion boys and chased 'em, but the dirty, Bullshevists beat us to it up the hill. But we've got 'em licked!"

"Keep 'em licked for the rest of the night," Morrison suggested. "I'll be down-town with you, right away!"

But Lanigan, in his raging excitement, was not amenable to hints or orders, nor was he cautious in his revelations. "We can handle things down-town, Your Honor! What we want to know is, what about up-town--up on Capitol Hill?"

"You've had my promise of what I'll do. And I'll do it!"

Senator Corson and his daughter had arrived in the ballroom. The Senator was promptly and intensely interested in this cocksure declaration by Morrison.

"Your promise is the same as hard cash for me and the level-headed ones," retorted Commander Lanigan. "But whether it's the Northern Lights in the skies or plain hellishness in folks or somebody underneath stirring and stirring trouble and starting lies, I don't know! Lots of good boys have stopped being level-headed! I'll hold the gang down if I can, sir. But what I want to know is, can we depend on you to tend to Capitol Hill? Are you still on the job? Can I tell 'em that you're still on the job?"

"You can tell 'em all that I'm on the job from now till morning," shouted the mayor. He was heard by the men outside. They gave his declaration a howl of approval.

"The people will be protected," shouted an unseen admirer.

Stewart hurried to Senator Corson and was not daunted by that gentleman's blazing countenance.

"I'm sorry, sir. This seems to be a flareback of some sort. I'll have police on guard at once!"

"You'll protect the people, eh? There's a flatterer in your mob, Morrison! You can't even give window-glass in this city suitable protection--a mayor like you! I'll have none of your soviet police around my premises." He turned to his secretary. "Call the adjutant-general at the State House and tell him to send a detachment of troops here."

"I trust they'll co-operate well with the police I shall send," stated the Mayor, stiffly. He hastened from the room.

When Stewart had donned hat and overcoat and was about to leave the mansion by the main door, Lana stepped in front of him. "Stewart, you must stop for a moment--you must deny it, what father has been saying to me about you just now!"

"Your father is angry--and in anger a man says a whole lot that he doesn't mean. I'm in a hurry--and a man in a hurry spoils anything he tries to tell. We must let it wait, Lana."

"But if you go on--go on as you're going--crushing Mr. Daunt's plans--spoiling your own grand prospects--antagonizing my father--paying no heed to my advice!" The girl's sentences were galloping breathlessly.

"We'll have time to talk it over, Lana!"

"What! Talk it over after you have been reckless enough to spoil everything? You must stand with your friends, I tell you! Father is wiser than you! Isn't he right?"

"I--I guess he thinks he is--but I can't talk about it." He was backing toward the door.

"You must know what it means--for us two--if you go headlong against him. I stand stanchly for my father--always!"

"I reckon you'll have to be sort of loyal to your father--but I can't talk about it! Not now!" he repeated. He was uncomfortably aware that he had no words to fit the case.

"But if you don't stand with him, you're in with the rabble--the rabble," she declared, indignantly. "He says you are! Stewart, I know you won't insult his wisdom and deny my prayer to you! Only a few moments ago I was ready----But I cannot say those words to you unless----You understand!"

This interview had been permitted only because Senator Corson's attention had been absorbed by Mrs. Stanton's hysterical questions. But the lady's fears did not affect her eyesight. She had noted Lana's departure and she caught a glimpse of the mayor when he strode past the ballroom door with his hat in his hand.

"Yes, I'll be calm, Senator! I'm sure that we'll be perfectly protected. Lana followed the mayor just now, and I suppose she is insisting on a double detail of police."

The Senator promptly followed, too, to find out more exactly what Lana was insisting on.

"Haven't you joined your rabble yet, Morrison?" Corson queried, insolently, when he came upon the two.

"I'm going, sir--going right along!"

Lana set her hands together, the fingers interlaced so tightly that the flesh was as white as her cheeks. "'Your rabble!' Stewart! Oh! Oh!" In spite of her thinly veiled threat of a few moments ago, there was piteous protest in her face and voice.

"According to suggestions from all quarters, I don't seem to fit any other kind of society just now," he replied, ruefully. He marched out into the night.

"Call my car," Senator Corson directed a servant.

In the reception-hall he encountered Silas Daunt, "Slip on your hat and coat. Come along with me to the State House. I'll show you how practical politics can settle a rumpus, after a visionary has tumbled down on his job!"

XII
RIFLES RULE IN THE PEOPLE'S HOUSE

At eleven o'clock Adj.-Gen. Amos Totten set up the cinch of his sword-belt by a couple of holes and began another tour of inspection of the State House. He considered that the parlous situation in state affairs demanded full dress. During the evening he had been going on his rounds at half-hour intervals. On each trip he had been much pleased by the strict, martial discipline and alertness displayed by his guardsmen. The alertness was especially noticeable; every soldier was tautly at 'tention when the boss warrior hove in sight. General Totten was portly and came down hard on his heels with an elderly man's slumping gait, and his sword clattered loudly and his movements were as well advertised as those of a belled cat in a country kitchen.

In the interims, between the tours of General Totten, Captain Danny Sweetsir did his best to keep his company up to duty pitch. But he was obliged to admit to himself that the boys were not taking the thing as seriously as soldiers should.

Squads were scattered all over the lower part of the great building, guarding the various entrances. While Captain Sweetsir was lecturing the tolerant listeners of one squad, he was irritably aware that the boys of the squads that were not under espionage were doing nigh about everything that a soldier on duty should not do, their diversions limited only by their lack of resources.

Therefore, when General Totten complimented him at eleven o'clock, Captain Sweetsir had no trouble at all in disguising his gratification and in assuming the approved, sour demeanor of military gravity. Even then his ears, sharpened by his indignation, caught the clicking of dice on tiles.

"Of course, there will be no actual trouble tonight," said the general, removing his cap and stroking his bald head complacently. "I have assured the boys that there will be no trouble. But this experience is excellent military training for them, and I'm pleased to note that they're thoroughly on the *qui vive*."

Captain Sweetsir, on his own part, did not apprehend trouble, either, but the A.-G.'s bland and unconscious encouragement of laxity was distinctly irritating, "Excuse me, sir, but I have been telling 'em right along that there will be a rumpus. I was trying to key 'em up!"

"Remember that you're a citizen as well as a soldier!" The general rebuked his subaltern sternly. "Don't defame the fair name of your city and state, sir! The guard has been called out by His Excellency, the Commander-in-Chief, merely as a precaution. The presence of troops in the State House--their mere presence here-- has cleared the whole situation. Mayor Morrison agrees with me perfectly on that point."

"He does?" demanded the captain, eagerly, showing relief. "Why, I was afraid--" He checked himself.

"Of what, sir?"

"He didn't look like giving three cheers when I told him in the mill office that we had been ordered out."

"Mayor Morrison called me on the telephone in the middle of the day and I explained to him why it was thought necessary to have the State House guarded."

"And what did he say?" urged the captain, still more eagerly. Again he caught himself. He saluted. "I beg your pardon, General Totten. I have no right to put questions to my superior officer."

But General Totten was not a military martinet. He was an amiable gentleman from civil life, strong with the proletariat because he had been through the chairs in many fraternal organizations and, therefore, handy in politics; and he was strong with the Governor on account of another fraternal tie--his sister was the Governor's wife. General Totten, as a professional mixer, enjoyed a chat.

"That's all right, Captain! What did the mayor say, you ask? He courteously made no comment. Official tact! He is well gifted in that line. His manner spoke for him--signified his complete agreement. He was cordially polite! Very!"

The general put on his cap and slanted it at a jaunty angle. "And he still approves. Is very grateful for the manner in which I'm handling the situation. He called me only a few minutes ago. From his residence! I informed him that all was serene on Capitol Hill."

"And what did he say when he called you this time?"

"Nothing! Oh, nothing by way of criticism! Distinctly affable!"

Captain Sweetsir did not display the enthusiasm that General Totten seemed to expect.

"Let's see, Captain! You are employed by him?"

"Not quite that way! I'm a mill student--learning the wool business at St. Ronan's."

"Aren't you and Mayor Morrison friendly?"

"Oh yes! Certainly, sir! But--" Captain Sweetsir appeared to be having much difficulty in completing his sentences, now that Stewart Morrison had become the topic of conversation.

"But what?"

"He didn't say anything, you tell me?"

"His cordiality spoke louder than words. And, of course, I was glad to meet him half-way. I have invited him to call at the State House, if he cares to do so, though the hour is late. And now I come to the matter of my business with you, Captain Sweetsir," stated the general, putting a degree of official sanction on his garrulity in the case of this subordinate. "If Mayor Morrison does come to the State House to-night, by any chance, you may admit him."

"Did he say anything about coming?"

"Mayor Morrison understands that I am handling everything so tactfully that an official visit by him might be considered a reflection on my capability. His politeness equals mine, Captain. Undoubtedly he will not trouble to come. If he should happen to call unofficially you will please see to it that politeness governs."

"Yes, sir! But the other orders hold good, do they, politeness or no politeness?"

"For mobs and meddling politicians, certainly! I put them all in the same class in a time like this."

General Totten clucked a stuffy chuckle and clanked on his official way.

Captain Sweetsir heard a sound that was as fully exasperating as the click of dice; somebody, somewhere in the dimly lighted rotunda, was snoring. He had previously found sluggards asleep on settees; he went in search of the latest offender. But his thoughts were occupied principally by reflection on that peculiar reticence of the Morrison of St. Ronan's; Mill-student Sweetsir was assailed by doubts of the correctness of General Totten's comfortable conclusions. Mr. Sweetsir, in the line of business, had had opportunity on previous occasions to observe the reaction of the Morrison's reticence.

The adjutant-general did not bother with the elevator. He marched up the middle of the grand stairway.

The State House was only partially illuminated with discreet stint of lights. All the outside incandescents of dome, porte-cochère, and vestibules had been extinguished. The inside lights were limited to those in the corridors and the lobbies. The great building on Capitol Hill seemed like a cowardly giant, clumsily intent on being inconspicuous.

General Totten did not harmonize with the hush. He was distinctly an. ambulatory noise in the corridor which led to the executive department. He was announced informally, therefore, to His Excellency. There was no way of announcing oneself formally to the Governor at that hour, except by rapping on the door of the private chamber. The reception-room was empty, the private secretary was not on duty, the messenger of the Governor and of the Executive Council had been informed by Governor North that his services would not be required for the rest of the evening.

Being both adjutant-general and brother-in-law, Totten did not bother to knock.

The Governor was at his broad table in the center of the room; the big chandelier above the table was ablaze, and the shadows of the grooves on North's face were accentuated. He was staring at the opening door with an expectancy that had been fully apprised as to the caller's identity, and he was not cordial. "You make a devilish noise lugging that meat-cleaver around, Amos. What's the use of all the full-dress nonsense?"

"Official example *and*"--the general bore down hard on the conjunction--"the absolute necessity of a civilian officer getting into uniform when he exercises authority. I know human nature!"

"All right! Maybe you do. But don't trip yourself up with that sword and fall down and break your neck," advised the Governor, satirically solicitous as one of the family. "Anything stirring down-stairs?"

"The situation is being handled perfectly. Everybody alert. It's wonderful training for the guards."

"I haven't liked the sound of reports from the city. Has any news come to you lately?"

"Nothing of special importance. Only a little disturbance, or the threat of one, in the vicinity of Senator Corson's residence. His secretary called up. I sent a few boys down there."

"A disturbance?" barked North.

"I didn't quite gather the details. The man ran his words together." General Totten helped himself to one of his brother-in-law's cigars.

"This sounds serious. Why the infernal blazes don't you wake up?"

"An officer commanding troops mustn't be thrown off his poise by every flurry. What would happen if I didn't keep my head?"

"When was this?"

"Oh, maybe half an hour ago," replied the adjutant-general, with martial indifference to any mere rumblings of popular discontent.

"That's probably the reason why Corson hasn't got along yet. I'm expecting him. I sent for him." North twitched his nose; his eye-glasses dropped off and dangled at the end of their cord. "I have sent explicit orders to Mayor Morrison to tend to that mob that he has been coddling. He's letting 'em get away from him, if what you say is so."

"Oh, the mayor and I are in perfect accord and are handling the situation. I have just been talking with him on the telephone." Totten settled his cigar into the corner of his mouth.

"Where is he?"

"At his residence! Showing that he isn't any more worried than I am."

"Well, if he has got the thing in hand again, I hope he'll stay at his residence. If reports are anything to go by, he didn't help matters by going down-town and making speeches to that rabble."

"Politeness wins in the long run, Lawrence, whether you're talking to the mob or the masters. I make it my principle in life. Tact and diplomacy. Harmony and--"

"Hell and repeat!" stormed North. "You and Morrison are not taking this thing the way you ought to! In accord, say you! He is torching 'em up and you are grinning while the fire burns! Fine team-work! Amos, you get in accord with me and my orders. You keep away from Morrison till I can make sure that he stands clean in his party loyalty."

His Excellency was stuttering in his wrath and the general determined to be discreetly silent as to his recent tender of politeness to Morrison through the captain of the guards. Furthermore, Totten's self-complacency assured him that the mayor of Marion was leaving the affairs on Capitol Hill in the hands of the accredited commander on Capitol Hill.

Governor North pulled open a drawer of the table. He threw a bunch of keys to his brother-in-law. "I had the messenger leave these with me. Lock up all the doors of the Council Chamber. Leave only my private door unlocked."

The adjutant-general caught the keys. "But you certainly don't expect any trouble up here, with my guards--"

"It's plenty enough of a job for a cat to watch one rat-hole! Lock up, I tell you!"

XIII
THE LINE-UP FORMS IN THE PEOPLE'S HOUSE

While General Totten was bruising his dignity in the menial work of a turnkey, Governor North received two visitors. They were furred gentlemen who entered abruptly by the private door--the before-mentioned rat-hole--but the waiting cat did not pounce. On the contrary, one of the furred intruders did the pouncing. It was Senator Corson and he was furiously angry.

"What kind of a damnable fool has been giving off orders to those soldiers? I have been tramping around outside this State House from door to door, held up everywhere and insulted by those young whelps."

"I don't see how that could happen," protested the Governor.

"Who gave off such orders?"

"There were no orders, not in your case. I didn't think it was necessary to specify anything in regard to you, Senator. Do you mean to tell me that there's a man down there who didn't recognize you--who refused to allow you to pass without question?"

"They all know me! Of course they know me. And that's the whole trouble. They made that the reason why they wouldn't let me in here."

"How in the devil's name could that be?" The Governor's anger that promised punishment for the offenders served Senator Corson in lieu of apology.

"I was informed that there were strict orders not to admit politicians. According to those lunkheads at the doors I came under that classification." The Senator threw off his coat. "And Daunt, here, was penalized on account of the company he was keeping. Find out who gave those orders."

General Totten had locked the doors and was nervously jangling the keys.

"Amos, what kind of a fool have you been making yourself with your orders?" the Governor demanded.

"I--I think some instructions of mine in regard to admitting any of those persons whose seats are in dispute--probably those orders were misconstrued. My guards are very zealous--very alert," affirmed the adjutant-general, putting as good a face on the matter as was possible. He fully realized that this was no time to mention that exception in favor of Mayor Morrison, or to explain that he had intended to have Captain Sweetsir accept humorously instead of literally the more recent statement about politicians.

"There are two of those alert patriots who have had their zeal dulled for the time being," stated the Senator, showing his teeth with a grim smile. "I stood the impertinence as long as I could and then I cuffed the ears of the fools and walked in."

"We did issue strict instructions, as Amos has intimated," the Governor pleaded. "Some of those Socialists and Progressives who are claiming their seats have hired counsel and they proposed to force their way into the House and Senate chambers and make a test case, inviting forcible expulsion. I'm reckoning that my plan of forcible exclusion leaves us in cleaner shape."

"I'm not sure just how clean the whole thing is going to leave us, North." The Senator tossed his coat upon a huge divan at one side of the chamber and invited Daunt to dispose of his own coat in like fashion. Corson came to the table and sat sidewise on one corner of it. "You know how I feel about your pressing the election statutes to the extent you have. But we've got the old nag right in the middle of the river, and we've got to attend to swimming instead of swapping. I think, in spite of all their howling, the other crowd will take their medicine, as the courts hand it to them, when the election cases go up for adjudication. But there's a gang in every community that always takes advantage of any signs of a mix-up in high authority. My house got merry hell from a mob a little while ago. There's no political significance in the matter, however!"

The Governor queried anxiously for details and Corson gave them. He bitterly arraigned Morrison's stand.

North came to his feet and banged his fist on the table. "What? Take that attitude toward a mob in his own city? Strike hands with a ringleader of a riot--do it under a violated roof? Do it after what he promised me in the way of co-operation for law and order? Has he completely lost his mind, Senator Corson?"

"I think so," stated the Senator, with sardonic venom. "I'll admit that the thing isn't exactly clear to me--what he's trying to do--what he's thinking. A crazy man's actions and whims seldom are understandable by a sane man. But, so I gather, after showing us, as he has this evening, a sample of his work in running municipal government, he now proposes to take full charge of state matters."

"What?" yelled the Governor.

"Yes! Promised the ringleader of the mob to come up here and run everything on Capitol Hill. In behalf of the people--as the people's protector!" The Senator's irony rasped like a file on metal.

Banker Daunt was provoked to add his evidence. "It's exactly as my friend Corson says, Governor. I have been hearing some fine soviet doctrines from the mouth of Morrison this evening. Not at all stingy about giving his help to all those who need it! Gave his pledge of assistance to the fellow in the ballroom, as Corson says. Understood him to say that he is coming up here to help you, too!"

"I rather expected to find him here," pursued the Senator. "He went away in a great hurry to go somewhere. But after my experience with your alert soldiers down-stairs, Totten, I'm afraid our generous savior is going to be bothered about getting in."

The adjutant-general pulled off his cap and scrubbed his palm nervously over the glossy surface that was revealed.

"You might give some special orders to admit him," suggested Corson. "He'll be a great help in an emergency."

"This settles it with me as to Morrison and his conception of law and order," affirmed Governor North. "I have been depending on him to handle his city. I'd as soon depend on Lenin and the kind of government he's running in Russia."

"According to the samples furnished by both, I think Lenin would rank higher as help," said the Senator. "At least he has shown that he knows how to handle a mob. But we may as well calm down, North, and attend to our own business. We are making altogether too much account of a silly nincompoop. Daunt and I let our feelings get away from us this evening on the same subject. But we woke up promptly. Morrison was in a position to help his friends and to amount to something as an aid in that line. Now that he is running with the rabble, for some purpose of his own, he can be ignored. He amounts to nothing--to that!" He snapped a derogatory finger into his palm. "We can handle that rabble, Morrison included." He turned to the adjutant-general. "Your men seem to be alert enough in keeping out gentlemen who ought to be let in. Do you think you can depend on them to keep out real intruders?"

"Oh yes!" faltered Totten, absent-mindedly. He was trying to clear his troubled thoughts in regard to the matter of Morrison, who was now presented in a light where politeness might not be allowed to govern the situation.

"Have they been put to any test of their courage and reliability? Have they been up against any actual threats from the outside, this evening?"

"No, but I can depend on them to the limit, Senator Corson. I have been on regular tours of inspection. They are a cool and nervy set of young men and I have impressed on them a sense of what a soldier on duty should be."

"Very well, Totten! Nevertheless, let us hope that the mob fools have gone home to bed, including our friend Morrison. He needs his sleep; I believe he still follows the family rule of being in his mill at seven in the morning. He's a good millman, even if he isn't much of a politician."

"And I don't look for any trouble, anyway," declared General Totten, adding in his thoughts, for his further consolation, the assurance that, at half past eleven, so the clock on the wall revealed to his gaze, such an early riser as Morrison must be abed and asleep; therefore, the exception for the sake of politeness did not threaten to complicate affairs!

But at that instant something else did threaten.

Through the arches and corridors of the State House rang the sounds of tumult, breaking on the hush with terrifying suddenness. One voice, shouting with frenzied violence, prefaced the general uproar; there was the crashing of shattered wood.

The rifles barked angrily.

"My God, North! I've been afraid of it!" Corson lamented. "You have crowded 'em too hard!"

"I'm going by the law, Corson! The election law! The statute law! And the riot laws of this state! The law says a mob must be put down!"

An immediate and reassuring silence suggested that the law had prevailed and that a mob had been put down in this instance. Corson, whose face was white and whose eyes were distended, voiced that conviction. "If a gang had been able to get in they'd be howling their heads off. But it was quick over!"

The men in the Executive Chamber stood in their tracks and exchanged troubled glances in silence.

"Amos, what are you waiting for?" demanded His Excellency.

"For a report--an official report on the matter," mumbled the adjutant-general, steadying his trembling hands by shoving them inside his sword-belt.

"Go down and find out what it all means."

"I can save time by telephoning to the watchman's room," demurred Totten.

"Incidentally saving your skin!" the Governor rapped back. "But I don't care how you get the information, if only you get it and get it sudden!"

Totten went to the house telephone in the private secretary's room and called and waited; he called again and waited.

"Nobody is on his job in this State House tonight!" His Excellency's fears had wire-edged his temper. "By gad! you go down there and tend to yours, as I have told you to do, Amos, or I'll take that sword and race you along the corridor on the point of it!"

"We must be informed on what this means," insisted the Senator.

There was a rap on the private door. Again the men in the Executive Chamber swapped uneasy glances. Corson's demeanor invited the Governor to assume the responsibility. His Excellency was manifestly shirking. He looked over his shoulder in the direction of the fireplace, as if he felt an impulse to arm himself with the ornamental poker and tongs.

"May I come in?" The voice was that of the mayor of Marion. The voice was deprecatory.

"Come in!" invited North.

Morrison entered. He greeted them with a wide smile that did not fit the seriousness of the situation, as they viewed it. There was humor behind the smile; it suggested suppressed hilarity; it hinted that he had something funny to tell them.

But their grim countenances did not encourage him.

"If I am intruding on important business----"

"Shut the door behind you! What is it? What happened?" demanded North.

Before shutting the door Morrison reached into the gloom behind him and pulled in a soldier.

Stewart had put off his evening garb. He wore a business suit of the shaggy gray mixture that was one of the staples among the products of St. Ronan's mill. His matter-of-fact attire was not the only element that set him out in sharp contrast among the claw-hammers and uniforms in the room; he was bubbling with undisguised merriment; Corson, Daunt, and the Governor were sullenly anxious; even the young soldier looked flustered and frightened.

"I have brought along Paul Duchesne so that you may have it from his own mouth! Go ahead, Duchesne! Let 'em in on the joke! Gentlemen, get ready for a laugh!" Stewart set an example for them by a suggestive chuckle.

"Your arrival in the State House seems to have been attended by considerable of a demonstration," commented Senator Corson, recovering himself sufficiently to indulge in his animosity. "Judging from your success in starting other riots this evening, I ought to have guessed that you were in the neighborhood."

"My arrival had nothing whatever to do with the demonstration, Senator. Go on, Duchesne!"

"I jomped myself," stammered the soldier, a particularly crestfallen Canuck.

"I see you don't grasp the idea," Morrison hastened to put in. "We mustn't have the flavor of the joke spoiled. I know Paul, here. He works in my mill. He has a little affliction that's rather common among French Canadians. He's a jumper." He suddenly clapped the youth on the shoulder and yelled "Hi!" so loudly that all the auditors leaped in trepidation. The soldier leaped the highest, flung his arms about wildly, and let out a resounding yelp.

"That's the idea!" explained Stewart. "A congenital nervous trouble. Jumpers, they are called!"

"What the devil is this all about?" raged the Governor.

"Tell 'em, Paul. Hurry up!"

"I gone off on de nap on a settee," muttered Duchesne, twisting his fingers together.

General Totten winced.

"Dere ban whole lot o' dem gone off on de nap, too," asserted the guard, offering defense for himself.

"By way of showing alertness, Totten!" growled the Senator.

"So I ban dream somet'ing! Ba gar! I dream dat t'ree or two bobcat he come--"

"Never mind the details of the dream, Paul!" interposed Morrison. "These gentlemen have business! Get 'em to the laugh, quick!"

"Ma big button on ma belt she caught on de crack between de slat of dat settee. And when I fight all dat bobcat dat jomp on maself, ba gee! it was de settee dat fall on me and I fight dat all over de floor. Dat's all! Oh yes! Dey all wake up and shoot!"

"And nobody hurt!" stated Morrison. He gazed at the sour faces of the listeners. "Great Scott! Doesn't Duchesne's battle to the death with a settee get even a grin? What's the matter with all of you?"

"We seem to be quite all right--in our normal senses," returned the Senator, icily. "I believe there are persons who gibber and giggle at mishaps to others--but I also believe that such a peculiar sense of humor is confined largely to institutions for the refuge of the feeble-minded."

"You may go back to your nap, Duchesne!" The mayor turned on the soldier and spoke sharply. He followed the young man to the door and closed it behind Duchesne.

He marched across the chamber and faced the surly Governor. "I brought the boy here, Your Excellency, so that you might get the thing straight. I hope you believe him, even if you don't take much stock in me!" Morrison's face matched the others in gravity. There was an incisive snap in his tone. "I happened to be in the rotunda when the--"

"How did you happen to be in the rotunda, sir--past the guards?"

"I walked in."

"By whose permission?"

"Why, I reckoned it must have been yours," returned Stewart, calmly.

"I gave no such permission."

"Well, at any rate, I was informed by the guards that a special exception had been made in my case. Furthermore, Governor North, you told me this evening that if I needed any specific information I could find you at the State House."

"By telephone, sir! By telephone! I distinctly stipulated that!"

"I'm sorry! I was considerably engrossed by other matters just then. Perhaps I didn't get you straight. However, telephone conferences are apt to be unsatisfactory for both parties. I'm glad I came up. I assure you it's no personal inconvenience to me, sir!"

"There's a fine system of military guard here, and a fine bunch to enforce it. That's what I've got on my mind to say!" whipped out the Senator. "If one man and a settee can show up your soldiers in that fashion, Totten, what will a real affair do to them?"

"Nobody sent for you, Mayor Morrison. Nobody understands why you're here," stated Governor North. "You're not needed."

The intruder hesitated for a few moments. His eyes found no welcome in any of the faces in the Executive Chamber. He swapped a whimsical smile for their frowns.

"Well, at all events, I'm here," he said, mildly.

He was carrying his overcoat on his arm, his hat in his hand. He went across the room and laid the garment carefully on the divan, smoothing its folds. His manner indicated that he felt that the coat might be lying there for some little time, and consideration for good cloth was ingrained in a Morrison.

XIV
THE IMPENDING SHAME OF A STATE

Morrison, returning from the shadows, standing in the light-flood from the great chandelier, confronted three men who were making no effort to disguise their angry hostility.

The adjutant-general, nervously neutral, dreading incautious words that would reveal his unfortunate policy of politeness, tiptoed to the table and laid there the bunch of keys. "I'm needed officially down-stairs, Your Excellency!"

"By Judas! I should think you were!"

Stewart placed a restraining hand on Totten's arm. "I beg your pardon, Governor, but we need the adjutant-general of the state in our conference."

"Conference about *what*?"

"About the situation that's developing outside, sir."

"I'm principally interested in the situation that has developed inside. In just what capacity do you appear here?"

There was offensive challenge in every intonation of North's voice. His eyes protruded, purple circlets made his cheek-bones look like little knobs, he shoved forward his eye-glasses as far as the cord permitted and waggled them with a hand that trembled.

Morrison's good humor continued; his calmness was giving him a distinct advantage, and North, still shaken by the panic of a few moments before, was forced farther off his poise by realization of that advantage.

"Allow me to be present simply as an unprejudiced constituent of yours, Governor North."

"Judging from all reports, I'm not sure whether you are a constituent or not. I'm considerably doubtful about your politics, Morrison."

"I hope you don't intend to read me out of the party, sir! But if that question is in doubt, please permit me to be here as the mayor of the city of Marion. There's no doubt about my being that!"

"Let me remind you that this is the State House, not City Hall."

"But tolerate me for a few minutes! I beg of you, sir! Both of us are sworn executives!"

"Your duties lie where you belong--down in your city. This is the State House, I repeat!"

"Do you absolutely refuse to give me a courteous hearing?"

"Under the circumstances, after your actions this evening, after your public alliance with the mob and your boasts of what you were coming up here to do, I'm taking no chances on you. You're only an intruder. Again, this is the State House!"

Morrison dropped his deference. He shot out a forefinger that was just as emphatic as the Governor's eye-glasses. "I accept your declaration as to what this place is! It is the State House. It is the Big House of the People. I'm a joint owner in it. I'm here on my own ground as a citizen, as a taxpayer in this state. I have personal business here. Let me inform you, Governor North, that I'm going to stay until I finish that business."

"That poppycock kind of reasoning would allow every mob-mucker in this state to rampage through here at his own sweet will. General Totten, call a corporal and his squad. Put this man out."

Senator Corson grunted his indorsement and went to a chair and sat down. His Excellency was pursuing his familiar tactics in an emergency--the rough tactics that were characteristic of him. In this case Senator Corson approved and allowed the Governor to boss the operation.

"I-I think, Mayor Morrison," ventured the adjutant-general, "considering that recent perfect understanding we had on the matter, that we'd do well to keep this on the plane of politeness."

"So do I," Stewart agreed.

"Then I hazard the guess that you'll accompany me down-stairs to the door. Calling a guard would be mutually embarrassing."

"It sure would," asserted Stewart, agreeing still.

"Then--" The general crooked a polite arm and offered it.

"But your guess was too much of a hazard! You don't win!"

However, Morrison turned on his heel and ran toward the private door. He appeared to be solving all difficulties by flight. It was plain that those in the room supposed so; their tension relaxed; the mayor of Marion was manifestly avoiding the ignominy of ejection from the Capitol by the militia--and that would be a fine piece of news to be bruited on the streets next day, if he had remained to force that issue!

Stewart flung open the door. But instead of stepping through he stepped back. "Come in," he called.

Paymaster Andrew Mac Tavish led the way, plodding stolidly, his neck particularly rigid. Delora Bunker, stenographer at St. Ronan's mill, followed. Last came Patrolman Rellihan, his bulk nigh filling the door, his helmeted head almost scraping the lintel. He carried a night-stick that resembled a flail-handle rather than the usual locust club. Morrison slammed the door and Rellihan put his back against it.

There was a profound hush in the Executive Chamber. The feet of those who entered made no sound on the thick carpet. Those who were in the chamber offered evidence of the truism that there are situations where words fail to do justice to the emotions.

Morrison was the first to speak. He walked to the table before uttering a word; on his way across the room his eyes were on the keys. When he leaned on the table he put one hand over them. "This invasion seems outrageous, gentlemen. Undoubtedly it is. But I have tried another plan with you and it did not succeed. I had hoped that I would not need these assistants whom I have just called in."

"Totten, go bring the guard!" North's voice was balefully subdued.

Rellihan looked straight ahead and twirled his stick.

"I apologize for stretching my special exception a bit, and introducing these guests past the boys at the door," Stewart went on. "I'm breaking the rules of politeness--and the rules of everything else, I'm afraid. But all rules seem to be suspended to-night!"

"Totten!" the Governor roared, pounding his fist on the arm of his chair.

Morrison gave the policeman a side-glance as if to inform himself that all was right with Rellihan.

Then he pulled a handy chair to the table and motioned to Miss Bunker. She sat down and opened her note-book.

"I have come here on business, gentlemen, and you must allow me to follow some of my business methods. The heat of argument often causes men to forget what has been said. I'm willing to leave what I may say to the record, and, in view of the fact that all this is public business, I trust I'll have your co-operation along the same line. And there's a young lady present," he added. "That fact will help us to get along wonderfully well together."

"What's that devilish policeman doing at my door?" demanded the Governor, finding that his frantic gestures were not starting the adjutant-general on his way.

"Insuring complete privacy!" The mayor beamed on the Governor. "Nothing gets in--nothing gets out!"

North grabbed the telephone instrument on his desk.

One of Stewart's hands was covering the keys; with the fingers of the other hand he had been fumbling under the edge of the desk. He suddenly pulled wires from the confining staples; he yanked a big mill-knife from his trousers pocket and cut the wires. North flung a dead instrument clattering on the broad table and found only oaths fit to apply to this perfectly amazing effrontery.

"You need not take, Miss Bunker!" The quiet dignity of Morrison and the rebuke the Governor found in the girl's contemplative eyes choked off the profanity as effectively as would gripping fingers at his throat.

"I realize that all this is absolutely unprecedented--has never been done before--is unadulterated gall on my part, Governor North. Perhaps I haven't a leg to stand on."

"Morrison, this infernal nonsense must cease!"

Senator Corson shouted, leaping from his chair and shaking both fists.

"You need not take, Miss Bunker!"

Corson gulped and surveyed the young lady, and found her eyes as disconcertingly rebuking as they had proved in the case of North.

"Not especially on account of the style of your language, Senator! But you are merely a visitor here, the same as I! At the present time your comments on the business between the Governor and myself can scarcely have any weight in the record."

"What in blazes is that business? Get it out of you!" commanded the other principal in the controversy.

"With pleasure! Thank you for coming down to the matter in hand. You may take, Miss Bunker.

"Governor North, I have been about among people this evening and--"

"You have been making incendiary speeches, and I demand to know what you have said and why you have said it!"

"I have no time now to go into those details. My business is more pressing, sir."

"You're in cahoots with a mob! I saw you operating, with my own eyes, under my own roof," asserted Senator Corson, violently.

"I have no time for discussing that matter." Morrison looked up at the clock on the wall. "This other business, I assert, is urgent."

Banker Daunt had been holding his peace, growling anathema to himself in the depths of a big chair.

He struggled to the edge of that chair. "I am in this building right now to warn the Governor of this state that you are playing your own selfish game to stifle enterprise and development and to discourage outside capital--hundreds of thousands of it--waiting to come in here."

"Pardon me, sir! I have no time to discuss water-power, either! Right now I'm submitting news instead of theories!" He faced the Governor again. "That's why I'm here--I'm bringing news. That news must put everything else to one side. We have minutes only to deal with the matter. And if we don't use those minutes with all the wisdom that's in us, the shame of our state will be on the wires of the world inside of an hour!"

His vehemence intimidated them. His manner as the bearer of ill tidings won what his appeals had not secured--an instant hearing.

"What I say will be a matter of record, and the blame will be placed where it belongs. You can't claim that you didn't have facts. I have been among the people. I have sent others among 'em and I have received reports and I know what I am talking about. There's a mob massing down-town--a mob made up of many different elements! That kind of mob can't be handled by mere arguments or by machine-guns. That mob must be shown! Talking won't do any good. Just a moment! You won't do what you ought to do, Governor, unless you have this thing driven straight at you! In that mob are the men who have voted for various members of the legislature who claim seats and whose seats are threatened. It's a personal matter with those men. You can't soft-soap 'em to-night with promises of what the courts will do. Several hundred huskies are on the way over here from the Agawam quarries Those men don't care about this or that candidate. They have been paid to grab in on general principles--and they're bringing sledge-hammers. In that mob, also, are the Red aliens who keep under cover till a row breaks out; any kind of trouble suits their purpose--and you know what their purpose is in regard to this government of ours. They're coming, I tell you. They're coming on to Capitol Hill!"

"And what have you been doing to stop 'em, after all your promises of what you'd do?" raged North.

"I've been doing the best I could, with what loyal boys I could depend on. But I want to know now what *you're* going to do?"

"Shoot every damnation thug of 'em who gets in range of our machine-guns. Totten, hustle yourself down-stairs and see that it's done!"

"Genera! Totten will not leave this room--not now! You're all wrong, Governor."

"That's the way a mob was handled in one state In this Union not so very long ago, and the Governor was right! He was hailed from one end of the country to the other as right!"

"The principle behind him was right--that's what you mean, Governor North. That was just the point he made!"

"Do you dare to stand there and intimate that I haven't got principle behind me? Statute law, election law?"

Morrison glanced again at the clock; then he tossed a bomb into the argument. "The principle in this instance is a pretty wabbly backing, sir. I'm afraid that even my loyal boys will join the mob if the news gets out about those election returns in certain districts--the returns that were sent back secretly to be corrected."

The bomb had all the effect that Morrison hoped for. His Excellency slumped back in his chair and "pittered" his lips wordlessly.

"I don't think the news has actually got out among the general public, but it's apt to leak any minute, sir. You can't afford to take chances."

"Such slander is preposterous!" Corson asserted. "What used to be done--reviving old stories--I say that our party will not lend its countenance to any such tricks." In his excitement he had dropped an admission as to the past in politics while offering a disclaimer as to the present.

"There's no time now for any political discussions," retorted Morrison, curtly. "It's a matter right now of side-tracking a fight. If that fight comes off, Governor North, the truth will come out. And you can't point to a principle in your case as an excuse for bloodshed!"

"If a mob attacks this State House there's got to be a fight."

"It takes two to make a fight, sir. Order General Totten to march his troops out of the State House. Machine-guns and all! Tell 'em to go home and go to bed."

That audacious advice was a second bomb!

After a few moments Senator Corson leaped out of his chair, strode across the room, and plucked his coat and hat from the divan. "Come along, Daunt!" he counseled, his voice cracking hoarsely.

"Hold on, Senator!" expostulated the Governor. "I need your help!"

"I won't allow myself to be mixed into this mess, North. I can't afford to help shoulder the blame where I have not been fully informed. And I won't allow a lunatic to endanger my life. Come on, Daunt, I tell you!"

"If you're bound to go, I'll go along, too," proffered the Governor, rising hastily. "This thing can be handled. It's got to be handled. We'll go where this infernal, clattering loom from St. Ronan's mill can't break up a gentlemen's conference."

Stewart did not suggest that the gentlemen remain; nor did he offer to go; nor did he plead for a decision. He stood quietly and watched them pull on their overcoats.

The Senator led the retreat toward the private door.

Morrison dropped the captured bunch of keys into his pocket.

Rellihan held his club horizontally in front of him with both hands.

"Get out of the way!" yelped Corson.

The officer shook his head.

"General Totten, open that door."

"No chance!" Rellihan growled.

North wagged his way close to the barring "fender" and shook an admonitory finger under the policeman's nose. "I'm the Governor of this state! I order you to move away from that door."

"I can't help what ye are! I'm taking me orders on'y fr'm the mayor o' Marion."

"You see, gentlemen!" suggested Morrison. "It looks as if we'd be obliged to settle our business right where we are--in this room. Time is short. Won't you come back here to the table?"

There was absolute silence in the Executive Chamber--a silence that continued. The dignitaries at the door deigned to accord to Morrison neither glance nor word; they would not indulge his incredible audacity to that extent. As to Rellihan, they did not feel like stooping so low as to waste words on the impassive giant who personified an ignorant insolence that made no account of personalities. They adventured in no move against that obstacle in their path, either by concerted attack or individual effort to pass. They looked like wakened sleepers who were struggling with the problems proposed in a nightmare. It was a situation which seemed beyond solution by the ordinary sensible methods.

After a time Governor North voiced in a coarse manner, inadequately, some expression of the emotion that was dominating the group. "What in hell is the matter with us, anyway?"

Again there was a prolonged silence.

"Seeing that nobody else seems to want to express an opinion on the subject, I'll tell you what the matter is, as I look at it," ventured Stewart, chattily matter-of-fact. "We're all native-born Americans in this room. Right down deep in our hearts we're not afraid of our soldiers. We good-naturedly indulge the boys when they are called on to exercise authority. But from the time an American youngster begins to steal apples and junk and throw snowballs and break windows a healthy fear of a regular cop is ingrained in him. It's a fear he doesn't stop to analyze. It's just there, that's all he knows. Even a perfectly law-abiding citizen walking home late feels a little tingle of anxiety in him when he marches past a cop. Puts on an air as much as to say, 'I hope you think I'm all right, officer--tending right to my own business!' So, in this case, it's only your ingrained American nature talking to you, gentlemen! You're all right! Nothing is the matter with you! It ought to please you because you feel that way! Proves you are truly American. 'Don't monkey with the cop!' Just as long as we obey that watchword we've got a good government!"

Senator Corson was more infuriated by that bland preachment than he would have been by vitriolic insult. While he marched back to the table he prefaced his arraignment of Morrison by calling him an impudent pup. He dwelt on that subject with all his power of invective for some minutes.

"I agree with you, Senator," admitted Morrison when Corson stopped to gather more ammunition of anathema. "But what are you going to do about it?"

He asked the same question after the Senator had finished a statement of his opinion on the obstinacy of the lunkhead at the door.

The Senator kept on in his objurgation. But whenever he looked at the door he found the policeman there, an immovable obstacle.

Whenever Corson looked at Morrison he met everlastingly that hateful query.

Both the question and the cop were impossible, impassable. Corson found the thing too outrageously ridiculous to be handled by sane argument; his insanity in declamation was getting him nowhere.

"There's only one subject before the meeting," insisted Stewart. "We've got to keep this state from being ashamed of itself when it wakes up to-morrow morning!"

Somewhere, in some hidden place in the room, a subdued buzzing began and continued persistently.

The understanding that passed between Corson and North in the glance which they exchanged was immediate and highly informative, even had the observer been obtuse. But in that crisis Stewart Morrison was not obtuse.

Whether it was deference, one to the other, or caution in general that was dominating the Senator and the Governor was not clearly revealed by their countenance. At any rate, they made no move.

"Pardon me, Senator Corson," said Stewart. "I'm quite sure I know where the other end of that telephone line is. I think your daughter is calling!" His inquisitive eyes were searching the walls of the chamber; the source of the buzzing was not easily to be located by the sound.

The Governor suddenly dumped himself out of his chair and started across the room.

Morrison strode into His Excellency's path and extended a restraining arm that was as authoritative as Rellihan's club. "I beg your pardon, too, Governor! But that call is undoubtedly for Senator Corson. I happen to know quite a lot about the conveniences in his residence!"

"And all the evening you have been using that knowledge to help you in violating my hospitality! Morrison, you're not much else than a sneak!" affirmed Corson.

The Governor struck his fist against the rigid arm and spat an oath in Morrison's face, "Get out of my way! I'm in my own office--I'll tend to that call!"

"No, you'll not!" was Morrison's quick rejoinder. "Senator Corson, if you want to inform your daughter that you're all safe--if you want to ask her not to worry, you'd better answer. But I must insist that a private line shall not be used to convey out of this room any of our public business!"

Corson then became the only moving figure in the tableau; he went to the wall, pushed aside a huge frame which held the state's coat of arms, and pulled from a niche a telephone on an extension arm. He proceeded to display his utter contempt for commands issuing from the absurd interloper who was presuming in such dictation to dignity "Yes! Lana! Call High-sheriff Dalton! As quickly as possible! Tell him to secure a posse. Tell him I'm in the State House, threatened by a lunatic. Tell him--"

By that time Morrison was at Corson's side and was wresting the instrument from the wall. He broke off the arm and the wires and flung them across the room.

"There's fight enough on the docket, as the thing stands, without calling in another bunch to make it three-sided, sir! Rellihan, open the door for Mac Tavish! Andy, run to the public booth in the corridor and call Dalton and tell him to pay no attention to any hullabaloo by hysterical women. Tell him I said so! Ask him to keep that to himself. And rush back!"

He turned on the Senator and the Governor.

There was no longer apology or compromise in the demeanor of the mayor of Marion. "I know I'm a rank outsider! You needn't try to tell me what I know myself. I didn't think I'd need to be so rank! But I'm just what you're forcing me to be. I have jumped in here to stop something that there's no more sense in than there is in a dog-fight. They may fight in spite of all I can do! But, by the gods! I'm not going to stand by and see men like you rub their ears! Senator Corson, I advise you and Governor North to go and sit down. You're only making spectacles of yourselves!"

XV
THE BOSS OF THE JOB

After Senator Corson had recovered his poise his dignity asserted itself and he sat down and assumed an attitude that suggested the frigidity of a statue on an ice-cake. He checked Governor North with an impatient flap of the hand. "You have had your innings as a manager, North!"

He proceeded frostily with Morrison. "There was never a situation in state history like this one you have precipitated, sir, and if I have made an ass of myself I was copying current manners."

"It is a strange situation, I'll admit, Senator," Morrison agreed.

"As a newsmonger, you say, do you, that minutes are valuable?"

"Yes, sir!"

"Well, we'd better find out how valuable they are. Will you send General Totten below to investigate?"

Morrison surveyed appraisingly the panoplied adjutant-general. "I'd never think of making General Totten an errand-boy, sir, if I'm to imply that I have any say in affairs just now."

"You have assumed all say! You have put gentlemen in a position where they can't help themselves." The Senator scowled in the direction of Rellihan. But Rellihan did not mind; right then he was opening the door to the returning Mac Tavish.

"I routed Mac Tavish out of bed and brought him along to attend to errands. He will go and see how matters are below, and outside," proffered Morrison, courteously.

The self-appointed manager gave Mac Tavish his new orders and added: "Inquire, please, if any telegrams have arrived for me. I'm expecting some."

Rellihan again deferentially opened the door for the messenger of the mayor of Marion; Mac Tavish had knocked and given his name. "It's all richt, sir!" he had reported on his arrival from his mission to the telephone.

The exasperated Governor viewed that free ingress and muttered.

Mac Tavish's unimpeded egress on the second errand provoked the Governor more acutely.

"Morrison, I'm now talking strictly for myself," went on the Senator. "I shall use plain words. By your attitude you directly accuse me of being a renegade in politics. To all intents and purposes I am under arrest, as a person dangerous to be at large in the affairs that are pressing."

"Senator Corson, I don't believe you ever did a deliberately wrong or wicked thing in your life, as an individual."

"I thank you!"

"But deliberately political methods can be wicked in their general results, even if those methods are sanctioned by usage. It's wicked to start a fight here to-night by allowing political misunderstandings to play fast and loose with the people."

"You're a confounded imbecile, that's what you are," shouted Governor North.

The mayor turned on him. "Replying in the same sort of language, so that you may understand right where you and I get off in our relations, I'll tell you that you're the kind of man who would use grandmothers in a matched fight to settle a political grudge--if the other fellow had a grandmother and you could borrow one. Now let me alone, sir! I am talking with Senator Corson!"

The Senator squelched the Governor with another gesture. "We have our laws, Morrison. We must abide by 'em. And the political game must be played according to the law."

"I think I have already expressed my opinion to you about that game, sir. I'll say again that in this country politics is no longer a mere game to be played for party advantage and the aggrandizement of individuals. The folks won't stand for that stuff any longer."

"I think you and North, both of you, are overexcited. You're going off half cocked. You are exaggerating a tempest in a teapot."

"If every community in this country gets right down to business and stops the teapot tempests by good sense in handling them when they start, we'll be able to prevent a general tornado that may sweep us all to Tophet, Senator Corson."

"Legislation on broad lines will remedy our troubles. We are busy in Washington on such matters."

"Good luck to the cure-all, sir! But in the mean time we need specific doses, right at home, in every community, early and often. That's what we ought to be tending to to-night, here in Marion. If every city and town does the same thing, the country at large won't have to worry."

Senator Corson kept his anxious gaze on the private door. "Well, let's have it, Morrison! You seem to be bossing matters, just as you threatened to do. What's your dose in this case?"

"I wasn't threatening! I was promising."

"Promising what?"

"That the people would get a square deal in this legislative matter."

"You don't underrate your abilities, I note!"

"Oh, I was not promising to do it myself. I have no power in state politics. I was promising that Governor North and his Executive Councilors who canvassed the election returns would give the folks a square deal."

In his rage the Governor, defying such presumptuous interference, was not fortunate in phrasing his declaration that Morrison had no right to promise any such thing.

The big millman surveyed His Excellency with a whimsical expression of distress. "Why, I supposed I had the right to promise that much on behalf of our Chief Executive. You aren't going to deny 'em a square deal--you don't mean that, do you, sir?"

"Confound your impudence, you have no right to twist my meaning. I'm going by the law--strictly by the statutes! The question will be put up to the court."

"Certainly!" affirmed Senator Corson. "It must go to the court."

Just then Rellihan slammed the private door with a sort of official violence.

Mac Tavish had entered. He marched straight to Morrison with the stiff jerkiness of an automaton. He carried a sealed telegram and held it as far in front of himself as possible. Stewart seized upon it and tore the envelope. "I'm glad to hear you say that about the court, gentlemen. I have taken a liberty this evening. Will you please wait a moment while I glance at this?"

It was plainly, so his manner indicated, something that had a bearing on the issue. They leaned forward and attended eagerly on him when he began to read aloud:

"My opinion hastily given for use if emergency is such as you mention is that mere technicalities, clerical errors that can be shown to be such or minor irregularities should not be allowed to negative will of voter when same has been shown beyond reasonable doubt. Signed, Davenport, Judge Supreme Judicial Court."

Morrison waited a few moments, gazing from face to face. Then he leaned across the table and gave the telegram into the hands of Miss Bunker. "Make it a part of the record, please," he directed.

"Well, I'll be eternally condemned!" roared the Governor. "You're a rank outsider. You don't know what you're talking about. How do you dare to involve the judges? They don't know what they're talking about, either, on a point of law, in this case."

"Perhaps Judge Davenport isn't talking law, wholly, in that telegram. He may be saying a word as an honest man who doesn't want to see his state disgraced by riot and bloodshed to-night." The mayor addressed Mac Tavish with eager emphasis. "What do you find down below, Andy?"

"Nae pairticular pother withindoors. Muckle powwow wi'out," reported the old man, tersely.

"Then you got a look outside?"

"Aye! When I took the message frae the telegraph laddie at the door."

"Was Joe Lanigan in sight?"

"Aye!"

"It's all right so far, gentlemen," the mayor assured his involuntary conferees. "Joe is on the job with his American Legion boys, as he promised me he'd be. Now I'm going to be perfectly frank and inform you that I have made a promise of my own in this case. I haven't meant to be presumptuous. I don't want you to feel that I've got a swelled head. I'm merely trying to keep my word and carry out a contract on a business oasis. It's only a matter of starting right; then everything can be kept right."

He whirled on Mac Tavish. "Trot down again, Andy. I'm expecting more messages. And keep us posted on happenings!"

"Are such humble persons as North and I are entitled to be let in on any details of your contract, Mister Boss-in-Chief?" inquired the Senator.

"I think the main contract is your own, sir--yours and the Governor's. I don't like to seem too forward in suggesting what it is."

"Nothing you can say or do from now on will seem forward, Morrison. Even if you should order that Hereford steer, there, at the door, to bang us over our heads with his shillalah, it would seem merely like an anticlimax, matched with the rest of your cheek! What's the contract?"

"You and North stated the terms of it, yourselves, when you were campaigning last election. You said that if you were elected you'd be the servants of the people."

"What in the devil do you claim we are now?"

"I make no assertion. But when I was down with the bunch this evening I was able to get into the spirit of the crowd. I found myself, feeling, just as they said they felt, that it's a queer state of affairs when servants barricade themselves in a master's castle and use other paid servants to threaten with rifles and machine-guns when the master demands entry."

"I'd be carrying out my contract, would I, by disbanding that militia and opening this State House to the mob?" demanded North.

"This is a peculiar emergency, sir," Morrison insisted. "Outside are massing all the elements of a know-nothing, rough-house mêlée. Even the Legion boys don't know just where they're at till there's a showdown. I can depend on 'em right now while they're waiting for that showdown. They'll fight their finger-nails off to hold the plain rowdies in line. Such boys have been showing their mettle in one city in this country, haven't they? But a mere licking, no matter which side wins, doesn't last long enough for any general good unless the licking is based on principle and the principle is thereby established as right! Now let me tell you, Governor North. You can't fool those Legion boys outside. They have come home with new conceptions of what is a square deal. They're plumb on to the old-fashioned tricks in cheap politics. They're not letting officeholders play checkers with 'em any longer.

"Governor--and you, Senator Corson--this is now a question of to-night--an emergency--an exigency! I have told those boys that they will be shown! You've got to show 'em. Show 'em that this State House is always open to decent citizens. Show 'em that you, as officeholders, don't need machine-guns to back you up in your stand." He emphasized each declaration by a resounding thump of his fist on the table. "Show 'em that it's a square deal, and that your cuffs are rolled up when you deal! Show 'ern that you're not bluffing honestly elected members of this incoming legislature out of their seats by closing the doors on 'em to-morrow. That's your contract! Are you going to keep it?"

Mac Tavish returned. He brought another telegram.

Morrison ripped the inclosure from the envelope.

"It's of the same purport as the other," he reported. "Signed, 'Madigan, Justice Supreme Judicial Court.' Back to the door, Mac Tavish. Here, Miss Bunker, insert this in the record."

"This is simply preposterous!" exploded the Senator.

"Rather irregular, certainly," Stewart confessed. "But I didn't ask 'em for red tape! I asked 'em for quick action to prevent bloodshed!"

Senator Corson's fresh fury did not allow him to reason with himself or argue with this interloper, this lunatic who was flailing about in that sanctuary of vested authority, knocking down hallowed procedure, sacred precedents--all the gods of the fane!

"Morrison, no such an outrage as this was ever perpetrated in American politics!"

"It surely does seem to be a new wrinkle, Senator! I'll confess that I don't know much about politics. It's all new to me. I apologize for the mistakes I'm making. Probably I'll know more when I've been in politics a little longer."

"You will, sir!"

Governor North agreed with that dictum, heartily, irefully.

"I do seem to be finding out new things every minute or so," went on Stewart, making the agreement unanimous. "Taking your opinion as experts, perhaps I may qualify as an expert, too, before the evening is over."

"Where is this infernal folly of yours heading you?" Corson permitted his wrath to dominate him still farther. He shook his fist under Morrison's nose.

"Straight toward a Bright Light, Senator! I'm putting no name on it. But I'm keeping my eyes on it. And I can't stop to notice what I'm knocking down or whose feet I'm treading on."

The Senator went to Governor North and struck his fist down on His Excellency's shoulder. "I've been having some doubts about your methods, sir, but now

I'm with you, shoulder to shoulder, to save this situation. Pay no attention to those telegrams. There's no telling what that idiot has wired to the justices. This man has not an atom of authority. You cannot legally share your authority with him. To defer to one of his demands will be breaking your oath to preserve order and protect state property."

"Exactly! I don't need that advice, Corson, but I do need your support. I shall go ahead strictly according to the constitution and the statutes."

"I am glad to hear you say that, Governor," stated Morrison.

"Did you expect that I was going to join you and your mob of lawbreakers?"

"Your explicit statement pleases me, I say. Shall you follow the constitution absolutely, in every detail?"

"Absolutely! In every detail."

"Right down to the last technical letter of it?"

"Good gad! what do you mean by asking me such fool questions?"

"I'm getting a direct statement from you on the point. For the record!" He pointed to the stenographer.

"I shall observe the constitution of this state to the last letter of it, absolutely, undeviatingly. And now, as Governor of this state, I shall proceed to exert my authority. Put that statement in the record! I order you to leave the State House immediately. Record that, too! Otherwise I shall prefer charges before the courts that will put you in state prison, Morrison!"

"Do you know exactly the provisions of the constitution relating to your office, sir?"

"I do."

"Don't you realize that, according to the technical stand you take, you have no more official right in this Capitol than I have, just now?"

His Excellency's silence, his stupefaction, suggested that his convictions as to Morrison's lunacy were finally clinched.

"The constitution, that you have invoked, expressly provides that a Governor's term of office expires at midnight, on the day preceding the assembling of the first session of the legislature. You will be Governor in the morning at ten-thirty o'clock, when you take your oath before the joint session. But by your own clock up there you ceased to be Governor of this state five minutes ago!" Morrison drawled that statement in a very placid manner. His forefinger pointed to the clock on the wall of the Executive Chamber.

Governor North did know the constitution, even if he did not know the time o' night until his attention had been drawn to it. He was disconcerted only for a moment; then he snorted his disgust, roused by this attempt of a tyro to read him a lesson in law.

Senator Corson expressed himself. "Don't bother us with such nonsense! Such a ridiculous point has never been raised."

"But this is a night of new wrinkles, as we have already agreed," insisted the mayor of Marion. "I'm right along with the Governor, neck and neck, in his observance of the letter of the law."

"Well, then, we'll stick to the letter," snapped His Excellency. "I have declared this State House under martial law. The adjutant-general, here, is in command of the troops and the situation."

"I'm glad to know that. I'll talk with General Totten in a moment!"

Again Mac Tavish came trotting past Rellihan.

Morrison snatched away the telegram that his agent proffered; but the master demanded news before proceeding to open the missive.

"There's summat in the air," reported Andrew. "Much blust'ring; the square is crowded! Whilst I was signing the laddie's book Lanigan cried me the word for ye to look sharp and keep the promise, else he wouldna answer for a'!"

"Gentlemen, I'll let you construe your own contracts according to your consciences. I have one of my own to carry out. Mac Tavish has just handed me a jolt on it!

"Governor North, seeing that your contract with the state is temporarily suspended, I suppose we'll have to excuse you to some extent, after all! Mac Tavish, step here, close to me!"

The old man obeyed; the two stood in the full glare of the chandelier.

Stewart held up his right hand. "You're a notary public, Andrew. Administer an oath! Like that one you administered to me when I was sworn in as mayor of Marion. You can remember the gist of it."

"In what capaceety do you serve, Master Morrison?" inquired Mac Tavish, stolidly.

Stewart hesitated a moment, taking thought. "I'm going to volunteer as a sort of an Executive, gentlemen," he explained, deferentially. "The exigency seems to need one. I have heard that a good Executive is one who acts quickly and is right--part of the time! I'm indebted to Senator Corson for a suggestion he made a little while ago. I think, Mac Tavish, you'd better swear me in as Boss of the Job."

XVI
THE CITY OF MARION SEEKS ITS MAYOR

Gaiety's glaring brilliancy on Corson Hill had been effectually snuffed by the onslaught of the mob. The mansion hid its lights behind shades and shutters. The men of the orchestra had packed their instruments; the dismayed guests put on their wraps and called for their carriages.

In the place of lilting violins and merry tongues, hammers clattered and saws rasped; the servants were boarding up the broken windows.

Lana Corson, closeted with Mrs. Stanton, found the discord below-stairs peculiarly hateful; it suggested so much, replacing the music.

The rude hand of circumstance had been laid so suddenly on the melody of life!

"And I'll say again--" pursued Mrs. Stanton, breaking a silence that had lain between the two.

"Don't say it again! Don't! Don't!" It was indignant expostulation instead of supplication and the matron instantly exhibited relief.

"Thank goodness, Lana! Your symptoms are fine! You're past the crisis and are on the mend. Get angrier! Stay angry! It's a healthy sign in any woman recovering from such a relapse as has been threatening you since you came back home."

"Will you not drop the topic?" demanded Miss Corson, with as much menace as a maiden could display by tone and demeanor.

"As your nurse in this period of convalescence," insisted the imperturbable lady, "I find your temperature encouraging. The higher the better, in a case like this! But I'd like to register on your chart a hard-and-fast declaration from you that you'll never again expose yourself to infection from the same quarter!"

Lana did not make that declaration; she did not reply to her friend.

The two were in the Senator's study. Lana had led the retreat to that apartment; its wainscoted walls and heavy door shut out in some measure the racket of hammers and saws.

She walked to the window and pulled aside the curtain and looked out into the night.

Between Corson Hill and Capitol Hill, in the broad bowl of a valley, most of the structures of the city of Marion were nested. The State House loomed darkly against the radiance of the winter sky.

She was still wondering what that blood-stained intruder had meant when he declaimed about the job waiting on Capitol Hill, and she found disquieting suggestiveness in the gloom which wrapped the distant State House. Even the calm in the neighborhood of the Corson mansion troubled her; the scene of the drama, whatever it was all about, had been shifted; the talk of men had been of prospective happenings at the State House, and that talk was ominous. Her father was there. She was fighting an impulse to hasten to the Capitol and she assured herself that the impulse was wholly concerned with her father.

"I'll admit that the thoughts of youth are long, long thoughts, just as that poet has said they are," Mrs. Stanton went on, one topic engrossing her. "But I'm assuming that there's an end to 'em, just as there is to the much-talked-of long lane. In poems there's a lot of nonsense about marrying one's own first love--and I suppose the thing is done, sometimes. Yes, I'm quite sure of it, because it's written up so often in the divorce cases. If I had married any one of the first five fellows I was engaged to, probably my own case would have been on record in the newspapers before this. Lana dear, why don't you come here and sit down and confide in a friend and assure her that you're safe and sane from now on?"

Miss Corson, as if suddenly made aware that somebody in the room was talking, snapped herself 'bout face.

"Doris, what are you saying to me?"

"I'm giving you a little soothing dissertation on love--the right kind of love-- the sensible kind--"

"How do you dare to annoy me with such silliness in a time like this?"

"Why, because this is just the right moment for you to tell me that you are forever done with the silly kind of love. Mushy boy-and-girl love is wholly made up of illusions. This Morrison man isn't leaving you any illusions in regard to himself, is he?"

Miss Corson came away from the window with a rush; her cheeks were danger-flags. "You seem to be absolutely determined to drive me to say something dreadful to you, Doris! I've been trying so hard to remember that you're my guest."

"Your friend, you mean!"

"You listen to me! I'm making my own declarations to myself about the men in this world--the ones I know. If I should say out loud what I think of them--or if I should say what I think of friends who meddle and maunder on about love--*love*--I'd be ashamed if I were overheard. Now not another word, Doris Stanton!" She stamped her foot and beat her hand hard on the table in a manner that smacked considerably of the Senator's violence when his emotions were stirred. "I'm ashamed of myself for acting like this. I hate such displays! But I mean to protect myself. And now keep quiet, if you please. I have something of real importance to attend to, even if you haven't."

She went to a niche in the wall and pulled out the private telephone instrument; the pressure of a button was required to put in a call. After the prolonged wait, Senator Corson's voice sounded, high-pitched, urgent. His appeal was broken short off.

Lana stared at Mrs. Stanton while making futile efforts to get a reply to frantic questions; fear paled the girl's face and widened her eyes.

"What has happened, Lana?"

"It's father! He asked for help! It's something--some danger--something dreadful." She clung to the telephone for several minutes, demanding, listening, hoping for further words--the completion of his orders to her.

Then, abandoning her efforts, she made haste to call the sheriff of the county, using the study extension of the regular telephone.

The customary rattle informed her that the line was in use, after she had called for the number, looking it up in the directory. When she finally did succeed in getting the ear of the sheriff she was informed in placatory orotund by that official that all her fears were groundless. "I have been talking with the State House just before you called me, Miss Corson. I am assured on the best of authority that everything is all right, there." He was plainly indulging what he accepted as the vagaries of hysteria--having been apprised by the matter-of-fact Mac Tavish that some nonsensical news might come through an excited female. "I think you must have misconstrued what your father said. My informant is known to me as reliable. Oh no, Miss Corson, I cannot give you his name. It's a rule of the sheriff's office that individuals who give information have their identities respected. If the Senator is at the State House you can undoubtedly reach him by 'phone in the Executive Chamber." He placidly bade her good night.

But Miss Corson was unable to communicate with the Executive Chamber.

After many delays she was informed that central had tried repeatedly and directly through the State House exchange, as was the custom after the departure of the exchange operators for the night; central officially reported, "Line out of order."

During her efforts to communicate, Coventry Daunt hastened into the study; he had tapped and he obeyed his sister's admonition, "Come in!"

"I tell you something terrible is the matter," Lana declared, giving up her efforts to get news over the wire. "Coventry, your looks tell me that you have heard bad news of some sort!"

"I don't want to be an alarmist," admitted young Daunt, "but all sorts of whip-whap stuff" seem to be in the air all of a sudden. I just took a run down to the foot of the hill. The bees are buzzing a little livelier there than they are in the neighborhood of the house. Up here some soldier boys are waving their bayonets and fat cops are swinging clubs. We're all right, ladies, but there are all sorts of stories about what's likely to happen up at the State House. I've come to tell you that if you can do without me I think I'll take a swing over to Capitol Hill. I don't want to miss anything good, and I'll bring back straight news."

"I can't endure to wait here for news, Coventry," Lana said. "Order the car; I'll go along with you."

"It's absolute folly!" declared Mrs. Stanton, aghast, "Haven't you had enough experience with mobs for one evening?"

"I am going to my father, mobs or no mobs! I know his voice and I know he's in trouble, no matter what that idiot of a sheriff tells me." She hurried to the door. "Order the car, I say! I'll get my wraps."

Mrs. Stanton divided rueful gaze between her own evening gown and Lana's. "Are you going with that dress on?"

"I certainly am!" Lana called from the corridor, running toward her apartments.

"Well," Mrs. Stanton informed her brother, "this gown has served me all evening during the political rally that somebody tried to pass off as a reception. Probably it will do very well for the mob-affair. I'll go for my furs."

"That's a brick!" was her brother's indorsement. "She needs us both. But don't be frightened, sis! It's only a political flurry, and such fusses are usually more fizz than fight. I'll have the car around to the door in a jab of a jiffy!"

By the time the limousine swung under the porte-cochère Lana was down and waiting; Mrs. Stanton came hurrying after, ready to defy a January midnight in a cocoon of kolinsky.

Coventry had ridden from the garage with the chauffeur. "I have been talking with Wallace. He thinks he'd better drive to the State House by detour through the parkway."

"Go straight down through the city," commanded the mistress. "I'm not afraid of my hometown folks. Besides, I have an errand. Stop at the Marion *Monitor* office, Wallace!"

The city certainly offered no cause for alarm when they traversed the streets of the business district. Nobody was in sight; they did not see even a patrolman.

"The bees seem to have hived all of a sudden," remarked young Daunt. "All fizz, as I told you, and now the fizz has fizzled."

When the car stopped in front of the newspaper office Lana asked her guests to wait in the automobile. "That is, if you don't mind!" Then Miss Corson revealed a bit of nerve strain; she allowed herself to copy some of the sarcasm that was characteristic of Doris Stanton. "One of those old friends whom we have been discussing so pleasantly this evening, Doris, is the city editor of the *Monitor*. Gossipy, of course, from the nature of his business. But I'm sure that he'll gossip more at his ease if there are no strangers present."

Coventry had opened the door of the car. Lana hastened past him and disappeared in the building.

"Dorrie, I'm afraid you are overtraining Lana," the brother complained. "I have never heard her speak like that before."

"I'm giving her special training for a special occasion which will present itself very soon, I hope. When she talks to a certain man I want to feel that my efforts haven't been thrown away."

"Oh, Morrison has botched everything for himself--all around!"

"Thank you! I'm glad to hear you admit that a caveman can be too much of a good thing with his stone hatchet or club or whatever he uses to bang and whack all heads with!"

Mrs. Stanton impatiently invited Coventry to step in and shut the door and make sure that the electric heater was doing business.

City Editor Tasper had a pompadour like a penwiper, round eyes, and a wide smile. He trotted out to Lana in the reception-room and gave her comradely greeting. "Any other night but this, Lana Corson, and I'd have been up to your house to pat Juba on the side-lines even if I couldn't squeeze in one assignment on your dance order. But as a Marionite you know what we're up against in this office the night before an inauguration. Afraid the reception-spread will be squeezed? Don't worry. It's a big night, but I'm giving you a first-page send-off just the same."

"Billy, I'm not here to talk about that reception. I don't care if there isn't a word about it."

"Oh, I get you! Don't worry about that fracas, either! I'm killing all mention of it. We're not advertising that Marion has Bolshevists. Hurts!"

"But I'm not trying to tell you your business about the paper!" the girl protested. "I'm here after news. What is the trouble at the State House?"

"I don't know," he confessed. "That is to say, I'm not on to the real inside of the proposition. We can't get our boys in and we can't get any news out! Those soldiers won't even admit the telephone crew to restore connection with the Executive Chamber."

"My father is there! He's there with the Governor."

"Well, I should say for a guess that the Senator is in the safest place in the city, judging from the way Danny Sweetsir and his warriors are on their jobs at those doors."

"Billy, who else is there with the Governor?" she questioned, anxiously, harrowed by that memory of her father's tone when he shouted the word "lunatic!"

"No know! No can tell!" returned Tasper. "But why all the excitement? There's a crowd outside the State House, but all my reports say that it's still orderly. It's only the old 'state steal' stuff warmed over by the sore-heads. But we're printing a statement from Governor North in the morning. The whole matter is going up to the full bench in the usual way. If the opposition starts any rough-stuff to-night, the gang hasn't got a Pekingese's chance in a bulldog convention. There are three machine-guns in that State House!"

A young chap who was trying hard to be professionally blasé bolted into the reception-room in search of his chief. "Excuse me! But four truck-loads of men from the Agawam quarries just went through toward the State House. They had crow-bars and sledge-hammers!"

"So? Warson is making a demonstration, is he? I'll be back there in a minute, Jack!" Tasper turned to Lana again. "Warson was turned down by North on the state-prison-wing stone contract. If Warson is setting up stone-cutters to be shot as rowdies, Warson and his party will be the ones who'll get hurt."

"But our state will be hurt most of all, Billy," the girl declared, with passionate earnestness. "We'll be ashamed and disgraced from one end of the country to the other. Just think of our own good state making a hideous exhibition when we're all trying so hard to get back to peace!"

"Must have law and order," Tasper insisted.

"Will Governor North tell those soldiers to shoot and kill?"

"Sure thing! His oath of office obliges him to protect state property. I've just been reading proof of an interview he gave us this afternoon."

Lana walked up and down the room, beating her hands together.

"I'll explain to you, Lana. There's quite a story goes with it. You haven't been in touch with conditions here at home. The election statutes provide that the Governor and his Council--"

"I haven't any time to listen to explanations! My father is in that State House! In the name of Heaven, Billy Tasper, isn't there some man in this state big enough, broad enough, honest enough to get between the fools who are threatening this thing?"

"He doesn't seem to be in sight--at any rate, just now."

She paused in her walk, hesitated, and then blurted, "What part is Stewart Morrison playing in all this?"

"I see you have some news about him, too!" Mr. Tasper fenced, eying her with some curiosity.

"Dealing in news is your business, not mine," she said, tartly. "But I did hear him declare in public to-night that he would give the people a square deal--or that he would see to it that it is done--or--or something!" She showed the embarrassment of a person who was dealing with affairs in the details of which she was not well informed.

"All right, I'll give you news as we get it in the office, here. Morrison has gone nuts over this People thing. He is bucking the corporations in this water-power dream of his. Playing to the people! I think it's bosh. Holds capital out of the state! But I see you're in a hurry! He made a speech to a hit-or-miss gang down-town to-night. It was snapped as a surprise and we didn't have our men there. But from what we gather he incited feeling against the State House crowd. Told his merry men he'd grab in and fix it for 'em. Bad foozle, Lana! Bad! When a mayor of a city talks like that he's putting a fool notion into the heads of unthinking irresponsibles, making 'em believe that there is really something to be fixed. He ought to have told 'em that everything was all right and to go home and go to bed. Your father would have told 'em that. That's good politics. But you and I know Stewart from the ground up! He is about as much a politician as I am parson--and I'd wreck a well-established parish in less than five minutes by the clock. He's taking a little more time as a wrecker in his line--but he's making a thorough job of it!"

When Tasper mentioned "job" he suggested a natural question to Miss Corson. "Where is he right now?"

This time the stare that the city editor gave the girl was distinctly peculiar. "According to what we can get in the way of reports, Lana, the last time Morrison was seen in public he was talking with you. If he has talked with anybody since then the folks he has talked with are keeping mighty mum about it. Perhaps he has told you where he was going."

Miss Corson exhibited an emotion that was more profound than mere embarrassment.

"Pardon me! But I'd like to know, Lana! It's mighty important to me in the line of my business right now."

"What? Can't you find the mayor of the city in a time like this?"

"He's not at home! He's not at City Hall. The chief of police won't say a word. And he's not in the crowd outside the State House."

Lana did not disclose the fact that she had suggested to the mayor, in a way, the rabble as Morrison's probable destination, and that he had agreed with her.

"And a fine chance he has of being let inside the State House," Tasper went on, with conviction, "after the attitude he has taken in regard to the administration!"

"He may be there, nevertheless!" Whether hope that he was there or fear that he might be there prompted Lana's suggestion was not clear from her manner.

"You'll sooner find a rat down the back of my neck than find Stewart Morrison inside that State House after the brags he has been making around this city in the past few hours," declared Tasper, with the breezy freedom of long friendship with the caller. "He is A Number One in the list of those who can't get in!"

"But Captain Sweetsir is his mill-student!"

"Captain Sweetsir, in this new importance of his, is leaning so far backward, in trying to stand straight, that he's scratching the back of his head on his heels. His own brother is one of our reporters and what Dan did to Dave when Dave made a holler at the door is a matter of record on the emergency-hospital blotter. That's straight! Inch of sword-blade. Not dangerous, but painful!"

All through this interview Lana had maintained the demeanor of one who was poised on tiptoes, ready to run. She gathered her coat's broad collar more tightly in its clasp of her throat, and started for the door. But she whirled and ran back to Tasper.

"You say that Stewart Morrison is no politician! But I noticed the queer flash in your eyes, Billy Tasper! Do you think he is a coward and has run away?"

"Tut, tut! Not so strong!" The newspaper man put up a protesting palm. "I simply state that His Honor the Mayor is under-somewhere! I never saw any signs of his being a coward--but a lot of us have never been tested by a real crisis, you know!"

"You say he has no power in politics! Could he do anything in a case like this?"

Tasper clawed his hand over his head and the crest of his pompadour bristled more horrently. "He could at least try to undo some of the trouble he has caused by his tongue. He could be at City Hall, where he belongs. The fact that he isn't there--that he can't be found--speaks a whole lot to the people of this city, Lana Corson! Why, there isn't a policeman to be seen on the streets of Marion to-night! We can't get any explanation from police headquarters. A devil of a mayor, say I!"

She turned and fled to the door.

"Lana!" called the editor. "He has made promises that he can't back up--and he has ducked. That's the story We're going to say so in the *Monitor*. We can't say anything else!"

She made no reply.

She did not wait for the elevator to take her down the single flight of stairs; she ran, holding her wrap about her.

Coventry Daunt, on the watch for her, opened the limousine's door and she plunged in. "Wallace! To the State House! Quick!" she commanded.

When Tasper returned to the city-room he was told that somebody was waiting on the telephone. It was one of the men assigned to the matter on Capitol Hill; he was calling from a drug-store booth in that neighborhood.

"Boss, it looks as if they're going to mix it. The tough mutts are ready to grab any excuse and they won't listen to men like Commander Lanigan of the Legion."

"If there's a fight pulled off all we can do is to see that we have a good story. What else?"

"I think I've located the mayor. I can't get anything at all out of those tin Napoleons at the doors, but Lanigan says that Morrison is in the State House--'on his job,' so Lanigan puts it."

"Lanigan is a liar!" the city editor yelped. "He has been a two-legged Hurrah-for-Morrison ever since his high-school days. I like a good lie when it's told to help a friend! This one isn't good enough! Stewart Morrison is in that State House like tissue-paper napkins are in Tophet."

"But sha'n't I send in what Lanigan says?" "We won't have any room for the joke column in the morning," returned the city editor, hanging up.

XVII
THE CAPITOL IN SHADOW

Capitol Square was choked with men. The gathering was characteristically a mob made up of diverse elements. It was not swayed by a set purpose and a common motive. It was not welded by coherence of intent. Its eddies rushed here or filtered there, according as arguments or protests gained attention by sharp clamor above the continuous diapason of voices. One who was versed in the natures and the moods of mobs would have found that mass particularly menacing by reason of the lack of unanimity. Too many men of the component elements did not know what it was all about! The arguments pro and con were developing animosities that were new, fresh, of the moment, creating factions, collecting groups that were ready to jump into an affray that would enable them to avoid embarrassing explanations of why they were there.

A mob of that sort is easily stampeded!

Some men who captained the factions did know why they were there! A few of them harangued; others went about, whispering and muttering, inciting malice by their counsel.

The scum of that yeasty gallimaufry was on the outskirts.

When the Corson limousine rolled into the square and sought to part its way through that scum somebody in the crowd made a proposition that was promptly favored as far as the votes by voices went: "Tip the lapdog kennel upside down!"

Chauffeur Wallace met the emergency with quick tactics. He reversed and drove the car backward. The fingers of the attackers slipped from the smooth varnish and the wheels threatened those who tried to grab the running-boards. Men who seized the fender-bar were dragged off their feet.

When Coventry Daunt showed a praiseworthy inclination to jump out and whip a few hundred of them, so he declared in his ire, he was pushed back into a corner by his sister.

The chauffeur made a long drive in reverse, circling, and then put the car ahead with a rush and they escaped into a side-street.

"Wallace, get us home as quick as the good Lord will let you!" Mrs. Stanton's command was hysterically shrill.

"Wallace, take the first turn to the left," countermanded the mistress. "Then around the State House to the west portico."

"You crazy girl, what--after that--why--what are you trying to do?" demanded Mrs. Stanton, fear making her furious.

"I'm trying to get into that building--and I'm going to get in!"

"You can't get in! They won't let you in! Lana Corson, you sha'n't endanger our lives again!"

"Here, Wallace! This turn!"

The driver obeyed.

Doris set rude hands upon Lana and shook her. "There's nothing sensible you can do if you do get in!"

"Perhaps not! But my father is there; he has asked me to help and I'm going to explain to him how I did my best. Doris, I must tell him, so that he won't get into worse danger by waiting and depending on that idiot of a sheriff."

"You are the idiot!"

"I may be. But I'm going in there!'

"Coventry, you are sitting like a prune glacé! Help me to prevail on this girl to use some common sense!"

"You'll help me very much if you'll do some prevailing with your sister, Coventry," affirmed Miss Corson, resentfully, trying to unclasp the chaperon's vigorous hands.

"After what has been happening, I don't think Lana needs any more shaking, Dorrie," the brother remonstrated. "Everything having been well shaken, it's time to do a little taking. Won't you take some advice, Lana?"

"If it's advice about going home and deserting my father I'll not take it."

"I was afraid you wouldn't. But do you really think you can get into the State House?"

The girl did not disclose the discouraging information given to her by Editor Tasper on the subject of effecting an entrance. "I'm going to try! And I warn you, Doris, that I'm about at the end of my endurance."

Mrs. Stanton sat back and gritted her teeth.

The car traversed a boulevard; the arc-lights showed that it was deserted. A narrow street, empty of humankind, led to the west portico. That entrance, so Lana knew, was used almost wholly by the State House employees. The door was closed; nobody was in sight.

"If you insist on the venture, I'll go with you, of course," offered the young man. When the car stopped he stepped out.

"I'm afraid you'll only make it harder for me, Coventry. I know the captain of the guard. But it will never do for me to bring a stranger."

She hurried into the shadow of the portico. "Get back into the car! You must! Wallace, drive Mrs. Stanton and Mr. Daunt to the house."

When Coventry protested indignantly she broke in: "I haven't any time to argue with you. We may be watched. Wait at the corner yonder with the car. If you see me go in, take Doris home and send the car back. Wallace, I'll find you down there at the fountain!" She designated with a toss of her hand the statuary, gleaming in the starlight, and when the car moved on she ran up the steps of the State House.

The big door had neither bell nor knocker. She turned her back on it and kicked with the heel of her slipper.

The voice that inquired "Who's there?" revealed that the warder was not wholly sure of his nerves.

"I am Senator Corson's daughter!"

She received no reply.

"I tell you I am Senator Corson's daughter! I want to come in. My father is there!"

She was answered by a different voice; she recognized it. It was the unmistakable drawl and nasal twang of Perley Wyman. Her girlhood memories of Perley's voice had been freshened very recently because he had been assigned to the Corson mansion by Thompson the florist as her chief aide in decorating for the reception. "Wal, I should say he was here--and then some! This was the door he came in through."

"Open it! Open it at once, Perley Wyman!"

"I dunno about that, Miss Corson! We've got orders about politicians and mobbers--"

"I'm neither. I command you to open this door."

"Who else is there?"

"I'm alone."

Soldier Wyman pulled the bolts and opened. "I ain't feeling like taking any more chances with the Corson family this evening," he admitted, with a grin that set his long jaw awry. "Your father nigh cuffed my head up to a peak when I tried to tell him what my orders were."

Miss Corson was not interested in the troubles of Guard Wyman. He was talking through a narrow crack; she set her hands against the door and pushed her way in. "Where is my father? What trouble is he in?"

"I reckon it can't be any kind of trouble but what he'll be capable of taking care of himself in it all right," opined the guard, fondling his cheek with the back of his hand. "But there ain't any trouble in here, Miss Corson. It's all serene as a canned sardine that was canned for the siege of Troy, as it said in the opery the High School Cadets put on that year you was in the--"

"There's a mob in front of the State House!"

"It'll stay there," stated Wyman, remaining as serene as the comestible he had mentioned. "The St. Ronan's Rifles can't be backed down by any mob. We have been ordered to shoot, and that kind of a gang in this city might as well learn its lesson to-night as any other night. It's getting time to do a lot of law-and-order shooting in this country."

The girl, harrowed by her apprehensions, was not in the mood to discuss affairs with this amateur belligerent. But his complacency in his bloodthirsty attitude was peculiarly exasperating in her case. He seemed to typify that unreasonable spirit of slaughter that disdained to employ the facilities of good sense first of all. This florist's clerk, whom she had last seen on a step-ladder with his mouth full of tacks, was talking of shooting down his fellow-civilians as if there were no other alternative.

"My father may be in danger in this State House, but I'm glad he is here. He is not condoning this! He is not allowing this shame! Who is the lunatic who is threatening my father and bringing disgrace on this state?" She remembered the Senator's assertion over the telephone and, in her eagerness for news, she was willing to start with the humble Soldier Wyman.

She realized suddenly that her spirit of fiery protest was provoking her into an argument that might seem rather ridiculous if somebody in real authority should overhear her talking to Wyman and his mate. The portico door opened into a remote corridor.

"The only lunatic, up to date, Miss Corson, has been a Canuck who had a knock-down and drag-out with a settee and--"

Lana was not finding Wyman's statement especially convincing in the way of establishing faith in his sanity. "I thank you for letting me in! I must find my father."

The interior of the Capitol building was familiar ground to her.

It occurred to her sense of discretion that it might be well to avoid Captain Sweetsir in his new exaltation as a military martinet. She found a narrow, curving stairway which served employees.

On the second floor, hastening along the dimly lighted corridors, turning several corners, she reached the spacious hall outside the Senate lobby. She paused for a moment. From the hall she could look down the broad, main stairway which conducted to the rotunda. The rumble of trucks had attracted her attention. Soldiers were moving a machine-gun; they lined it up with two others that were already facing the great doors of the main entrance. She had half hoped that her father was in the rotunda, using his influence and his wisdom, now that the mob was threatening the building outside those great doors. She did not understand just how the Senator would be able to operate, she admitted to herself, but she felt that his manly advice could prevail in keeping his fellow-citizens from murdering one another!

In the gloom below her she saw only soldiers and uniformed Capitol watchmen.

Across from her in the upper hall where she waited there was the entrance to the wing which contained the Executive Chambers. Two men, one of whom was talking earnestly, came along the corridor from the direction of the chambers. Still mindful of what Tasper had said about the State House rules of that evening, she did not want to take chances with others who might be less amenable than Florist-Clerk Wyman. There were high-backed chairs in the corners of the hall; she hid herself behind the nearest chair. Her dark fur coat and the twilight concealed her effectually.

"General Totten, if you don't fully comprehend your plain duty in this crisis, you'd better stop right here with me until you do. We can't afford to have those soldiers overhear. Are you going to order them to march out of this State House?" This peremptory gentleman was Stewart Morrison!

Lana choked back what threatened to be an exclamation.

"I refuse to take that responsibility on myself."

"You must! Such a command to state troops must come from you, the adjutant-general."

"This is a political exigency, Mister Mayor!"

"It seems like that to me!"

"It requires martial law."

"But not civil war."

"This building is threatened by a mob."

"That's because you have put it in a state of siege against citizens."

"There's no telling what those men will do if they are allowed to enter."

"They'll do worse if they are kept out by guns."

"It means wreck and rampage if they are permitted to come through those doors."

"Look here, Totten, this State House has stood here for a good many years, with the citizens coming and going in it at will. I don't see any dents!"

"This is an exigency, and it's different, sir. The state must assert its authority."

"I'll not argue against the state and authority with you, Totten, for you're right and there's no time for argument. But when you said political exigency you said a whole lot--and we'll let this particular skunk cabbage go under that name. Don't try that law-and-order and state-authority bluff with me in such a case as this is. You're right in with the bunch and you know just as well as I do what the game is this time. Probably those folks outside there don't know what they want, but they do know that something is wrong! Something is almighty wrong when elected servants are obliged to get behind closed doors to transact public affairs. I'm putting this on a business basis because business is my strong point. These red-tape fellows go to war and use the people for the goats to settle a matter that could be settled peaceably by hard-headed every-day men in five minutes. Now with these few words, and admitting that I'm all that you want to tell me I am--and confessing to a whole lot more that I personally know about my unadulterated brass cheek in the whole thing--we'll close debate. Order those militia boys to march out!"

"I--"

Morrison held a little sheaf of papers in his hand. He flapped the papers violently under General Totten's nose. "Do you dare to ignore these telegrams--the opinions of the justices of the supreme judicial court of this state?"

"I don't--"

The papers flicked the end of the general's nose and he shuffled slowly backward. "Do you dare, I say?"

"This exigency--"

"That's the name we've agreed on--for a dirty political trick without an atom of principle behind it. These telegrams will make great reading on the same page with the list of names in the hospitals and the morgue!" General Totten was retreating more rapidly, but the vibrating papers inexorably kept pace with his nose.

"But to leave this State House unguarded--"

"I have already shown you what I can do with one single cop! I gave you a little lecture on cops in general back yonder. You fully understand how one cop handled the adjutant-general of a state. I'll answer for the guarding of this State House. Send away your militia!"

"I'm afraid to do it!" wailed Totten.

"Then you're afraid of a shadow, sir! But I'll tell you what you may well be afraid of. I'm giving you your chance to save your face and your dignity. Order away those boys or I'll go and stand on the main stairway and tell 'em just how they're being used as tools by political tricksters. And then even your tricksters will land on your back and blame you for forcing an exposure. I'll tell the boys! I swear I'll do it! And I'll bet you gold-dust against sawdust that they'll refuse to commit murder. Totten, this exigency is now working under a full head of steam. You can hear that mob now! This thing is getting down to minutes, I'll give you just one of those minutes to tramp down into that rotunda and issue your orders."

"But what--" The general's tone unmistakably indicated surrender; the Governor had already shifted the onus; Totten knew his brother-in-law's nature; the

Governor would just as soon shift the odium after such an explosion as this wild Scotchman threatened.

"You needn't bother about the what, sir. You give the order. And as soon as the thing is on a business basis I'll tend to it."

Stewart took the liberty of hooking his arm inside the general's. The officer seemed to be experiencing some difficulty in getting his feet started. The two hurried along and trudged down the middle of the main stairway.

Lana followed. She halted at the gallery rail and surveyed the scene below.

Even in her absorption in the affair between Stewart and the adjutant-general she had been aware of the rising tumult outside.

The bellow of voices had settled into a sort of chant of, "Time's up--time's up!"

Captain Sweetsir had deployed his men across the rotunda behind the machine-guns.

When he beheld the mayor and the general on the stairs he saluted nervously. "They're getting ready to use sledge-hammers, sir. Shall I hand 'em the rifle-fire first or let loose with the machine-guns?"

Stewart still held to the general's arm.

Totten hesitated. His face was white and his lips quivered.

Morrison's gaze was set straight ahead, but a twist of his face indicated that he said something through the corner of his mouth.

The general made his plunge.

"Captain Sweetsir, instruct your men to empty their magazines, assemble accoutrements, and stand at ease in marching order."

The captain came onto his tiptoes in order to elongate himself as a human interrogation-point.

"Captain Sweetsir, order your bugler to sound retreat!"

The officer forced an amazed croak out of his throat by way of a command, and on the hush within the rotunda the clarion of the bugle rang out. It echoed in the high arches. Its sharp notes cut into the clamor outdoors.

Morrison recognized a voice that was keyed to a pitch almost as high as the bugle's strains. "Hold your yawp! Don't you hear that?" Lanigan screamed. "Don't you know the difference between that and a fish-peddler's horn? That's the tune we fellers heard the Huns play just before Armistice Day. That's retreat! Come on,

Legion!" he urged, frantically. "Ram back those sledgehammers!"

Morrison grinned and released the general's arm.

"You hear that, do you, sir? When you can convince fair men that you're on the right slant, the fair men will proceed to show rough-necks where they get off if they go to trying on the wrong thing!"

"There's going to be the devil to pay!" insisted the adjutant-general. "You're going to let that mob into the State House, and they'll fight all over the place."

"We'll see what they'll do after the showdown, sir! And you can't make much of a showdown in the dark."

He left General Totten on the stairs, leaped down the remaining steps, and ran to a group of watchmen and night employees of the State House who were bulwarking the soldiers.

"I'm beginning to see that it's some advantage, after all, to be the mayor of this city," Stewart informed himself. One of Marion's aldermen was chief electrician of the Capitol building and was in the group, very much on duty on a night like that. "Torrey has always backed me in the city government meetings, at any rate!"

The alderman came out of the ranks, obeying the mayor's gesture.

"Alderman, I'm in the minority here, right now, but I hope you're going to vote with me for more light on the subject."

Torrey did not understand what this quick shift in all plans signified, and said so, showing deference to the mayor at the same time.

"If we've got to fight that gang we need these soldiers, Mayor Morrison!"

"Our kind of men, Alderman, fight best in the light; the cowards like the dark so that they can get in their dirty work. Do you get me? Yes! Thanks! Excuse me for hurrying you. But get to that switchboard! We need quick action. You and I represent the city of Marion right now. Must keep her name clean! I'll explain later. But give 'er the juice! Jam on every switch. Dome to cellar! Lots of it! Put their night-beetle eyes out with it."

He was hustling along with Torrey toward the electrician's room. He was clapping his hand on the alderman's shoulder.

"I'm going outside there, Torrey! Touch up the old dome and give me all the front lights. If the bricks begin to whiz I want to see who's throwing 'em!"

XVIII
THE CAPITOL ALIGHT

First of all, within the State House, there was burgeoning of the separate lights of the wall brackets and then the great chandeliers burst into bloom. Electrician Torrey possessed a quick understanding and was in the habit of doing a thorough job whenever he tackled anything. He threw in the switches as rapidly as he could operate them.

Story by story the great building was flooded with glory that mounted to the upper windows and overflowed into the night with a veritable cascade of brilliancy when the thousand bulbs of the dome's circlet flashed their splendor against the sky. The lamps of the broad front portico and its approaches added the final, dazzling touch to the general illumination.

From a sullen, gloomy hulk of a building, with its few lights showing like glowering eyes in ambush, the State House was transformed into a temple of glory, thrust into the heavens from the top of Capitol Hill, a torch that signaled comforting candor, a reassuring beacon.

The surprise of the happening stilled the uproar.

Neither Morrison, inside, nor the mob, outside, was bothering with the mental analysis of the psychology of the thing!

Something had happened! There was The Light! It threw into sharp relief every upturned face in the massed throng. Their voices remained hushed.

Commander Lanigan, standing above them on a marble rail, his figure outlined against a pergola column, did his best to put some of his emotions into speech. He shouted, "*Some* night-blooming cereus, I'll tell the world!"

The great doors swung open slowly. They remained open.

Now curiosity replaced astonishment and held the rioters in their tracks; their mouths were wide, the voices mute.

The mayor of Marion walked into view.

The columns of the porte-cochère were supported on a broad base, and he climbed up and was elevated in the radiance high above their heads.

He smiled hospitably. "Boys, it's open house, and the house is yours. Hope you like its looks! But what's the big idea of the surprise party?"

No one took it on himself to reply. He waited tolerantly.

"Well, out with it!" he suggested.

Somebody with a raucous voice ventured. "You probably know what they've been trying to hide away from the people inside there. Suppose you do the talking."

"I'm not here to make a speech."

"Well, answer a question, then!" This was a shrill voice. "What about those soldiers and those machine-guns in there?"

"Not a word!"

With yells, oaths, and catcalls the crowd offered comment on that declaration.

His demeanor as a statue of patience was more effective than remonstrance in quieting them.

"Any other gentlemen wish to offer more remarks? Get it all out of you!"

He utilized the hush. "Boys, I'm going to give you something better than words. Hearing can't always be trusted. But seeing is believing!"

He pulled a police whistle from his pocket and shrilled a signal.

For a time there was no answer or demonstration of any sort.

Then the tramp of marching feet was heard on the pavement of the square.

It was Marion's police force, issuing from some point of mobilization near at hand; it was the force in full strength, led by the chief; he was in dress-parade garb and the radiance of the square was reflected in imposing high-lights by his gold braid.

The crowd was shaken by eddies and was convulsed by quickly formed vortices. Morrison was studying that mob with his keen gaze, watching the movements as they sufficed to reveal an expression of emotions.

"Hold on, boys! Don't run away!" he counseled. "Wait for the big show! No arrests intended! Only cowards and guilty men will run!"

The light that was shed from the State House was pitilessly revealing; men could not hide their movements. Morrison reiterated his promise and dwelt hard on the "coward and guilty" part of his declaration.

The chief of police waved his hand and the crowd parted obediently and the officers marched up the lane, four abreast.

"Hold open that passage as you stand, fellow-citizens!" the mayor commanded. "There's more to this show! You haven't seen all of it! Hold open, I tell you!"

Men whom he recognized as Lanigan's Legion members were jumping in on the side-lines as the policemen passed. With arms extended the veterans held back those whom Morrison's commands were not restraining.

"That's good team-work, Joe," Stewart informed Lanigan when the latter hurried past to take his place as a helper.

The advent of the police had provoked a flurry; their movements after their arrival caused a genuine surprise. They gave no indication of being interested in the crowd that was packed into Capitol Square. The ears of the mob were out for orders of dispersal! Eyes watched to see the officers post themselves and operate according to the usual routine in such matters.

But the policemen marched straight into the State House, preserving their solid formation.

The bugle sounded again within.

With a promptness that indicated a good understanding of the procedure to be followed, the St. Ronan's Rifles came marching out.

Captain Sweetsir saluted smartly as he passed the place where the mayor of Marion was perched.

"How about three cheers for the boys?" Morrison shouted. "What's the matter with you down there?"

He led them off as cheer-leader. He marked the sullen groups, the voiceless malcontents as best he was able. The Legion boys were vehemently enthusiastic in their acclaim.

The guards marched briskly. The machine-guns clanged along the pavement, bringing up the rear.

"That's all!" Stewart declared, when the soldiers were well on their way. "Now you don't need any words, do you? I'll merely state that your State House is open to the people!"

"Like blazes it is," bawled somebody.

He pointed to the open doors, his reply to that challenge.

"How about those cops?" demanded somebody else.

"Your State House is open, I tell you. If you want to go in, go ahead. It's open for straight business, and it will stay open. There are no dark corners for dirty tricks or lying whispers. It's your property. If there's any whelp mean enough to damage his own property, he'll be taken care of by a policeman. That's why they're in there. That's what you're paying taxes for, to have policemen who'll take care of sneaks who can't be made decent in any other way. Some other gentleman like to ask a question?"

Morrison realized that he had not won over the elements that were determined to make trouble. His searching eyes were marking the groups of the rebels.

He directed an accusatory finger at one man, a Marion politician. "Matthewson, what's on your mind? Don't keep it all to yourself and those chaps you're buzzing with!"

Matthewson, thus singled out, was embarrassed and incensed at the same time. "What have they been trying to put over with that militia, anyway?"

"Put protection over state property because such mouths as yours have been making threats ever since election. But just as soon as it was realized that good citizens, like the most of these here, were misunderstanding the situation and were likely to be used as tools of gangsters, out went the militia! You saw it go, didn't you?"

"I'd like to know who did all that realizing you're speaking of!"

"It's not in good taste for an errand-boy of my caliber to gossip about the business of those for whom he is doing errands. I'll merely say, Matthewson, that the people of this state can always depend on the broad-gaged good sense of United States Senator Corson to suggest a solution of a political difficulty. And you may be sure that the state government will back him up. Go down-town and ask the boys of the guard who it was that gave the command for them to leave the State House. After that you'd better go home to bed. That's good advice for all of you."

A shrill voice from the center of the massed throng cut in sharply. "Go home like chickens and wait to have your necks wrung! Go home like sheep and wait for the shearer and the butcher."

The mayor leaned forward and tried to locate the agitator. "Hasn't the gentleman anything to say about goats? He's missing an excellent opportunity!" Morrison showed the alert air of a hunter trying to flush game in a covert.

The provoking query had its effect. "Yes, that's what you call us-all you rulers call us the goats!"

A brandished fist marked the man's position in the mob.

"Ah, there you are, my friend! What else have you on your mind?"

"I'll tell you what you have on your face. You have the mark of an honest man's hand there! I saw him plant that mark!"

"And what's the answer?" asked Stewart, pleasantly.

"You're a coward! You're not fit to advise real men what to do!"

"I'm afraid you have me sized up all too well!" There was something like wistful apology in Morrison's smile.

Lanigan had forced his way close to the foot of the plinth where the mayor was elevated. The commander's head was tipped back, his goggling eyes were full of anguished rebuke, and his mouth was wide open.

The man in the crowd yelped again, encouraged by his distance and by Morrison's passivity under attack. "You think you own a mill. Your honest workmen own it. You are a thief!"

"My Gawd!" Lanigan squawked, hoarsely. "Ain't it in you? Ain't a spark of it in you?"

Morrison delivered sharp retort in an undertone. "Don't you know better than to tangle my lines when I'm playing a fish? Shut up!" He tossed his hand at the individual in the crowd, inviting him to speak further.

"You're a liar, too!" responded the disturber.

"That's a tame epithet, my friend. Commonly used in debate. I'm afraid you're running out of ammunition. Haven't you anything really important to say, now that I'm giving you the floor?"

Men were beginning to remonstrate and to threaten in behalf of the mayor of the city.

"Hold on, boys!" Morrison entreated. "We must give our friend a minute more if he really has anything to say. Otherwise we'll adjourn--"

The bait had been dangled ingratiatingly; a movement had been made to jerk it away--the "fish" bit, promptly and energetically.

"I'll say it--I'll say what ought to be said--I'll shame the cowards here!"

"Let Brother What's-his-name come along, boys! Please! Please!" The mayor stretched forth his arms and urged persuasively. "Keep your hands off him! Let him come!"

"They're going over him for a gat, Mister Mayor," called Lanigan. "I've given 'em one lesson in that line this evening, already!"

The volunteers who were patting the disturber released him. The patting had not been in the way of encouragement. "Nothing on him! Let him go!" commanded one of the searchers.

The man who came forcing his way through the press, his clinched fists waving over his head, was young, pallid, typically an academic devotee of radicalism, a frenetic disciple, obsessed by *furor loquendi* He was calling to the mob, trying to rouse followers. "You have been standing here, freezing in the night, damning tyrants, boasting what you would do. Why don't you do it? Do you let a smirking ruler bluff all the courage of real men out of you? He's only doing the bidding of those higher up. He admits it! He's a tool, too! He's a fool, along with you, if he tries to excuse tyranny. You have your chance, now, and all the provocation that honest men need. The rulers tried to scare you with guns. But you have called the bluff. Their hired soldiers have run away. Now is your time! Take your government into your hands! Down with aristocrats! Smash 'em like we smash their windows. They hold up an idol and ask you to bow down and be slaves to it; but you're only bowing to the drivers of slaves! They hide behind that idol and work it for all it's worth. They point to it and tell you that you must empty your pockets to add to their wealth, and work your fingers off for their selfish ends."

He halted a short distance from the plinth, declaiming furiously.

Morrison broke in, snapping out his words. "Down to cases, now! What is the idol?"

"A patchwork of red, white, and blue rags!"

Morrison whirled, crouched on his hands and knees, set his fingers on the edge of the plinth, and slid down the side. He swung for an instant at the end of his arms and dropped the rest of the way to the pavement.

Lanigan had started for the man, but Stewart overtook the commander, seized him by the collar and coattail slack, and tossed him to one side.

"Here's a case at last where I don't need any help or advice from you, Joe!"

"Punch the face offn him!" adjured Lanigan, even while he was floundering among the legs of the men against whom he had been thrown.

The mayor plunged through the crowd in the direction of the vilifier.

The man did not attempt to escape. "Strike me! Strike me down. I offer myself for my cause to shame these cowards!"

But Morrison did not use his fists, though Lanigan continued to exhort.

"There are altogether too many of you would-be martyrs around this city to-night. I can't accommodate you all!" Stewart made the same tackle he had used in the case of Lanigan and Spanish-walked his captive back toward the porte-cochère.

"I reckon I do need your help, after all, Joe!" confessed Morrison, noting that Lanigan was on his feet again. "Give me your back and a boost!"

Then the captor suddenly tripped the captive and laid him sprawling at Lanigan's feet; before the fallen man was up, Morrison, using the commander's sturdy shoulders and the thrust of the willing arms of his helper, had swung himself back to the top of the plinth. He kneeled and reached down his hands. "Up with him, Joe! Toss! I won't miss him!"

Lanigan was helped by a comrade in making the toss. Morrison grasped the man and yanked him upright and held him in a firm clutch.

The mayor was receiving plenty of advice from the crowd by that time. The gist of the counsel followed Lanigan's suggestion about punching off the fellow's face. But the mob was by no means unanimous. Men were daring to voice threats against Morrison.

As it had availed before that evening, Morrison's imperturbable silence secured quiet on the part of others.

"The opinion of the meeting seems to be divided," he said. He had recovered his poise along with his breath. "But no matter! I shall not adopt the advice of either side. I shall not let this fellow go until I have finished my business with him. I shall not punch his face off him. I'll not flatter him to that extent. A good American reserves his fists for a man-fight with a real man." He shook the captive, holding him at arm's-length. "Here's a young fool who has been throwing stones at windows. Here's a fresh rowdy who has been sticking out his tongue at authority. I know exactly what he needs!"

"He insulted the flag of this country! Turn him over to the police!" somebody insisted, and a roar of indorsement hailed the demand.

"Citizens, that would be like giving a mongrel cur a court trial for sheep-killing! This perverted infant simply needs--***dingbats!***" He shouted the last word. He twisted the radical off his feet, stooped, and laid the victim across a knee that was as solid as a tree-trunk, and with the flat of a broad hand began to whale the culprit with all his might.

The onlookers were silent for a few moments. Then there was a chorus of jeering approbation.

When the shamed, humiliated, agonized radical--thus made a mark for gibes instead of winning honor as a martyr for the cause--began to wail and plead the men who were nearest the scene of flagellation started to laugh. The laughter spread like a fire through dry brambles. It ran crackling from side to side of the great square. It mounted into higher bursts of merriment. It became hilarity that was expended by a swelling roar that split wide the night silence and came beating back in riotous echoes from the façade of the State House. That amazing method of handling anarchy had snapped the tense strain of a situation which had been holding men's emotions in leash for hours. The ludicrousness of the thing was heightened by the nervous solemnity immediately preceding. Men beat their neighbors on the back in instant comradeship of convulsed, rollicking jubilation.

"Always leave 'em laughing when you say good-by!" Morrison advised the chap whom he was manhandling. He held the fellow over the edge of the plinth by the collar and dropped him, wilted and whimpering, into the waiting arms of the appreciative Lanigan. "Dry his eyes, Joe, and wipe his nose, and see that he gets started for home all right."

Morrison stood straight and secured a hearing after a time. "Boys, those of you who are in the right mind--and I hope all of you are that way now, after a good laugh--I've given you a sample of how to handle the Bolshevist blatherskites when you come across 'em in this country. Look around and if you find any more of 'em in the crowd go ahead and dose 'em with dingbats! Fine remedy for childish folly! I reckon all of us have found out that much for ourselves in the old days. I won't keep you standing in the cold here any longer. Good night!"

He leaped down on to the porch and went into the State House.

General Totten was near the big door.

The men outside were guffawing again.

Morrison was dusting his palms with the air of a man who had finished a rather unpleasant job. "Do you hear 'em, Totten? Sounds better than howls of a crowd bored by machine-gun bullets, eh? How much chance do you think there is of starting a civil war among men who are laughing like that?"

XIX
LANA CORSON HAS HER DOUBTS

The chief of police had distributed his officers to posts of duty and was patrolling the rotunda.

He saluted the mayor when Morrison came hurrying in through the main entrance.

"All is fine, Chief! I thank you for your work. I don't look for anything out of the way, after this. But keep your men on till further orders."

At the foot of the grand stairway Stewart's self-possession left him.

Lana Corson was standing half-way up the stairs. Her furs were thrown back, revealing her festival attire. Her beauty was heightened by the flush on her cheeks and by the vivid animation in her luminous eyes.

He paused for a moment, his gaze meeting hers, and then he hastened to her.

"How did it happen--that you're here, Lana?"

"I'm here--let that be an answer for now. But this, Stewart--this what I have been seeing and hearing! Does it mean what it seems to mean?"

"I'll have to admit that I don't know exactly how it does show up from the side-lines. Suppose you say!"

"I heard you talk to General Totten. I heard you talk to that mob. I saw what you did. But I heard you give all the credit to my father." She searched Stewart's face with more earnest stare. "You have saved the state from disgracing itself, haven't you? Isn't that what you have done--you yourself?"

"Oh, nonsense! Tell me! How did you get in and who came with you?"

"I'm here alone, Stewart, and it's of no importance how I got in. The question I have asked you is the important one just now."

Her insistence was disconcerting; he had not recovered from the astonishment of the sudden meeting; he felt that he ought to lie to that daughter, in the interests of her family pride, but he was conscious of his inability to lie glibly just then.

"Where is your car?"

"Waiting for me in the little park."

"Lana, there'll be no more excitement here--not a bit. Nothing to see! Suppose you allow me to take you to the car. Come!" He put out his arm.

"Certainly not! Not till I see my father! He is in danger!"

"I assure you he is not. I left him with the Governor only a few minutes ago, and the Senator was never better in his life--nor safer!" In spite of his best endeavor to be consolatory and matter-of-fact he was not able to keep a certain significance out of his tone.

From where she stood she could look across the rotunda and down into the square. The glare of the lights made all movements visible. The crowd was melting away.

"Stewart, brains and tact have accomplished wonders here to-night. I want to know all the truth. Why shouldn't you be as candid to me as you seemed to be with those men when you were talking to them? I want to give my gratitude to somebody! The name of our good state has been kept clean. You're not fair to me if you leave me in the dark any longer."

"I did my little bit, that's all! I'm only one of the cogs!"

"I know how I'll make you tell. I propose to give you all the credit. And I never knew you to keep anything that didn't belong to you."

"Now you're not fair yourself, Lana! We just put our heads together--the whole of us--that's all! Put our heads together! You know! As men will!" His stammering eagerness did not satisfy her feminine penetration. Her daughterly interest in the Senator's political standing was stirred as she reflected.

"My father is down here to see that his fences are in good shape," she declared, with true Washington sapience. "I think it was his duty and privilege to step out there and make the speech. I'm surprised because he let such an opportunity slip. With all due respect to the mayor of Marion, you were not at all dignified, Stewart. They laughed at you--and I didn't blame them!"

"I can't blame 'em, either," he confessed. "I--I--I guess I lost my head. I'm not used to making speeches. I have made two since supper, and both of 'em have seemed to stir up a lot of trouble for me."

"I think, myself, that you're rather unfortunate as a speechmaker," she returned, dryly. "I suppose you're going back to report to father. I'll go with you." In her manner there was implied promise that she would proceed to learn more definitely in what quarters her especial gratitude ought to be expended.

"Lana," he urged, "I wish you'd go home and wait for your talk with your father when he comes. He'll be coming right along. I'll see that he does. There's nothing--not much of anything to keep him here. But I need to have a little private confab with him."

"So private that I mustn't listen? I hope that we're still old friends, Stewart, you and I, though your attitude in regard to father's affairs has made all else between us impossible."

He did not pursue the topic she had broached. There was a certain finality about her deliverance of the statement, a decisiveness that afforded no hint that she would consider any compromise or reconsideration. His face was very grave. "I have a little business--a few loose ends to take up with the Senator. Once more I beg that you will defer--"

"I will go with you to the Executive Chamber. I'll be grateful for your escort. If you don't care to have me go along with you, I can easily find my way there alone."

Her manner left no opportunity for further appeal.

He bowed. He did not offer his arm. They walked together up the stairway. With side-glances she surveyed his countenance wonderingly; in his expression true distress was mingled with apprehensiveness. He had the air of an unwilling guide detailed to conduct an unsuspecting innocent to be shocked by the revelations of a chamber of horrors; she put it that way to herself in jesting hyperbole.

The newspaper men, who had followed Mayor Morrison into the State House, had been holding aloof, politely, from a conference which seemed to have no bearing on the political situation. They hurried behind and overtook Stewart and the young lady at the head of the stairway; their spokesman asked for a statement.

"I made it! Out there a few minutes ago! Boys, you heard what I said, didn't you?"

"Yes."

"Well, I talked more than I intended to! Boil it down to a few lines and let it go at that!"

"We want to get the matter just right, Mister Mayor, and give credit where it's due."

"I covered the matter of credit. There's nothing more to say," replied Stewart, curtly.

The reporters surveyed him with considerable wonderment; his manner in times past had always been distinguished by frank graciousness.

"We'd like to see Senator Corson and Governor North."

That request seemed to provoke the mayor's irritability still more. "I'm not the guardian of those gentlemen or of this State House!" He turned on his heel abruptly. "Miss Corson!" She was waiting a few paces away. He rejoined her and by a gesture invited her to walk along. "I'm sorry! I did not mean to delay you!"

The newspaper men followed on as far as the door of the Executive Chamber.

Morrison faced them there. "I don't mean to interfere with you, boys, in any way. And you mustn't interfere with me. As soon as the Senator and the Governor finish with me they'll give you all the time you want, no doubt! Please wait out-side!" He tapped on the door and gave his name. Rellihan opened. Morrison seized the officer's arm and pulled him outside. "Keep everybody away from the door for a few moments--till further orders."

Stewart escorted Miss Corson into the chamber with almost as much celerity as he had employed in escorting Rellihan out; and he promptly banged the door. He walked slowly across the room toward the big table, following Lana, who hastened toward her father. The Senator was standing behind the table, flanked by North and Daunt. The three of them formed a portentous battery. Morrison did not speak. His expression indicated humility. He drooped his shoulders. There was appeal in his eyes. "Here I am!" the eyes informed the glowering Senator. But a side-glance hinted: "Here is your daughter, too. Use judgment!"

Lana was manifestly perplexed by what she saw. Three distinguished gentle-men were presenting the visages of masculine Furies. She looked away from them and received a little comfort from the placid countenances of Andrew Mac Tavish and Delora Bunker, but their presence in that place and at that hour only made her mystification more complete.

She had been allowing her imagination to paint pictures before she stepped into the Executive Chamber; she had expected to find her father virtuously trium-phant, serenely a successful molder of pacific plans. His scowl was so forbidding that she stopped short.

"Father, it's wonderful--perfectly wonderful, isn't it?" She tried to speak joy-ously, but she faltered. "I saw it all! I saw how your plan succeeded."

"Damn you, Morrison! What has happened?" The Senator did not merely de-mand--he exploded.

The silence which followed became oppressive. Miss Corson was too thorough-ly horrified to proceed. Apparently Governor North and Daunt had selected their spokesman and had nothing to say for themselves. Morrison seemed to be especially helpless as an informant; he wagged his head and pointed to Lana.

"Answer my question, Morrison!"

"I think Miss Corson better tell you, sir. She was an impartial observer."

"Perhaps she *had* better tell me! You're right! After this night I wouldn't take your word as to the wetness of water. Lana, speak out!"

"I don't know what I can tell you--you have been right here all the time in the State House--"

The Senator jammed a retort between the links of her stammering speech. "Yes, I have been right here! What has happened below, I ask you?"

"Why, the troops marched out. They went away! Right through the mob! And it's all calm and quiet."

Governor North stamped his way a half-dozen paces to the rear, and whirled and marched back into line.

"Morrison, have you--have you--" Senator Corson choked. Not knowing ex-actly what to say, he shook his fist.

"Father, what's the matter? It was only carrying out your orders."

"Orders--my orders?"

"Stewart Morrison, why don't you say something?" she demanded.

"I'm sure your father prefers to hear from you."

"Confound it! I do want to hear, and hear immediately!"

Lana displayed some of the paternal ire. "Stewart, I asked you to be candid with me. You're leaving me to flounder around disgracefully in this matter."

The Senator advanced on his daughter and seized her arm. "I don't want that renegade to say another word to me as long as I live--and he knows it. I'll tell you later what has been going on here. But now tell me to what orders of mine you are referring! Quick and short!"

"Mayor Morrison made a little speech to the mob and said that you thought it was best to send away the troops to prevent bad feelings and misunderstanding, and said you were backed up by the Governor."

The Senator swapped looks with the goggling North over Lana's head.

"And the mob has gone home, and the State House is thrown wide open, and the policemen are on duty, and I say again that it's wonderful," insisted the girl.

"Morrison, did you say that? Have you done that?"

Stewart was fully aware that he had allowed the men in the square to draw an inference from a compliment that he had paid to Senator Corson's sagacity, and had refrained from making a direct declaration. But he was not minded to embarrass the girl any further. He bowed. "I thank Miss Corson for giving the gist of the thing so neatly."

"I know I don't understand it all yet, father!" Lana was both frightened and wistful. The Senator had turned from her and was striding to and fro, scuffing his feet hard on the carpet. "If you're blaming Mayor Morrison for revealing confidences, I'm sorry. But you can't help being proud when it is spread abroad how your handling of the dreadful affair prevented bloodshed and shame in this state."

"Spread abroad!" Senator Corson brought down his feet more violently.

The situation, if it remained bottled up there in the Executive Chamber any longer, threatened to explode in still more damaging fashion, was Stewart's uncomfortable thought. The Senator's remark suggested a diversion in the way of topics, at any rate.

"That reminds me that the newspaper boys are waiting outside in the corridor, Senator Corson. I asked them to be patient for a few minutes. Please allow me to say that I have added no statement to what I said to the crowd in the square. I shall not add any."

"I don't see how you could add anything!" retorted the Senator with venom.

He continued his promenade.

Again the silence in the room became oppressive.

Morrison was scrutinizing Governor North with especial intentness.

His Excellency was giving unmistakable evidence that he was surcharged. He was working his elbows and was whispering to himself with a fizzling sound. He had turned his back on Lana Corson as if he were resolved to ignore the fact of her presence.

Stewart, exhibiting deference while a United States Senator was pondering, strolled leisurely across the room to North and fondled the lapel of the Governor's coat. "I beg your pardon, and I hope you'll excuse curiosity in a chap who makes cloth, Governor. But this is as fine a piece of worsted as I've seen in many a day."

North lifted his arm as if to knock the presumptuous hand away; but Stewart slowly clenched his fist, holding the fabric in his close clutch, exerting a strength that dominated the man upon whom his hold was fastened. The mayor went on in an undertone, as if anxious to show additional deference in the presence of the senatorial ponderings. "Governor, petty politics haven't been allowed to make a bad mess of what has been turned into an open proposition. Now don't allow your tongue to make a mess of this new development as it stands right now. Humor Miss Corson's notions! And let me tell you! My policemen are going to stay on the job until after the legislature assembles."

"Morrison, you're a coward!" grated North. "You brought Corson's girl here so that you can sneak behind her petticoats."

Stewart released his hold, clapped His Excellency on the shoulder, raised his voice, and cried, heartily:

"Thank you. Governor! You're right. You have an excellent idea of a piece of goods, yourself."

Senator Corson arrived at a decision which he did not confide to anybody. He spoke to Daunt and the two of them went to the divan and dragged on the overcoats which they had discarded when Rellihan's obstinacy had been found to be unassailable.

Lana, studying the faces of the men, drew her furs about her.

"The car is waiting near the west portico, father," she ventured to say.

Corson took his time about buttoning his coat. Lana had her heritage of dark eyes from her father; his wrath had settled into cold malevolence and his eyes above his white cheeks were not pleasant objects. He surveyed the various persons in the room. He took his time in that process, too!

"For the present--for now--for to-night," he said, quietly, elaborating his mention of the moment with significance, "we seem to have cleaned up all the business before us. In view of that interregnum, Governor, of which you have been so kindly reminded, I suppose you feel that you can go to your hotel and rest for the remainder of the night so as to be in good trim for the inaugural ceremonies. Allow me to offer you a lift in my car."

The Governor trudged toward, a massive wardrobe in a corner of the chamber.

"I do not presume to offer you the convenience of my car, Mayor Morrison," the Senator went on.

"I take it that your recent oath as supreme Executive during the aforesaid interregnum obliges you to stay on the job. Ah--er--do we require a countersign in order to get out of the building?"

The mayor was walking toward the private door. "No, sir!" he said, mildly.

"I hope you hear that, Governor North! I was compelled to give countersigns to your soldiers--quite emphatic countersigns. The new regime is to be complimented."

Morrison threw open the door. "That's all, Rellihan! Report to the chief!"

The newspaper men came crowding to the threshold.

"You have interviewed Mayor Morrison on the situation, haven't you?" demanded the Senator, breaking in on their questions.

"Yes!"

"To-night--for the time being--for now," returned Corson, dwelling on the point as emphatically as he had when he spoke before, "Mayor Morrison seems to be doing very well in all that has been undertaken. I have no statement to make--absolutely no word to say!"

He stepped back and allowed the Governor to lead the retreat; His Excellency collided with two of the more persistent news-gatherers. With volleyed "No! Nothing!" he marked time for the thudding of his feet.

Apparently Lana had entered into the spirit of that armed truce which, so her father's manner informed her, was merely a rearrangement of the battle-front. She hurried out of the chamber without even a glance in Morrison's direction.

Stewart's grim countenance intimidated the reporters; they went away.

For a long time the mayor paced up and down the Executive Chamber, his hands clasped behind him.

Miss Bunker thumbed the leaves of her note-book, putting on an air of complete absorption in that matter.

Mac Tavish studied the mayor's face; Morrison was wearing that expression which indicated a mood strange for him. Mac Tavish had seen it on the master's face altogether too many times since the Morrison had come from the mill in the forenoon. It was not the look he wore when matters of business engrossed him. The old paymaster liked to see Morrison pondering on mill affairs; it was meditation that always meant solution of difficulties, and the solution was instantly followed by a laugh and good cheer.

But it was plain that Morrison had not solved anything when he turned to Mac Tavish.

"Not much like honest, real business--this, eh, Andy?"

"Naething like, sir!"

"Doesn't seem to be a polite job, either--politics--if you go in and fight the other fellow on his own ground."

"I've e'er hated the sculch and the scalawags!"

"Totten calls this a political exigency."

"I'll no name it for mysel' in the hearing o' the lass!"

"Seems to need a lot of fancy lying when a greenhorn like me starts late and is obliged to do things in a hurry. Gives business methods an awful wrench, Andy!"

"Aye!" The old Scotchman was emphatic.

"In fact, in a political exigency, according to what I've found out this evening, the quickest liar wins!" He walked to Miss Bunker's side. "You might jot that down as sort of summing the thing up and consider the record closed."

"Do ye think it's all closed and that ye're weel out of it?" inquired Mac Tavish, anxiously.

"I think, Andy," drawled the mayor, a wry smile beginning to twist at the corners of his mouth, "that I may have the militia and the people and the politicians well out of it, but considering the mess, as it concerns me, myself, I'm only beginning to be good and properly in it."

"Ye hae the record, as jotted by the lass, and I heard ye say naething but what was to your credit. And the words o' the high judges! Ye're well backed!"

"Oh, that reminds me, Andy. That boy who brought the telegrams to the door! He'll come to the mill in the morning. Pay him ten dollars. I didn't have the money in my clothes when I hired him."

"And that reminds me, too, Mr. Morrison!" said Miss Bunker. "Do you want me to keep the telegrams with the record? You remember you took them when you went out with the general."

Morrison reached into his breast pocket for the papers, tore them slowly across, and stuffed the scraps back into a side-pocket. "I reckon they won't do the record much good. It's more of the political exigency stuff, Andy! I wrote 'em myself!"

His hands had touched his pipe when he had shoved the bits of paper into his pocket. He took it out and peered into the bowl. There was tobacco there and he fumbled for a match.

"Andy, usually I like to have morning come, for there's always business waiting for me in the mornings and honest daylight helps any matter of clean business. But I'm not looking ahead to this next sunrise with a great deal of relish. Those telegrams were clinchers in the case of Totten, but I don't know what the judges will say. What I said about Senator Corson to the mob helped a lot--but I don't know what the Senator is going to say in the morning. And I don't know what Governor North proposes to say. Or what--" He checked himself and shook his head. "Well, there's considerable going to be said, at any rate! I'll run over the thing in my mind right now while I have time and everything is quiet. Mac Tavish, take Miss Bunker to the car and tell Jock to carry you and her home and to come back here for me."

After they had gone he lighted his pipe and sat down in the Governor's big chair and smoked and pondered. Every little while he thrust his forefinger and thumb into his vest pocket and ransacked without avail. "I must have left it in my dress clothes," he muttered. "But no matter! I'm not in the right frame of mind to enjoy poetry. However, merely in the way of taking a new clinch on the proposition I do remember this much, 'But I will marry my own first love!' There's truth in poetry if you go after it hard enough. And, on second thought, I'd better keep my mind on poetry as closely as I can! I certainly don't dare to think of politics right now!"

XX
IN THE COLD AND CANDID DAYLIGHT

For the first time in his life Governor North had his breakfast served to him in his room at his hotel; he ate alone, chewing savagely and studying newspapers. He did not welcome this method of breakfasting as a pleasing indulgence. Rugged Lawrence North was no sybarite; he hated all assumptions of exclusiveness; he loved to mingle and mix, and his morning levees in the hotel breakfast-room catered to all his vanity as a public functionary. He did not own up squarely to himself that he was afraid to go down and face men and answer questions. He had ordered the hotel telephone exchange to give him no calls; he had told the desk clerk to state to all inquirers that the Governor was too busy to be seen; he paid no attention to raps on his door. His self-exculpation in this unwonted privacy was that he could not afford to allow himself to be bothered by questioners until he and Senator Corson could arrange for effectual team-work by another conference. When he and the Senator parted they agreed to get together at the Corson mansion the first thing after breakfast.

While the Governor ground his food between his teeth he also chewed on the savage realization that he had nothing sensible to say in public on the situation, considering his uncompromising declarations of the day before; there were those declarations thrusting up at him from the newspaper page like derisive fingers; by the reports in parallel columns he was represented as saying one thing and doing another! And a bumptious, blundering, bull-headed Scotchman had put the Governor of a state in that tongue-tied, skulking position on the proud day of inauguration!

His Excellency slashed his ham, and stabbed his eggs, making his food atone vicariously.

He did not order his car over the hotel telephone. The hotel attachés were obsequious and would be waiting to escort him in state across the main office. The politicians would surround the car. And he was perfectly sure that some of the big men of an amazed State House lobby might step into that car along with him and seek to know what in the name o' mischief had happened overnight to change all the sane and conservative plans in the way of making a legislature safe!

He bundled himself and his raw pride into his overcoat, turned the fur collar up around his head, and went down a staircase. He was sneaking and he knew it and no paltering self-assurance that he was handling a touchy situation with necessary tact helped his feelings in the least. He stepped into a taxicab and was glad because the breath of previous passengers that morning had frosted the windows. That consolation was merely a back-fire in the rest of the conflagration that raged in him.

It was a dull morning, somber and cold.

When he stamped up the broad walk from the gate of the Corson mansion he beheld the boarded windows of the ballroom, and the spectacle added to his sense of chill. But his anger was not cooled.

Senator Corson's secretary was waiting in the hall; he showed the Governor up to the Senator's study.

Either because the outdoors was not cheerful that morning or because the Senator had been too much engrossed in meditation to remember that daylight would serve him, the curtains of the study were drawn and the electric lamps were on.

Corson was walking up and down the room, chewing on one end of a cigar and making a soggy torch of the other end. He continued to pace while North pulled off his coat.

"I have sent word to Morrison to come here," reported the host.

The mantel clock reported the hour as nine; His Excellency scowled at the clock's face. "And you got word back, I suppose, that after he has come out of his mill at ten o'clock and has washed his hands and--"

"He's at City Hall," snapped Corson, with an acerbity that matched the Governor's. "I called the mill and was referred to Morrison at City Hall. He's on his way up here! At any rate, he said he'd start at once."

"Did he condescend to intimate in what capacity he proposes to land on us this time?"

"I'm going to allow you to draw your own conclusions. I've been trying to draw some of my own from what he said."

"What did he say?"

"Apologized because I was put to any trouble in locating him. Said he was expecting to be called by me and thought he would go to City Hall and await my summons in order to put himself and the whole situation on a strictly official basis." The Senator delivered that information sullenly.

"What kind of a devilish basis does he think he's been operating on?"

"Look here, North! If you have come up here to fight with me after the row you have been having down-town this morning I warn you--"

"I have had no row down-town. I wouldn't see anybody. I wouldn't talk with anybody. Blast it! Corson, I don't know what to say to anybody!"

"Well, that's one point, at least, on which you and I can get together even if we can't agree on anything else. If you have been so cursedly exclusive as all that, North, perhaps you haven't been in touch with any of the justices of the supreme court, as I have."

"You have, eh?"

"I called Davenport and Madigan on the telephone."

"What excuse could they give for sending their snap opinions over the wire on the inquiry of a fool?"

"They offered no excuse. They couldn't. They knew nothing about any telegrams till I informed 'em. They received no inquiry. They sent no replies, naturally."

"That--that--Did that--" The Governor pawed at his scraggly neck. "He faked all that stuff?"

"Absolutely!"

Comment which could not have been expressed in long speeches and violent denunciation was put into the pregnant stare exchanged by the two men.

Then the Senator took another grip on his cigar with bared teeth and began to march again.

"Corson, what's going to be done with that blue-blazed understudy of Ananias?"

"Depend on the wrath of Heaven, perhaps," said the Senator, sarcastically. "I haven't had time to look in Holy Writ this morning and ascertain just what kind of a He Ananias told. But whatever it was, it was tame beside what Morrison told that mob about me last night."

"You've had your fling at me about my exclusiveness! What are you putting out yourself this morning in the way of statements?" The Governor banged his fist down on the newspapers which littered the study table.

"Nothing! Not yet!"

"I've got to have my self-respect with me when I deliver my inaugural address this forenoon. The only way I can possess it is by ramming Morrison into jail."

"On what ground, may I ask?"

"Interference with the Chief Executive of this state! Inciting the mob against the militia! Putting state property in danger. Forgery--contempt of court! I'll appeal to the judges to act. I'll call in the attorney-general. You and I were forcibly detained!"

"Yes, we might allege abduction," was Corson's dry rejoinder. "Our helplessness in the hands of a usurper would win a lot of public sympathy."

"I tell you, we would have the sympathy of the people," asserted the Governor, too angry to be anything else than literal.

"And they'd express it by giving us the biggest laugh ever tendered to two public men in this state, North. We've got to look this thing straight in the eye. I told Morrison last night that no such preposterous thing was ever put over in American politics, and he agreed with me. You must agree, too! That makes us unanimous on one point, and that's something gained, because it's an essential point. We can't afford to let the public know just how preposterous the situation was. A man in American public life can get away with almost any kind of a fix, if it's taken seriously. But the right sort of a general laugh will snuff him like that!" He snapped his finger. "We're not dealing with politics and procedure in the case of Morrison,"

"We're dealing with a fool and his folly!" the Governor shouted.

It was another of those cases where the expected guest under discussion becomes an eavesdropper at just the wrong moment; Morrison was not deliberately an eavesdropper. He had followed the instructed secretary to the study door, and the Governor had declared himself with a violence that was heard outside the room.

The mayor stepped in when the secretary opened the door

After the secretary had closed the door and departed Morrison stepped forward. "Governor North, you're perfectly right, and I agree with you without resenting your remark. I did make quite a fool of myself last night. Perhaps you are not ready to concede that the ends justify the means."

"I do not, sir!"

"A result built on falsehoods is a pretty poor proposition," declared the Senator. "I refer especially to those fake telegrams and to your impudent assertion to the mob that I said this or that!"

"Yes, that telegram job was a pretty raw one, sir," Morrison admitted. "But I really didn't lie straight out to those men in the square about your participation. I let 'em draw an inference from the way I complimented your fairness and good sense. I was a little hasty last night--but I didn't have much time to do advance thinking."

"I'm going to express myself about last night," stated Senator Corson.

"Will you wait a moment, sir?" Morrison had not removed his overcoat; he had not even unbuttoned it; he afforded the impression of a man who intended to transact business and be on his way with the least possible delay. He glanced at the electric lights and at the shaded windows. "This seems too much like last night. Won't you allow me? It's a little indulgence to my state of mind!"

He hurried across the room and snapped up the shades and pulled apart the curtains. He reached his hand to the wall-switch and turned off the lights.

"This isn't last night--it's this morning--and there's nothing like honest daylight on a proposition, gentlemen! Nothing like it! Last night things looked sort of tragic. This morning the same things will look comical if"--he raised his forefinger--"if the inside of 'em is reported. If the real story is told, the people in this state will laugh their heads off." Again the Governor and the Senator put a lot of expression into the look which they exchanged. "I got that mob to laughing last night and, as I told General Totten, that settled the civil war. If the people get to laughing over what happened when Con Rellihan took his orders only from the mayor of Marion, it will--well, it'll be apt to settle some political hash."

"Do you threaten?" demanded North. He was blinking into the matter-of-fact daylight where Morrison stood, framed in a window.

"Governor North, take a good look at me. I'm not a pirate chief. I'm merely a business man up here to do a little dickering. I can't trade on my political influence, because I haven't any. You have all the politics on your side. I propose to do the best I can with the little stock in trade I have brought." He walked to the table and flapped on it his hand, palm up. "You are two almighty keen and discerning gentlemen. I don't need to itemize the stock in trade I have laid down here. You see what I've got!"

He paused and, his eyes glinting with a suppressed emotion that the discerning gentlemen understood, he glanced from one to the other of them.

"You've got a cock-and-bull yarn in which you are shown up as a liar and a lawbreaker," the Governor declared. "You've got some guess--so about errors in returns--"

"Hold on! Hold on, North!" protested Senator Corson. "It's just as Morrison says--we don't need to itemize his stock in trade. I can estimate it for myself. Morrison, you say you're ready to dicker. What do you want?"

"A legislature that's organized open and above-board, with all claimants in their seats and having their word to say as to the sort of questions that will be sent up to the court. Staying in their seats, gentlemen, till the decisions are handed down! Let the legislature, as a whole, draft the questions about the status of its membership. I've got my own interest in this--and I'll be perfectly frank in stating it. I have a report on water-power to submit. I don't want that report to go to a committee that has been doctored up by a hand-picked House and Senate."

"You don't expect that Governor North and myself are going to stand here and give you guaranties as to proposed legislation, do you?"

"You are asking me, as an executive, to interfere with the legislative branch," expostulated His Excellency.

"Gentlemen, I don't expect to settle the problems of the world here this morning, or even this water-power question. I'm simply demanding that the thing be given a fair start on the right track." There was a great deal of significance in his tone when he added: "I hope there'll be no need of going into unpleasant details, gentlemen. All three of us know exactly what is meant."

Senator Corson was distinctly without enthusiasm; he maintained his air of chilly dignity. "What legislation is contemplated under that report that you will submit?"

"Some of the lawyers say that a general law prohibiting the shipping of power over wires out of the state must be backed by a change in our constitution. Until we can secure that change there must be a prohibitive clause on every water-power charter granted by the legislature--a clause that restricts all the developed power for consumption in this state."

"A policy of selfishness, sir."

"No, Senator Corson, a policy that protects our own development until we can create a surplus of power. Sell our surplus, perhaps! That's a sound rule of business. If you'll allow me to volunteer a word or two more as to plans, I'll say that eventually I hope to see the state pay just compensation and take back and control the water-power that was given away by our forefathers.

"As to power that is still undeveloped, I consider it the heritage of the people, and I refuse to be a party to putting a mortgage on it. My ideas may be a little crude just now--I say again that everything can't be settled and made right in a moment, but I have stated the principle of the thing and we fellows who believe in it are going ahead on that line. I realize perfectly well, sir, that this plan discourages the kind of capital that Mr. Daunt represents, but if there is one thing in this God's country of ours that should not be put into the hands of monopoly it's the power in the currents of the rivers that are fed by the lakes owned by the people. I'm a little warm on the subject, Senator Corson, I'll confess. I have been stubbing my toes around in pretty awkward shape. But I had to do the best I could on short notice."

"You have been very active in the affair," was the Senator's uncompromising rejoinder.

Governor North continued to be frankly a skeptic and had been expressing his emotions by wagging his head and grunting. In the line of his general disbelief in every declaration and in everybody, he pulled his watch from his pocket as if to assure himself as to the real time; he had scowled at the Senator's mantel clock as if he suspected that even the timepiece might be trying to put something over on him. "I must be moving on toward the State House." He wore the air of a defendant headed for the court-room instead of a Governor about to be inaugurated. "I must know where I stand! Morrison, what's it all about, anyway?"

The Governor was convincingly sincere in his query. He had the manner of one who had decided, all of a sudden, to come into the open. There was something almost wistful in this new candor. Stewart's poise was plainly jarred.

"What's it all about?" He blinked with bewilderment. "Why, I have been telling you, Governor!"

"Do you think for one minute that I believe all that Righteous Rollo rant?"

"I have been stating my principles and--"

"Hold on! I've had all the statements that I can absorb. What's behind 'em? That's what I want to know. Wait, I tell you! Don't insult my intelligence any more by telling me it's altruism, high-minded unselfishness in behalf of the people! I have heard others and myself talk that line of punk to a finish. Are you going to run for Governor next election?"

"Absolutely not!"

"Are you grooming a man?"

"No, sir!"

"Building up a political machine?"

"Certainly I am not,"

"Going to organize a water-power syndicate of your own after you get legislation that will give you a clear field against outside capital?"

"No--no, most positively!"

"Senator Corson, you claim you know Morrison better than I do. How much is he lying?"

"I think he means what he says."

North picked up his overcoat and plunged his arms into the sleeves. "If I should think so--if I should place implicit faith in any man who talks that way--I'd be ashamed of my weakness--and I've got too many things about myself to be ashamed of, all the way from table manners to morals! There's one thing that I'm sort of holding on to, and that's the fact that my intellect seems to be unimpaired in my old age. Morrison, I don't believe half what you say."

The mayor of Marion made no reply for some moments. Corson, surveying him, showed uneasiness. A retort that would fit the provocation was likely to lead to results that would embarrass the host of the two Executives.

"Oh, by the way, Governor," said Stewart, quietly, "I just came from City Hall. I really did not intend to drift so far from strictly official business when I came up here. I want to assure you that there will be no expense to the state connected with the police guard at the Capitol. They are at your service till after the inaugural ceremonies. Do you think you will need the officers on duty at your residence any longer, Senator Corson?"

"No, sir!"

"I agree with you that everything seems to have quieted down beautifully. Governor, you have my best wishes for your second term. I'm sorry I'll not be able to go to the State House to hear your address."

He went to the Governor and put out his hand, an act which compelled response in kind.

"I'm much obliged!" His Excellency was curt and caustic. "After the vaudeville show of last night there won't be much to-day at the State House to suit anybody who is fond of excitement."

Before North, departing, reached the door Senator Corson's secretary tapped and entered. He gave several telegrams into the hand of his employer.

"Pardon me, gentlemen!" apologized the Senator, tearing open an envelope. "Wait a moment, North. These messages may bear on the situation."

He read them in silence one after the other, his face betraying nothing of his thoughts.

He stacked the sheets on the table. "Evidently several notable gentlemen in our state rise early, read the newspapers before breakfast, and are handy to telegraph offices," he remarked, leveling steady gaze at Stewart. "These telegrams are addressed to me, but by good rights they belong to you, Mister Mayor, I'm inclined to believe."

There was irony in the Senator's tone; Morrison offered no reply.

"They're all of the same tenor, North," explained Senator Corson. "I'm bracketed with you. You'll probably find some of your own waiting at the State House for you. And more to come!"

"Well, what are they--what are they?"

"Compliments for the sane, safe, and statesmanlike way we handled a crisis and saved the good name of the state."

"Now, Morrison," raged the Governor, "you can begin to understand what kind of a damnable mess you've jammed me into along with Corson, here! That steer of a policeman will blab, that Scotchman will snarl, and that loose-mouthed girl will babble!"

"Governor, I haven't resented anything you have said to me, personally. You can go ahead and say a lot more to me, and I'll not resent it. But let me tell you that I can depend on the business loyalty of the folks who serve me; and if you go to classing my kind of helpers in with the cheap politicians with whom you have been associating, I shall say something to you that will break up this friendly party. My folks will not talk! Save your sarcasm for your agents who have been running around getting you into a real scrape by telling about those election returns."

He snapped about face, on his heels, and walked out of the door.

XXI
A WOMAN CHOOSES HER MATE

The haste displayed by Mayor Morrison in getting away from the study door suggested that he was glad to escape and was not fishing for any invitation to return for further parley.

But when he approached the head of the stairway he moved more slowly. His demeanor hinted that he would welcome some excuse, outside of politics, to keep him longer in the Corson mansion. He paused on the stairs and made an elaborate arrangement of a neck muffler as if he expected to confront polar temperature outside. He pulled on his gloves, inspected them critically as if to assure himself that there were no crevices where the cold could enter. He looked over the banisters. There was nobody in the reception-hall. He arranged the muffler some more. Step by step, very slowly, he descended as far as the landing where he had met Lana Corson joyously the night before. Not expectantly, with visage downcast, he looked behind him.

Lana was framed in the library door at the head of the stairs.

"I was trying to make up my mind to call to you. But you seemed to be in so much of a hurry! I suppose you have a great deal to attend to this morning."

"The principal rush seems to be over. Was it anything--Did you want to speak to me?"

"Perhaps it isn't of much importance. It did seem to be, for a moment. But it's something of a family matter. I think, after all, it will be imprudent to mention it."

He waited for her to go on.

"Probably under the circumstances you'll not be especially interested," she ventured.

"The trouble is, I'm afraid I'll show too much interest and seem to be prying."

"Will you please step up here where I'll not be obliged to shout at you?"

He obeyed so promptly that he fairly scrambled up the stairs.

"You said down there in the hall last evening that my father was angry and that an angry man says a great deal that he doesn't mean. My father was very, very angry when he and. I arrived home last night."

"I reckoned he would be."

"In his anger he talked to me very freely about you. The question is, should I believe anything he said?"

"I--I don't know," he stammered, "You're not going back on your own statement about an angry man, are you?"

"I don't think it's fair to accept all his statements."

"I'm sorry you still hold that opinion. You see I drew some conclusions of my own from what my father said to me, and those conclusions urge me to apologize to you for the Corson family. I'm afraid you didn't find my father in an apologetic mood this morning."

"Not exactly."

"Doris tells me that I have a New England conscience. I'm not sure. At any rate, I'm feeling very uncomfortable about something! It may be because you're misunderstood by our family. Do I seem forward?"

"No! Of course you don't. But you're putting me in a terrible position. I don't know what to say. I don't want any apologies. They'd make me feel like a fool-- more of a fool than I have been."

"Are you admitting now that you were wrong in the stand you took about the water-power and--and--well, about everything?"

He had been listening in distress and perplexity, striving to understand her, groping for the meaning she was hiding behind her quiet manner. But her question struck fire from the flint of his resolution. "That power matter is a principle, and I am not wrong in it. As to the means I used last night, it was brass and blunder and I'm ashamed of acting that way."

"There's no need of going into the matter. I received a great deal of information from my father--when he was angry. And I woke up early this morning and began to consider the evidence. I was hard at it when you drove up in your car. I have been waiting for you to come from your talk with my father and the Governor. I want to say, Stewart, that when I stood up last night, like a fool, and lectured you about neglecting your opportunities in life I was considering you only as the boss of St. Ronan's mill. But my father told me what you really are. I have always respected him as a very truthful man, even when he is well worked up by any subject. I must take his word in this matter, though he didn't realize just how complimentary he was in your case. And if you can spare me a few moments, I want you to come into the library."

She walked ahead of him toward the door.

"I think I'll leave the Corson family right out of it, Stewart. I'm a loyal daughter of this state. I'm home again and I've waked up. Humor me in a little conceit, won't you? Let me make believe that I'm the state and listen to me while I tell you what a big, brave, unselfish--"

They were inside the door and he put his arm about her and led her toward the big screen and broke in on her little speech that she was making tremulously, apprehensively, with a sob in her voice, trying to hide her deeper emotions under her mock-dramatics.

"Hush, dear! I don't want to hear any state talk to me! I want to hear only Lana Corson talk. I didn't understand her last night! Now, bless her honest, true heart, I do understand her."

Speech, long repressed, was rushing from his mouth. Then he struggled with words; his excitement choked him. He looked down at her through his tears. "The bit poem, lassie! You remember it. The poem you recited, and when I sent you the big basket o' posies! All the time since yesterday it has been running in my head. I sat alone in the State House last night and all I could remember was, 'But I will marry my own first love!' I tried to say it out like a man, believing that God has meant you for me. But I couldn't think I'd be forgiven!"

Lana took his hand between her palms and stopped him at the edge of the screen. She quoted, meeting his adoring eyes with full understanding:

"And I think, in the lives of most women and men,   There's a moment when all would go smooth and even--"

She drew him gently with her when she stepped backward.

She had heard the Senator's voice in the corridor; he was escorting Governor North.

On the panels of the screen were embroidered some particularly grotesque Japanese countenances. Those pictured personages seemed to be making up faces at the dignitaries who passed the open door.

"But I must go to your father, sweetheart," Stewart insisted. "I'd best do it this morning and have it all over with."

This declaration as to duty and deference was not made while Senator Corson was passing the door; nor was it made with anything like the promptitude the Senator might have expected in a matter which was so vitally concerned with a father's interests. In fact it was a long, long time before Stewart had anything to say on that subject. If Senator Corson had been listening again on the other side of the screen, he, no doubt, would have been mightily offended by a delay which seemed to make the father an afterthought in the whole business.

If he had been eavesdropping he would not have heard much, anyway, of an informing nature. He would have heard two voices, tenderly low and incoherent, interrupting eagerly, breaking in on each other to explain and protest and plead. If Stewart's protracted neglect of the interests of a father would have availed to rouse resentment, Lana's reply to Stewart's rueful declaration more surely would have exasperated the Senator; she emphatically commanded Stewart to say not one word on the subject to her father.

"Why, Stewart Morrison, for twenty-four hours you have been taking away my breath by doing the unexpected! You have been grand. Now are you going to spoil everything by dropping right back into the conventional, every-day way of doing things? You shall not! You shall not spoil my new worship of a hero!"

"Well, I won't seem much like a hero if I act as though I'm afraid of your father!"

She raised her voice in amazed query. "For mercy's sake, haven't you been proving that you're not afraid of him?" Once more, jubilantly, teasingly, wrought upon by the revived spirit of the intimacy of the old days, she assumed a playful pose with him, but this time her sincerity of soul was behind the situation. "Don't you realize, sir, that the calendar of the Hon. Jodrey Wadsworth Corson, on this day and date, is crowded with strictly new business? He is due at the State House very soon. Do you think he can afford to be bothered with unfinished business?"

He worshiped her with silence and a smile.

"Yes, Mister Mayor of Marion, unfinished business--yours and mine! Our business of the old days. But the honorable Senator is perfectly well aware that the business aforesaid is on the calendar. He had been supposing that we had forgotten it. I see a big question in your eyes, Stewart dear! Well, now that you're a party to the action and interested in the matter to be presented, I'll say that after Senator Corson had done his talking to me last evening, or very early this morning, to be more exact, I called on my family grit of which he's so proud and I did a little talking to Senator Corson. And he knows that the business is unfinished--he knows it will be brought duly to his attention--and he'll be in a better frame of mind after his present petulance has worn off."

"Petulance!" Morrison was rather skeptical.

"Exactly! He's just as much of a big child as most men are when another big child tries to take away a plaything. Oh, he was furious, Stewart! But let me tell you something for your comfort. He dwelt most savagely on the fact that you had grabbed in single-handed and beaten a Governor and a United States Senator at their own game! Wonderful, isn't it--admission like that? He has always patronized you as a countryman who knew how to make good cloth and who didn't amount to anything else in the world. Why, in a few days he'll be admitting that he admires you and respects you!"

She paused. After a few moments she went on, her tones low and thrilling. "I've been trying to explain myself to you, Stewart. You know, now, that I have always loved you. I have told you so in a way that leaves no doubts in a man such as you are. You have forgiven me for being simply human and silly before I woke up to understand you. And you don't misunderstand me any more, do you?" she pleaded, wistfully. "Last night I saw--your big *self*!"

"Lana, it was a wonderful night--more wonderful than I realized till now!"

After a time they became aware of a stir below-stairs and they came out from behind the screen where the Japanese faces grinned knowingly.

"Please obey me, Stewart; you must! It's really my trial of you to see if you're obedient when I know it's for your own good. Go down and wait for me." She left him in the corridor and ran away.

He marched down the stairs with as much self-possession as he could command.

Below him he saw Senator Corson, Mrs. Stanton, Silas Daunt, and the banker's son. All were garbed for outdoors and the Senator was inquiring of Mrs. Stanton why Lana was not ready.

From the landing down to the hall Stewart found the ordeal an exacting one. Those below surveyed him with an open astonishment that was more disconcerting than hostility; he was in a mood to fight for himself and his own; but to deal in mere polite explanations, after Lana's imperious command to keep silent on an important matter, was beyond any sagacity he possessed in that period of abashed wonder what to say or do.

It was his thought that Miss Corson, in her efforts to avoid an anticlimax of conventional procedure, was making a rather too severe test of him in forcing him to endure the unusual.

He did manage to say, "Good morning!" and smiled at them in a deprecatory way.

Coventry Daunt amiably responded as a spokesman for the group; but he had waited deferentially for his elders to make some response.

The Senator held a packet of telegrams in his hand. After Stewart had halted in the hall, putting on the best face he could and evincing a determination to stick the thing out, Senator Corson walked over and offered to give the mayor the telegrams. "They're beginning to arrive from Washington, sir. Better read 'em. They'll afford you a great deal of joy, I'm sure."

Stewart shook his head, declining to receive the missives. He wanted to tell the Senator that more joy right at that moment would overtask the Morrison capacity.

"I wish I were younger and more of an opportunist," Corson avowed. "In these guessing times among the booms, here is gas enough to inflate a pretty good-sized presidential balloon." He waved the papers.

The Senator's tone was still rather ironical, but Stewart was seeking for straws to buoy his new hopes; whether he was so recently away from Lana's dark eyes that the encouragement in them lingered with him, he was not sure. He felt, however, that the Senator's eyes did seem a little less hard than the polished ebony they had resembled.

An awkward silence ensued. The Senator stood in front of the caller and queried uncompromisingly with those eyes.

The caller, having been enjoined from babbling about the business that had been transacted behind the screen in the library, had no excuse to offer for hanging around there. "I--I suppose you're going to the State House," he suggested, after he decided that the weather called for no comments.

"We are! We are waiting for my daughter," stated Corson, with a severity which indicated that he was determined, then and there, to rebuke the cause of her delay.

"I'm so sorry you have waited!" Lana called to them from the landing, and came hurrying down, fastening the clasp of her furs.

She went to Mrs. Stanton, her face expressing apologetic distress. "It's so comforting, Doris, to know that you and I don't need to bother with all these guest and hostess niceties. You'll understand--because you're a dear friend! Father will make the doors of the Capitol fly open for his party--and you'll be looked after wonderfully." She bestowed her gracious glances on the others of the Daunt family, "I know you'll all forgive me if I don't come along."

She did not allow her amazed father to embarrass the situation by the outburst that he threatened. She fled past him, patting his arm with a swift caress. "I'm going with Stewart--over to Jeanie Mac Dougal Morrison's house. It's really dreadfully important. You know why, father. I'll tell you all about it later. Come, Stewart! We must hurry!"

Young Mr. Daunt was near the door. He opened it for her. When Stewart passed, following the girl closely, the volunteer door-tender qualified as a good sport. He whispered, "Good luck, old man!"

When Coventry closed the door he gave his sister a prolonged and pregnant stare of actual triumph.

It was only a look, but he put into it more significance than sufficed for Doris's perspicacity.

He had confided to his sister, the evening before, his hopeful reliance on a girl's heart.

But the Lana Corson who came down the stairs, who confronted them, who had fearlessly chosen her mate before their hostile eyes, was a woman.

And Coventry's gaze told his sister boastingly that he had made good in one respect--he had called the turn in his estimate of a woman.

The Codes Of Hammurabi And Moses
W. W. Davies

QTY

The discovery of the Hammurabi Code is one of the greatest achievements of archaeology, and is of paramount interest, not only to the student of the Bible, but also to all those interested in ancient history...

Religion   ISBN: *1-59462-338-4*   Pages:132
MSRP $12.95

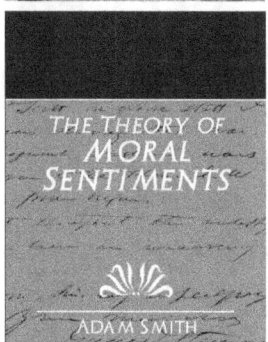

The Theory of Moral Sentiments
Adam Smith

QTY

This work from 1749. contains original theories of conscience amd moral judgment and it is the foundation for systemof morals.

Philosophy ISBN: *1-59462-777-0*   Pages:536
MSRP $19.95

Jessica's First Prayer
Hesba Stretton

QTY

In a screened and secluded corner of one of the many railway-bridges which span the streets of London there could be seen a few years ago, from five o'clock every morning until half past eight, a tidily set-out coffee-stall, consisting of a trestle and board, upon which stood two large tin cans, with a small fire of charcoal burning under each so as to keep the coffee boiling during the early hours of the morning when the work-people were thronging into the city on their way to their daily toil...

Childrens   ISBN: *1-59462-373-2*   Pages:84
MSRP $9.95

My Life and Work
Henry Ford

QTY

Henry Ford revolutionized the world with his implementation of mass production for the Model T automobile. Gain valuable business insight into his life and work with his own auto-biography... "We have only started on our development of our country we have not as yet, with all our talk of wonderful progress, done more than scratch the surface. The progress has been wonderful enough but..."

Biographies/   ISBN: *1-59462-198-5*   Pages:300
MSRP $21.95

The Art of Cross-Examination
Francis Wellman

QTY

I presume it is the experience of every author, after his first book is published upon an important subject, to be almost overwhelmed with a wealth of ideas and illustrations which could readily have been included in his book, and which to his own mind, at least, seem to make a second edition inevitable. Such certainly was the case with me; and when the first edition had reached its sixth impression in five months, I rejoiced to learn that it seemed to my publishers that the book had met with a sufficiently favorable reception to justify a second and considerably enlarged edition. ..

Pages:412

Reference   ISBN: *1-59462-647-2*   *MSRP $19.95*

On the Duty of Civil Disobedience
Henry David Thoreau

QTY

Thoreau wrote his famous essay, On the Duty of Civil Disobedience, as a protest against an unjust but popular war and the immoral but popular institution of slave-owning. He did more than write—he declined to pay his taxes, and was hauled off to gaol in consequence. Who can say how much this refusal of his hastened the end of the war and of slavery ?

Law   ISBN: *1-59462-747-9*   **Pages:48**
MSRP $7.45

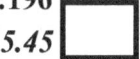

Dream Psychology Psychoanalysis for Beginners
Sigmund Freud

QTY

Sigmund Freud, born Sigismund Schlomo Freud (May 6, 1856 - September 23, 1939), was a Jewish-Austrian neurologist and psychiatrist who co-founded the psychoanalytic school of psychology. Freud is best known for his theories of the unconscious mind, especially involving the mechanism of repression; his redefinition of sexual desire as mobile and directed towards a wide variety of objects; and his therapeutic techniques, especially his understanding of transference in the therapeutic relationship and the presumed value of dreams as sources of insight into unconscious desires.

Pages:196

Psychology   ISBN: *1-59462-905-6*   *MSRP $15.45*

The Miracle of Right Thought
Orison Swett Marden

QTY

Believe with all of your heart that you will do what you were made to do. When the mind has once formed the habit of holding cheerful, happy, prosperous pictures, it will not be easy to form the opposite habit. It does not matter how improbable or how far away this realization may see, or how dark the prospects may be, if we visualize them as best we can, as vividly as possible, hold tenaciously to them and vigorously struggle to attain them, they will gradually become actualized, realized in the life. But a desire, a longing without endeavor, a yearning abandoned or held indifferently will vanish without realization.

Pages:360

Self Help   ISBN: *1-59462-644-8*   *MSRP $25.45*

The Rosicrucian Cosmo-Conception Mystic Christianity *by Max Heindel*   ISBN: *1-59462-188-8*   **$38.95**
The Rosicrucian Cosmo-conception is not dogmatic, neither does it appeal to any other authority than the reason of the student. It is: not controversial, but is: sent forth in the, hope that it may help to clear...   New Age/Religion Pages 646

Abandonment To Divine Providence *by Jean-Pierre de Caussade*   ISBN: *1-59462-228-0*   **$25.95**
"The Rev. Jean Pierre de Caussade was one of the most remarkable spiritual writers of the Society of Jesus in France in the 18th Century. His death took place at Toulouse in 1751. His works have gone through many editions and have been republished...   Inspirational/Religion Pages 400

Mental Chemistry *by Charles Haanel*   ISBN: *1-59462-192-6*   **$23.95**
Mental Chemistry allows the change of material conditions by combining and appropriately utilizing the power of the mind. Much like applied chemistry creates something new and unique out of careful combinations of chemicals the mastery of mental chemistry...   New Age Pages 354

The Letters of Robert Browning and Elizabeth Barret Barrett 1845-1846 vol II   ISBN: *1-59462-193-4*   **$35.95**
by Robert Browning and Elizabeth Barrett   Biographies Pages 596

Gleanings In Genesis (volume I) *by Arthur W. Pink*   ISBN: *1-59462-130-6*   **$27.45**
Appropriately has Genesis been termed "the seed plot of the Bible" for in it we have, in germ form, almost all of the great doctrines which are afterwards fully developed in the books of Scripture which follow...   Religion/Inspirational Pages 420

The Master Key *by L. W. de Laurence*   ISBN: *1-59462-001-6*   **$30.95**
In no branch of human knowledge has there been a more lively increase of the spirit of research during the past few years than in the study of Psychology, Concentration and Mental Discipline. The requests for authentic lessons in Thought Control, Mental Discipline and...   New Age/Business Pages 422

The Lesser Key Of Solomon Goetia *by L. W. de Laurence*   ISBN: *1-59462-092-X*   **$9.95**
This translation of the first book of the "Lernegton" which is now for the first time made accessible to students of Talismanic Magic was done, after careful collation and edition, from numerous Ancient Manuscripts in Hebrew, Latin, and French...   New Age/Occult Pages 92

Rubaiyat Of Omar Khayyam *by Edward Fitzgerald*   ISBN:*1-59462-332-5* **$13.95**
Edward Fitzgerald, whom the world has already learned, in spite of his own efforts to remain within the shadow of anonymity, to look upon as one of the rarest poets of the century, was born at Bredfield, in Suffolk, on the 31st of March, 1809. He was the third son of John Purcell...   Music Pages 172

Ancient Law *by Henry Maine*   ISBN: *1-59462-128-4*   **$29.95**
The chief object of the following pages is to indicate some of the earliest ideas of mankind, as they are reflected in Ancient Law, and to point out the relation of those ideas to modern thought.   Religion/History Pages 452

Far-Away Stories *by William J. Locke*   ISBN: *1-59462-129-2*   **$19.45**
"Good wine needs no bush, but a collection of mixed vintages does. And this book is just such a collection. Some of the stories I do not want to remain buried for ever in the museum files of dead magazine-numbers an author's not unpardonable vanity..."   Fiction Pages 272

Life of David Crockett *by David Crockett*   ISBN: *1-59462-250-7*   **$27.45**
"Colonel David Crockett was one of the most remarkable men of the times in which he lived. Born in humble life, but gifted with a strong will, an indomitable courage, and unremitting perseverance...   Biographies/New Age Pages 424

Lip-Reading *by Edward Nitchie*   ISBN: *1-59462-206-X*   **$25.95**
Edward B. Nitchie, founder of the New York School for the Hard of Hearing, now the Nitchie School of Lip-Reading, Inc, wrote "LIP-READING Principles and Practice". The development and perfecting of this meritorious work on lip-reading was an undertaking...   How-to Pages 400

A Handbook of Suggestive Therapeutics, Applied Hypnotism, Psychic Science   ISBN: *1-59462-214-0*   **$24.95**
by Henry Munro   Health/New Age/Health/Self-help Pages 376

A Doll's House: and Two Other Plays *by Henrik Ibsen*   ISBN: *1-59462-112-8*   **$19.95**
Henrik Ibsen created this classic when in revolutionary 1848 Rome. Introducing some striking concepts in playwriting for the realist genre, this play has been studied the world over.   Fiction/Classics/Plays 308

The Light of Asia *by sir Edwin Arnold*   ISBN: *1-59462-204-3*   **$13.95**
In this poetic masterpiece, Edwin Arnold describes the life and teachings of Buddha. The man who was to become known as Buddha to the world was born as Prince Gautama of India but he rejected the worldly riches and abandoned the reigns of power when... Religion/History/Biographies Pages 170

The Complete Works of Guy de Maupassant *by Guy de Maupassant*   ISBN: *1-59462-157-8*   **$16.95**
"For days and days, nights and nights, I had dreamed of that first kiss which was to consecrate our engagement, and I knew not on what spot I should put my lips..."   Fiction/Classics Pages 240

The Art of Cross-Examination *by Francis L. Wellman*   ISBN: *1-59462-309-0*   **$26.95**
Written by a renowned trial lawyer, Wellman imparts his experience and uses case studies to explain how to use psychology to extract desired information through questioning.   How-to/Science/Reference Pages 408

Answered or Unanswered? *by Louisa Vaughan*   ISBN: *1-59462-248-5*   **$10.95**
Miracles of Faith in China   Religion Pages 112

The Edinburgh Lectures on Mental Science (1909) *by Thomas*   ISBN: *1-59462-008-3*   **$11.95**
This book contains the substance of a course of lectures recently given by the writer in the Queen Street Hall, Edinburgh. Its purpose is to indicate the Natural Principles governing the relation between Mental Action and Material Conditions...   New Age/Psychology Pages 148

Ayesha *by H. Rider Haggard*   ISBN: *1-59462-301-5*   **$24.95**
Verily and indeed it is the unexpected that happens! Probably if there was one person upon the earth from whom the Editor of this, and of a certain previous history, did not expect to hear again...   Classics Pages 380

Ayala's Angel *by Anthony Trollope*   ISBN: *1-59462-352-X*   **$29.95**
The two girls were both pretty, but Lucy who was twenty-one who supposed to be simple and comparatively unattractive, whereas Ayala was credited, as her Bombwhat romantic name might show, with poetic charm and a taste for romance. Ayala when her father died was nineteen...   Fiction Pages 484

The American Commonwealth *by James Bryce*   ISBN: *1-59462-286-8*   **$34.45**
An interpretation of American democratic political theory. It examines political mechanics and society from the perspective of Scotsman James Bryce   Politics Pages 572

Stories of the Pilgrims *by Margaret P. Pumphrey*   ISBN: *1-59462-116-0*   **$17.95**
This book explores pilgrims religious oppression in England as well as their escape to Holland and eventual crossing to America on the Mayflower, and their early days in New England...   History Pages 268

QTY

The Fasting Cure *by Sinclair Upton*   ISBN: *1-59462-222-1*   **$13.95**
In the Cosmopolitan Magazine for May, 1910, and in the Contemporary Review (London) for April, 1910, I published an article dealing with my experiences in fasting. I have written a great many magazine articles, but never one which attracted so much attention... New Age/Self Help/Health Pages 164

Hebrew Astrology *by Sepharial*   ISBN: *1-59462-308-2*   **$13.45**
In these days of advanced thinking it is a matter of common observation that we have left many of the old landmarks behind and that we are now pressing forward to greater heights and to a wider horizon than that which represented the mind-content of our progenitors...   Astrology Pages 144

Thought Vibration or The Law of Attraction in the Thought World   ISBN: *1-59462-127-6*   **$12.95**
by William Walker Atkinson   *Psychology/Religion Pages 144*

Optimism *by Helen Keller*   ISBN: *1-59462-108-X*   **$15.95**
Helen Keller was blind, deaf, and mute since 19 months old, yet famously learned how to overcome these handicaps, communicate with the world, and spread her lectures promoting optimism. An inspiring read for everyone...   Biographies/Inspirational Pages 84

Sara Crewe *by Frances Burnett*   ISBN: *1-59462-360-0*   **$9.45**
In the first place, Miss Minchin lived in London. Her home was a large, dull, tall one, in a large, dull square, where all the houses were alike, and all the sparrows were alike, and where all the door-knockers made the same heavy sound...   Childrens/Classic Pages 88

The Autobiography of Benjamin Franklin *by Benjamin Franklin*   ISBN: *1-59462-135-7*   **$24.95**
The Autobiography of Benjamin Franklin has probably been more extensively read than any other American historical work, and no other book of its kind has had such ups and downs of fortune. Franklin lived for many years in England, where he was agent...   Biographies/History Pages 332

Name	
Email	
Telephone	
Address	
City, State ZIP	

☐ **Credit Card**   ☐ **Check / Money Order**

Credit Card Number	
Expiration Date	
Signature	

Please Mail to: Book Jungle
PO Box 2226
Champaign, IL 61825
or Fax to: 630-214-0564

ORDERING INFORMATION
web: *www.bookjungle.com*
email: *sales@bookjungle.com*
fax: *630-214-0564*
mail: *Book Jungle PO Box 2226 Champaign, IL 61825*
or PayPal *to sales@bookjungle.com*

Please contact us for bulk discounts

DIRECT-ORDER TERMS

**20% Discount if You Order
Two or More Books**
Free Domestic Shipping!
Accepted: Master Card, Visa,
Discover, American Express

www.ingramcontent.com/pod-product-compliance
Lightning Source LLC
Chambersburg PA
CBHW080904020726
47502CB00008B/2348

9 7 8 1 4 3 8 5 9 4 0 5 7